Blood or Mead

Blood or Mead

Alan Alexander Beck

Copyright © 2008 by Alan Alexander Beck.

ISBN: Softcover   1440420815

EAN-13 9781440420818

All rights reserved. No part of this book may be reproduced or transmitted in any form or by any means, electronic or mechanical, including photocopying, recording, or by any information storage and retrieval system, without permission in writing from the copyright owner.

This is a work of fiction. Names, characters, places and incidents either are the product of the author's imagination or are used fictitiously, and any resemblance to any actual persons, living or dead, events, or locales is entirely coincidental.

This book was printed in the United States of America.

My thanks to Suzanne Hansen for her help editing this novel and to my teacher, Baret Yoshida, for his support in all my endeavors.

Prologue

Analysis is the only virtue
Hate Validates love
Life is an act of war on the Universe
Death is its only possible outcome

—Michael John Pratt

I'm finishing off a bottle of Jamison as I take one last drag off my cigarette. I take my pistol out and point it at my head. I'm praying to my gods for the strength to pull the trigger. The solace, whatever hell I arrive in has to be better than this life. The phone rings, the voice on the other line asks me why I am late. I lose my resolve and put the pistol down.

I shower and look into the mirror. Only a couple days away from 40 but I look a decade older. My face is etched and worn from a life of abuse and fights. Some fights were in the ring, but most came from the street or the bar. My eyes had the yellow miasma that only comes from decades of living one whiskey bottle to the next.

I look down at my body. It is covered in scars from a life of hard living and unnecessary risks. I try to remember a time when I didn't wake to a body that felt like it was going to die and a spirit that was more hollow than whole; in the end I can't even imagine the time.

Despite all this, while I know my best days are behind me, I'm still a force in a fight. While brooding, I remember the moment I gave up on doing something meaningful in my life, the day I put on a suit and traded my dreams for a 401k. I put on my clothes and then I don my Odhroeri amulet, which is comprised of three interlocked drinking horns. It's the sign of Odin, Chief god of the Norse and Germanic people. Then I put on a jade necklace of the Lord Buddha. My name is John Tran and this is my life.

Having donned the symbols of my two of faiths, I am now ready. I get into my car and go to the only place that makes me feel whole, my gym, the only place that really appreciates a fuck up like me. It's the oldest martial arts gym in town. We're not the place that caters to yuppies, either. It is small, dank, and you can always find new spots of blood on the floor illuminated by the handful of dim lights that work most of the time. We've got a sparring ring and some mats but the only ornamentation we have is a mural on the back wall depicting a black tiger in honor of our founder. He was in the Laotian Special Forces, the Black Tigers, and the mural is a memorial to him.

The yuppies tend to prefer the air conditioned gyms that make their members feel good instead of pushing them. We occasionally get the young punk that wants to prove something. Scanning the faces, I see there's a new kid here today. He must be about 21 and has a bodybuilder's physique. A thousand kids like him have passed through my life; just another muscle-bound kid who thinks he can be a fighter after one day's training.

Our gym specializes in Muay Thai kickboxing and submission wrestling. The former is a type of kickboxing from South East Asia that specializes in knee and elbow strikes. The latter is a form of wrestling that specializes in joint dislocation and chokes. I finish my routines and join a few my gym mates to talk about my unrequited affections for a certain women. They tell me, for what must be the thousandth time, to forget her and focus on my upcoming fight.

The new kid sees me. I can tell he thinks I'm easy game. Kids like him always need to make a big impression. He asks me to spar and tells me, "Don't worry, I'll go easy on you, old timer."

Some of the other guys start laughing. He hasn't caught on yet, so I decide to teach him about the pecking order here.

I let him get in a couple of punches. With his confidence growing, I know it is time to go after him. I start to pick him apart, and he staggers on his feet from a barrage of kicks and punches. He does what beginners always do when pressed; he tries to football tackle me to the mat. I go with the motion; but on our way down I wrap my left arm over his exposed throat and around his neck. I grab my left wrist with my right hand and squeeze. The pressure around his carotid arteries stops the flow of oxygenated blood to his brain. In just seconds he falls unconscious, a victim of the guillotine choke hold. It's the one that gets all the new wrestlers. The kid struggles to his feet after a couple of minutes. I made sure not to cause any unnecessary damage. The only thing hurt is his pride, and he storms out like all the rest.

The kid was just another muscular body with no technique. Dedication to the Art is necessary to become a fighter; a good physique is not enough.

Then one of my gym mates mentions, "Hey, don't you have a case you need to finish for your firm?"

I concede the truth of the point, but reply, "You're right, but goddamn it I wish I could just get the balls to say fuck it and just train full-time." I head to the showers then off to my firm.

At my office, I finish memorizing oral arguments for a trademark infringement case I have later today.

I think to myself, "How did it come to this? I'm just another corporate lawyer. There were a thousand other options." For a moment, I reminisce about my days in the Marine Corps. I would have been so much happier had I stayed. Despite all the crap I had to put up with, at least my life felt like it had a purpose back then.

One of my colleagues pokes his nose into my daydream and reminds me that I'm going to be late for court. I open up my desk drawer and pull out a bottle of Jamison. Finishing the remainder, I mutter to myself, "That's better; at least I can forget I'm alive, for awhile".

Court goes well. I win my case. Another million dollars made for a corporate client already worth billions. What was the point? At least I could take a little professional pride in winning; I am good at what I do. I never showboat or perform courtroom antics. Judge or jury, I show the arbiter of fact, the law and why the law is on my side. That's why my firm lets a 40 year old alcoholic fighter stay on. I am good at my job even if continually covered in bruises and managing the subtleties of drink.

I gather my accoutrement and step out of the courtroom. Then I see her. Leah Conley, she's an extraordinary woman; beautiful to watch with her straight brunette hair gently sliding over her pale skin and amber eyes reminiscent of a starry nebula. I've been pining over her for years and every time I see her strong sleek body I think how she just keeps getting more appealing. She is there in the hall with several of her associates. Working for the biggest firm in town, she just made partner.

Gratefully, or at least a part of me thinks that, she knows how I feel and is always polite enough to ignore it. We chat for awhile. It turns out she's just completed her own successful case. She congratulates me on my victory, and invites me to a party in celebration of her firm's victory. As if my agent, she thinks it will be good networking for me amid all the top lawyers.

I flashback to our first encounter and then think of the men she's chosen over me since then. Even knowing all the first picks will be there and that this will only make me feel worse, I agree to go. I've never really felt comfortable in this elite crowd, outside of work, but I can't say no to her. As she leaves, I drink in the last bits of her scent.

To make Leah's party a little less painful, I call up some of my gym mates asking if they'd like to go with me to this event. Even if only one guy shows up, at least we can chat over good booze on someone else's tab.

I am at the party, drinking heavily. It is like some gaudy, yet pricey night club that probably rents for what most people make in one month. There is a shitty band playing some noisy pop shit.

To my surprise I recognize some people. Two of my gym mates show up to spend the evening here. Both of them have the same bizarre misshapen cauliflower ears that I possess. The disfigurement comes with the brutal art we practice. Decades of grinding our heads against the mat and taking punches to the ears create bulging cartilage deposits where ears once were. It freaks most people out, but for us it's just the sign of an experienced fighter.

Usually my friends dress their heavily tattooed bodies in a way to show as much skin art as possible. But tonight, they are dressed for "social" acceptance, covering their tattoos. I'm just covering scars, no tattoos. My friend, Linh Nguyen, is a slim yet powerful Vietnamese man. His muscular biceps are covered with various Buddhist tattoos, and if he took off his shirt, you would see the Lord Buddha and the God of Luck tattooed on his chest. Most of the Buddhist symbols were inked by monks using a hammer and needle. Each tattoo is blessed to ward off spirits, give the wearer luck, also blessings specific to each image. Linh's other tattoos are from his gang in his youth. In the suit he is wearing, one would never know he was covered with tattoos.

My other friend is Bobby Pierson; the Nordic blood runs true within him. Blonde hair, blue eyes, he stands 6'3", and with his 250 lbs of muscle he has the look of a man that could easily break you in half. Under his blonde locks, he has the hammer of Thor, Mjolnir, tattooed on top on his skull. As a bounty hunter, he is altogether an intimidating man.

As we talk about the roust of the kid this morning another friend, Rodney, joins us. He is a quiet man of Chinese descent, who looks his part as a man whose trade is patent law. He's helped me out on a few strict product liability cases and in exchange, I taught him some hand-to-hand. Average height and build, he is a man you might walk right past without taking notice. However, I remember an incident some years back when a prisoner escaped from a court room, grabbed a gun from a police officer, and held the court at bay. Rodney, this unassuming patent lawyer tackled the man, and while pinning the man to the floor, he took a round to the chest that saved the life of the cop. Although he would never say anything, he had the bullet wound to show it.

As the night and the drinking go on, I'm on the brink of unconsciousness. I'm too drunk. My senses are so obliterated, I don't even notice the wails until my own screaming rips open my consciousness. I'm trapped in the fire with Leah, Linh, Bobby, and people I can barely see through the smoke. My skin burns. The horrifying sounds, the repulsive smells of smoldering flesh and boiling blood fill my senses. Pain, heat, the hell of burning to death momentarily overwhelms me. I hear my own voice cry out with those who are still alive. But I am lifted away from the sensations and I start laughing, loud raucous laughter. The louder I laugh the more it overpowers the wails of the burning. This crazy sounding laughter from a man burning to death is so bizarre that even some that are burning notice.

I roar out, "Thank you, Odin, for giving me death. It is the one thing I could not do myself."

Convergence I

Yet in the midst of the tragic dying out of sounds, I hear a clear, thundering voice, "You have yet to earn your place in Valhalla, but I will give you one more chance." Then my world starts to fade until I become aware that I am falling through an impossibly long tunnel. Am I really seeing this, a one eyed, white bearded man with a raven on each shoulder? He has a spear in one hand and is riding a six legged horse. I shudder a moment as I realize that there is a conversation going on.

"You're taking a risk, Odin, their souls are beyond our domain now," says the bodiless hissing voice of Lucifer, "and we'll have to pay a tremendous cost to send them on the retrieval mission."

Odin responds, "Not so, old friend; the risk is worth this unique opportunity and it is worth the cost!"

Another figure emerges, "Lucifer you're always a pessimist," Atlas blurts out, strutting his bulging muscles that are bared and bronzed.

"Would you care to place a wager on their failure?" Lucifer snorts, his body beginning to take shape. "Atlas, if these humans die, you bring me Gabriel's trumpet of Yahweh's Armageddon and Schrödinger's cat—the real one that went through the wormhole, not that scruffy stand-in that Einstein bought to replace the original, which he lost, I might add."

Atlas, annoyed by the wager, complains, "The trumpet's one thing; I see the use in having that, but why the cat?"

Lucifer hisses back, "Even Hell's got a rat problem, and since the cat's already immortal because of that quantum whatever experiment, that's less work for me. With all those damned rats, well, it's a bitch getting feline replacements all the time."

Atlas bargains, "Alright, the trumpet's no problem considering last time when a few glasses of absinth spiked with Dionysus's specialty got Gabriel and Michael so blasted, they missed out on getting Armageddon rolling. And they didn't even know what dimension they were in let alone where that stupid trumpet went when they lost it. The cat's another story. I'm going to have to go through a black hole to get the cat. So when I win, you better have something sweet for me; say, talk Lilith into spending some time with me," he smiled. "Do we have a bet? Or do you give?" Atlas challenges.

"I'm the Morning Star, remember; I'll get it done," Lucifer slyly assures him.

Atlas asks, scratching under his long black beard, "What do you need the trumpet for anyway?"

Lucifer's beauty continues to enchant them all as he explains, "It's part of Buddha's and Odin's plan to stop Yahweh's hordes from taking another shot at Armageddon, next time causality lines up. That old wise guy thinks we might be able to stop them for good if we play it right. We were lucky last time. If Monkey hadn't found out the location of the Holy Grail who knows what would have happened." Lucifer yawns, "Anyway, Yahweh's crew wants to end the world, and, well, I'm the Devil. I'm always interested in the power more souls would bring."

Odin, impatient, yells, "Look, we're trying to save this world and you two are making bets on whether or not they'll fail. Be still so we can get this plan going."

Chapter 1

> Then Grimhild handed me a full horn to drink
>   cool and bitter, that cast out grief;
>   in it was mixed the might of Earth
>   the ice-cold sea, and the blood of swine.
> Carved on the horn were many runes
>   painted red—I could not read them—
>   a long serpent out of the sea,
>   an ear of corn, entrails of beasts.
> Baleful things were mixed in that beer,
>   herbs from the forest, fire-blackened acorns,
>   the hearth's dew, soot, entrails of sacrifices,
>   boiled swine's liver, soothing to sorrow
>   —From the Elder Edda

I'm awakened to a throbbing head. So entranced by the pain, I don't realize I'm just staring at the ground. I vaguely remember falling, seeing things that could not possibly be true. Dusting myself off, I notice subtle changes to my body. I feel stronger, more powerful than I ever have. What is most evident but strange are the changes in my perceptions. I'm seeing things I don't think I should be seeing. And all around me I can feel or intuit what is there. For a moment, there seems like a ripple or tear, in what, in reality? Then it's as if I am looking through one glass bowl into another, or is it one reality into another.

    I mutter aloud, "Woe, I must have had some acid last night. Hope I didn't do anything too crazy." What's more, I think I'm in a forest. Well, forest-ish, is the closest thing I can come up with. What looks like trees are tree-shaped and are a flaxen color of paraffin, I guess. The leaves sparkle with a lavender crystalline tint like amethyst in spider webs, and they give off a faint luminescent glow. Here and there are strange ethereal shapes flitting in the sky; balls of light streaking at odd angles seem to move through impossible vector-like changes. The sky is the ever-changing and entrancing color of fox fire. There are sounds and smells unlike anything I've ever experienced and they're so vivid, almost visceral. The plants are even emanating a low hum?

I realize I'm not alone. There are bodies all around me and some are beginning to rouse. I leap up to a fighting stance; but wait, I think I recognize . . . These are the people from Leah's party, and my friends, Linh, Bobby, and Rodney. But they are different, not quite themselves, and I can feel that neither am I the same person. A few, including Leah, are slimmer and have ears pointed like the Vulcan's of TV's Star Trek. Their skin is paraffin-like and their eyes are altered. The pupils are thin and elongated like a cat's with the colors constantly in a state of flux. Little lines of gold, silver, and emerald stream across the ever-changing irises. They seem almost ethereal in essence. Each of them radiates a preternatural beauty. They look like the elves from Norse mythology.

I see my gym mates but at first I barely recognize them. There's Linh, but his skin has turned ashen gray. His face is long and gaunt. His eyes are entirely black like ebony, the kind that absorbs the light from anything it gazes upon. The strangest thing is wherever his body touches a shadow; the edges of his outline vibrate and become fuzzy. He seems to be merging with the shadows, becoming part of the absence of light.

Bobby is here, too. At least I think it's him. He has doubled in girth, and his skin seems to have hardened like a carapace; already developed muscles look larger and coiled. I'm thinking he could bench a truck if he so chose. Besides that, I swear he has vestigial fangs. I always thought he had something weird about him, but this is really out there.

Linh and Bobby are, and for that matter, everyone else is still in a sort of walking stupor. I wonder if anyone besides me is cogent enough to see what is charging over the hill towards us. A large group of riders is drawing down on us, and I realize we're about to be attacked. The time for action is upon us. I just hope that everyone with me, even the more bizarre unrecognizable, seemingly defenseless ones still on the ground, are from Leah's party or are at least not hostile towards me.

The riders mounts pull up sharply and not in unison as they stamp and paw at some unseen boundary. Instead of charging us, the riders dismount from their seemingly translucent yet crystalline equines. I realize what's happening; the rider's mounts stopped short, unwilling, or unable to come any closer.

The riders all look similar to the tall, thin, pointy-eared creatures around me. But, they are dressed in metal armor and are carrying serious swords and spears, unlike my "colleagues." Both the weapons and armor are unlike anything I have ever seen before. I can tell the metal is not metal and can almost feel its substance: It is more like the lavender organic crystals of the tree leaves. Moreover, I can detect a strange energy visibly coursing through the weapons and armor. It is as if I can see inside the substance and into the guardsmen, too. One of the guardsmen was obviously their leader, wearing more ornate armor than the others. He starts to approach me.

"I'm Captain Nefree of the 3rd Imperial Guard." His language was strange, and I could not put a name to it, but I could understand it.

"This land is reserved for the Nobility only. The penalty for trespass is death," Nefree said with a somber tone. "Do you have documents from the Nobility, permitting you to use these lands?"

He is a dangerous looking being. With the face of a person that has been in his share of fights, he is covered with deep noticeable scars across his face and arms. And he clearly held my gaze with murderous intent in his eyes.

The attackers are a squad with twenty-one guardsmen in their ranks of seven abreast with one Captain. Their horses are nervous and randomly cluster to the rear of the regiment. Without moving my head or eyes, I scan behind me, in front of me, and in all directions, simultaneously. I take in the whole scene as if from some vantage point far above me. Even if every one of the people on my side can fight we are still heavily outnumbered. Plus, help from my "colleagues" seems unlikely since many of them are still huddled over, coming to terms with what, and where, and who they are. And those whose awareness I touch, are not going to be much help, since if they are the ones form Leah's party, they are likely to be lawyers without martial arts training.

Quickly realizing I have no special papers, and that we are trespassing on the Nobles' land, it is clear that talking is not going to be an option. So, I take the initiative. Punching him by surprise, I hit the Captain square in the bare trachea, crushing it. He crumples over; he'll be dead in minutes.

Luckily, it seems as if some of the enemy guardsmen have not yet come to terms with the single blow from an unaided and unarmed man, killing their leader. They are slow to the quick. But I realize that I'm likely to die anyway, so I might as well go down fighting.

I try to reach for the captain's sword, but his guardsmen are on me too fast. Dodging blows from both sides, I come up with a flying knee to one of the guards, breaking his jaw and shattering most of his teeth. The guard's blood is green. A sword is thrust at me, and it's too late to fully dodge. I lurch to the side, but I'm cut a deep wound across my left shoulder. As the blade cuts me I feel both electricity and intense heat shocking and burning me at the same time. The strange energy in the swords carries quite a wallop.

Another guard comes up behind me ready to skewer me. Bobby, alert at last, grabs the guardsman from behind like in a Heimlich maneuver, but suplexing him and throwing him back over his shoulder right into the trees. I'm not alone in this fight.

Some part of me notices that as the guard slams into the tree, areas of his unarmored body touch the tree. The leaves immediately extend out like little spear-tipped webs, entangling the guardsman and quickly devouring him. I see that the blood from the guard I had kneed was drawing the attention of local flora, as well. Attracted to the green blood on his face, vines sprout from the ground and start to feast on him until he is nothing more than bones. Even then the skeleton's being dragged into the ground, presumably for a marrow feast. Great! On top of the guardsmen attacking us, we are in the middle of a carnivorous forest. Alright, three attackers down; only nineteen more to go.

I see Linh is now in the fight and is trying to pick up one of the slain guard's swords. He howls in pain as a blast of some energy shoots through him. I can feel that the weapons are specifically linked to each one's owner therefore only the proper person does not receive a tremendous shock trying to pick it up.

Now it's nineteen armed guards against three unarmed men. Not the best odds! The guards' training finally breaks through their shock of being attacked, and they form a semicircle around us. Bobby's to my right and Linh is on my left, or at least I sense them now. We all know we are going to die, and I could care less. I feel stronger, more alert than I have in years. I'm relishing every moment of it and yell, "Let's get 'em." But part of me watches Bobby start to convulse. "Bobby," I shout, "what's wrong?"

He responds, "I have no idea." The big man is phasing and shaking, his muscles stretch against his skin. In just moments, Bobby doubles in size!

My own heart beats wildly with my first hint of panic. Then my perceptions begin to change again. It's as if I'm becoming aware of everything around me. Not only can I see and feel all around me, but I can read the life forces of all the beings around me.

Bobby and I continue to transform while Linh is playing with the shadows. Bobby is now well over 1000 pounds. Fangs and claws spring from his face and hands and his skin is no longer skin but thickened hide. On my other side, my friend Linh actually disappears and then reappears out from another shadow. Linh engages, striking a guard, then disappears again. It was fantastic; he kept getting a cut in and disappearing before they could touch him. He injures a number of them and the plants go after the bloodied guards.

Bobby is now fully transformed into a 1500 pound creature covered in fur with a prehensile tail that looks like it has a stinger at the end. His head resembles the Norse gods fox head, his maw lined with two rows of sharp teeth and brutally large fangs. He also has grown an extra set of arms just as big as the others and a crown full of horns with two huge ones in the middle.

To the guardsmen credit, they didn't look afraid. They seemed to maintain an alert and controlled status, moving away from obvious shadows after realizing Linh's power over the shadows. They form their semi-circle and much to my surprise, shields of energy nearly the size of a man, appear out of bracelets on their arms. They fall into a phalanx pattern identical to the ancient Greek formation, in which spearmen line up in very close order, lock their shields together, and the first few ranks of soldiers project their spears out over the first rank of shields. They try to gain the upper hand in the battle early on, and as a result allow for the first few ranks of spearmen to engage their spears against us, the enemy. I'd never seen one before and the phalanx looks like a massive spear and shield wall.

With my heightened awareness, and even with my back to the party, I can tell a number of the sleepers are coming to. I feel each one's identity and energy aura.

Undaunted and charged up by his new body, Bobby rams the phalanx formation. His ferocious strength forces them back but amazingly they did not break formation. Moving back out, his tail snags one of the guardsmen in the hand. As I had sensed, the tip was poison. The guard's hand immediately turns black and he drops his spear. He drifts into the back where I sense he cuts off own hand to keep the fast moving poison from spreading or he assuredly will die. Where the guard's blade cuts, the energy in the sword cauterizes the wound so there is no blood for the plants to go after. All of this I know but I don't actually see it. Then I realize that my wound, too, is not bleeding.

Bobby charges again and again. But now wary of his tail, the phalanx deflects its sting with their shields that seem impenetrable. So all he's doing is pushing them back, again and again. I feel his energies waning as he is growing tired. With each charge he is getting more spear nicks, the brutal energy of the spears slowing him down nick by nick; but no blood loss.

Linh is having little luck either. Every time he gets close to the guardsmen, they close their ranks in on him and strike. With only his lethal hands he's no match for those spears. I sensed that a chest-crushing blow to Linh while in the shadows, would go right through him like it would a shadow. If Linh escapes into the shadow, the parts of him not in the shadow become exposed targets; and he too is taking damage. If we break off the attack, we won't stand a chance against their thrown spears. If that doesn't finish us, the guards' swords will. There still isn't any obvious help coming from any of Leah's partier's. So it is up to the three of us to come up with a plan. Then I remembered the devouring of the guard's body. I thought that if I could get the plants to attack the guardsmen, we might stand a chance.

"Bobby," I call, "Stop! I have a plan." I am afraid not only his body but his mind has turned beastlike. Even if his brain is still "normal" I wonder if he has the vocal chords and can actually speak. Surprisingly, not only does he reply he responds in English! Good to know. But can the guardsmen understand us as we can them? I am hoping that whatever power allows us to speak and understand the guard's language does not allow the guards to understand English.

"Bobby, Linh, if we can get the trees to attack them, we might be able to cut their numbers. Bobby, get ready to attack on my signal. Linh, distract them by moving from shadow to shadow tossing rocks and yelling. I'll get the plants' attention." I instruct. I hide behind Bobby's 1500 pound frame which is rather an easy task.

One guard yells out, "Look, he's a coward running and hiding behind the beast!"

Good that will buy me the time I need. "Damn, Bobby's charges have pushed the formation too far back," I say to myself as I look back at Captain Nefree's body. "There's no way I'll be able to carry his body this far without blowing my cover." If they see me doing to him what I'm thinking, that will also blow my cover and infuriate them even more.

"I guess I'll have to do this the hard way," I groan. First, I make sure Bobby is set to go. Then I take off my shirt. I bite into the meaty portion of my left hand. Human teeth can be powerful tools. The tear is extensive and bleeds greatly . . . red blood! I let the blood drench my shirt, careful to keep it from spilling on the ground. When the shirt is soaked in blood, I mutter to myself, "One good chance."

"Bobby, charge!" I yell. Bobby bulls his way forward, the ground shuddering with every step. The guardsmen, alerted to Bobby, defend against his attack and barely notice me, if at all. We get to within a few feet of the formation and I lob the blood-soaked shirt towards the guards. It lands on the ground in front of the guards' phalanx, splattering onto a few guards as I had planned. The guards' spear points are within reach so intentionally I thrust my palm into an oncoming spear tip. I yelp as the tip slices through my flesh cauterizing the teeth wound and giving me one of those holy hell shocks. But, it stops the bleeding.

Meanwhile, the vines wind out of the ground to drink the spilt blood and the needle-sharp thorns pierce the flesh of any guardsman, splattered with blood. The struggling guards howl in pain as the vines start to entangle them, pierce them, and drain their blood. I watch horrified to see the helpless guards being devoured and pulled into the ground. For a moment, the guards break discipline and try to rescue their doomed comrades. They thrust their spears at the vines, trying to cut free their comrades from the carnivorous vines. In that moment I shout, "Linh, Bobby, Now! Attack!"

Bobby charges in, ripping through the weakened formation. He manages to break the phalanx and skewer one guard through the throat with his head of horns.

Linh grabs one guard, wraps one arm around his neck, and grabs the wrapping arm's wrist with the other. The guard goes limp after a few moments from the maneuver, a rear naked choke.

"Thank you, fate!" Linh calls out for he has gambled that the armor will not defend like the guardsmen's weapons or else he would have been shocked and burned seriously. As the guard falls unconscious Linh grabs the guard and pushes his face into a tree. Linh watches with morbid fascination for a moment as the tree satiates its appetite. Then Linh falls once more into the shadows.

I feel like I'm in automatic mode defending against the attacks of two guardsmen; in my head I count, "Five more down, fourteen more to go. This is getting fun." My hyper-enhanced perceptions make me able to visualize each attack much quicker and I dodge a dozen hits that should have killed me.

Bobby, seeing how much fun I was having, leaps over some guards making a 25-foot jump in one bound. He mutters to himself, "This is not possible. How did I turn into this being?"

"Later, Bobby," I key in on his voice, "we'll think about that later." I tell him. "I don't know about you, but I'm a little busy right now."

Bobby grabs the two guards with decidedly inhuman strength and slams them again and again into each other. Then he gives the trees a meal.

With my increased perceptions I clearly hear every voice and separate out ones I key on. So that even in the din of battle, I hear the guards speaking to each other. One says, "You have to use it!"

The other replies, "But it's punishable by death to use magic on Noble land."

"The Imperial Source will protect us," says someone bravely.

Another joined in, "You and I are the only ones left that know combat spells. I'm using mine. We're dead anyway if we don't. We have to finish them off before their friends get up. Who knows what they can do."

The other guard finally agrees.

Counting the guard Linh killed, that leaves eleven. But, I have a bad feeling about what I heard. They may very well be able to cast magic spells. Part of me saw the two magic-user guards whose looks had changed from concern to fairly confident.

Bobby starts another charge! I cry out, "Bobby, Stop!" but it is too late. The magic casters produce some sort of energy and that blasts right into the huge beast. Bobby falls with a thunderous thud ten feet back, unconscious. I knew that force would have disintegrated any normal-sized human.

I try to rush the magic guards' positions, but the other nine guards are protecting the magic casters. One caster conjures a ball of light that destroys all the shadows nearby. Linh immediately pops out of the shadows and is a perfect target. As the second magic-user prepares to use his arcane energy again I grab a spear that's on the ground. Ignoring the burning flesh and pain I throw it at one caster and miss. The caster is jolted just enough so that his bolt of energy does not hit Linh, directly. Yet it was still enough to severely injure him; my senses read his life force weakening. We are all likely to be killed; yet again, that doesn't really matter to me. I hope that some of the others from Leah's party have enough time to awaken and run away. If they don't, they'll soon be plant food.

Suddenly both casters direct their arcane power on me. Nothing happens. Again they cast and nothing happens. Together they curse and one yells, "Why can't we hit him?"

"It's as if he is shielded, but I can't sense his aura at all. I can't lock on to his presence," says one.

Even as the guards start to panic for a moment since the magic didn't work on me, they realize that they still outnumber me eleven to one and to them, I am still unarmed. They reform their phalanx towards me and begin to advance. But I sense a presence approaching from behind me. I can feel that mind and recognize it is one of the party members. The figure is tall, Asian, with an energy about him that was like radiant light. Every step or two, the energy literally crackles around him. His eyes are completely opaque, yet I can sense he sees just fine. Over six feet tall, well muscled, he seems like a young god with his extraordinary aura. The figure announces, "It's me, Rodney."

"Just as we're about to be destroyed, just as I am about to die, Rodney emerges from the shadows. Weird," I thought. His looks and his "gift," are not by human design; much like the rest, he looks different. Everyone I've seen looks different, except me. It occurs to me that my body hasn't changed much, at least not as dramatically. "Rodney, I'm glad you're here," I shout. "You look, well, different. Do I look as different as you and Linh and Bobby?" I ask?

I am not surprised to hear him say no. But, why is this so? I know I have some protection from these people's magic. Why is my body much the same as before? I seem to have changed so little compared to my companions. I'm not sure whether to be relieved or angered by that, but this question could carry me to my impending death, if I don't stop my musing.

This time the magician guards send their combined energy force to attack Rodney. Feeling no fear, I jump in the way and once again the blasts dissolve harmlessly. "Cool!" I blurt out.

Rodney laughs and looks up at the sky. He says, "Do you see the lights in the sky, my friend? I can sense them; they're energy beings." He raises his arms to the sky, "I believe I can control them". Rodney seems to fall into a trance. "Oh Lights of Light, Oh Stars of Right, Let day away and come hither to night," he calls to the lights. And they succumb to his will circling down from the sky. They attack from above the guards' heads blasting one of the magician casters. Still, the caster's armor and shield protect him from such a potent attack. Only his exposed, unarmed skin is hit. But his armor and shield aren't enough. The orbs come in from this angle then that and finally the dozens of different angles prove his armor ineffective. Piece by piece his body is scorched until he dies screaming.

The other magician is next. But he is able to cast some sort of security ward that rebuffs the light beings. Rodney, still unsure of all of his abilities, decides to command the light beings to attack any guard. I sense again that in commanding the light beings it is taking an obvious toll on him. He is perspiring heavily and blood is dripping from his eyes, nose, and mouth.

"Rodney, don't let any of your blood hit the ground." I warn.

Two more guards are killed by the orbs. Then the remaining magician and two other guardsmen circle around beginning what appears to be a spell. Just as the light beings finish off a third guard, the guardsmen's spell is cast against the light beings. The balls of light cannot contend with this magic and disperse in a swirling flash of light.

Just as the light beings disappear, one of the other guards aims and throws his spear striking Rodney in the stomach. I feel him struggle as the unbearable strain of the surging eldritch energy from the spear floods through him. I cannot reach Rodney in time to save him, but just then, another figure emerges from the dark.

This being is stout, just shy of five feet tall, and yet he is probably close to 300 pounds of bunched muscle twisted into obscenely bulging cords. He pulses over to Rodney and pulls the spear out of the patent lawyer's stomach, then hurls it back at the guardsmen. Such is his strength that the spear slices right through the guard like paper. If he had actually intended to do so, his aim was uncanny, as the spear missed the area protected by the shield by a fraction of an inch. The point struck the guard through his helmet piercing his skull; six left.

The dwarf-like creature calls out, "Hey, calm the fuck down. It's Harvey Bivens, man," identifying himself. He is a detective that moonlights as an investigator for a number of law firms. His reputation for getting results and arrests is not without consequence: A member of his team was killed two years back. He tracked down the killer but since the murders had been ordered by well connected drug lords who paid off everyone, the court dismissed the case on a technicality then refused to go after the men who had given the orders. Distraught, Harvey had taken a six month leave of absence. While he was on leave, over forty people, known to be part of the drug ring or associated with the death of Harvey's man, ended up missing or dead. The deaths ranged from Colombia to Mexico to the states. And no one had ever proved anything connected with Harvey.

"What the hell's going on? What are those things?" Harvey blustered.

I give Harvey a quick rundown of the situation, but even as I'm explaining, he's figuring out how to take out the rest of the guards. If even one gets away, no doubt there'll be a hundred more coming. I look back to see if any of the others from the party are fit to fight yet. There is one figure rising whose form is definitely not human. Harvey was doing something quite odd. Out of some new felt instinct, he sticks his hands in the soil. Around his hands begin to form a hammer and an axe that are part of his body. The guards charge again. We gauge our assets; my friends are all badly injured and unconscious. If we don't get help soon they will die; we all will.

Then the odd figure I sense rising up from the party, comes to us out of the shadows. Its form is much like that of a plant, but it moves and grows at the same time. Amazingly, a human-sized, rose bud grows out from the stem and hangs down from the top of the plant. The beautiful pale green bud starts opening, blossoming, and out of it steps a figure that looks almost human. The figure is pure white, female, and has pale green petal-like hair. Other than the pointed ears, petal green hair, and the occasional plant part growing from it, most notably a vermilion bouquet on the right side of its head, it appeared to be a tall beautiful woman. I also notice, with my newly heightened senses, she does not have a hint of human scent. Instead, smells of lavender and roses emanate from her body. I don't recognize her as one of the partiers, which doesn't necessarily mean anything, but since we are in a carnivorous forest, I'll keep my guard up.

She calls out, "What the hell is going on?" in English.

I soon realize she is the environmental lawyer that various firms contracted to handle environmental cases. Her name is Michelle Lujan. She only works for the big firms to fund her various pro bono cases. She'd graduated from Yale Law and turned down everything that implied she would work for Green Peace. I respect her. She has not given up on her dream, and is willing to forge her own way.

"No time to explain. Look, all you need to know is those guys in armor are trying to kill us and I think we're in another dimension," I shout. "Other than me, every one of our group, so far as I've seen, is visibly changed. So, if you feel you have some sort of new power or can help in any other way, jump in. If not run. But don't touch any of the plants or they'll literally eat you," I warn.

She replies, "I can sense the plants all around us. It's wonderful, I can talk to them."

By this point I was willing to believe anything, so I told her, "Tell them to help us, then."

She communicates with the plants and then says, "They see me as a leader and want to obey my will." Then Michelle took control of the forest. Merging with it, she lashes out. It's a macabre scene. Horrible plants come out of the ground, out of the trunks of trees, out of the leaves. Harvey and I jump at the opportunity to attack the remaining guardsmen. Harvey rushes in brandishing his hammer and axe arms and cleaves a guardsman right down the middle, armor and all. The alien forest of paraffin-colored plants has come alive, bizarre mixtures of things that only were supposed to exist in novels and nightmares. One guard is eaten by what can only be described as a Venus flytrap. Another dies screaming as a flower releases a pollen that eats away his face. I grab one of the guards by the shoulder and throw him into a tree giving it another feast. Harvey and the plants have taken out 5 more guards, but the fifth one stabs his sword right through Harvey's torso just as Harvey bashes in his skull. They both fall to the ground.

The remaining magician finally realizes who is controlling the trees and sends out another bolt. Michelle raises plants around her as shields, but it is not enough. The bolt rips right through her. She bleeds green like the mixture of a human's and a plant's blood. The plants gently cover her and pull her into the ground.

Two guards left. At once, they both come at me; one wielding a sword, the other a spear. One guard attacks me with a huge swing of his sword. I am quite aware I have not dodged enough. Then the impossible happens: I have that strange feeling that I'm looking at ripples in reality, again. Everything is in slow motion and the blow that should decapitate me misses by a whisker. It's as if reality is bending just enough so that the blade misses me. I strike the first guardsman like I had the Captain, in the trachea; but as his trachea collapses he lands a final blow that thrusts his blade down to my clavicle. I feel my consciousness fading, and I know I am on the verge of death. With one more surge of effort, I pull the blade out of my torso smelling the burn of cauterized flesh. My senses take over and I see the last guard, the magician that had overtaken my friends. One left; pretty good, we took out twenty-one.

For all my fallen friends and for the sake of the win, I gather up the last bit of my strength and charge. The magician, taken off guard by the ferocity of this suicidal attack, does the only logical move. He jams his spear piercing right through my chest. I grin and keep coming, grabbing the shaft of the spear and ramming it through me. I use the spear to pull myself towards the last guard. Grimacing and screaming, the pain of the spear's power begins to stimulate me, waking me enough to finish my task. I cram the shaft deeper and deeper, closer and closer until I am eye-to-eye with the magician. I sink my snarling teeth into the guard's jugular, then laugh as I see the life blood of my enemy drain out, feeding the forest. And that makes twenty-two. Good enough to get me to Valhalla I'd say. Then I fall. Everything begins to fade. The sky and all its lights go black.

Convergence II

"So that went well. Less than an hour into the plan and they're already goners," says Lucifer. "Looks like you owe me a trumpet and an immortal cat, Atlas."

"Hey, they're not dead yet," Atlas replies. "Besides, how do you know the cat is immortal; what makes it immortal? I thought that quantum immortality stuff had to do with do with parallel versions of you."

"Well sure, that's the general idea, but they did something wacky. I don't know what those physicists did, but that specific-in-this-time-stream cat can't die. If there's a chance no matter how infinitesimal that the cat could live, he will. Since there's a chance anything can happen he basically can't die," explains Lucifer.

"That's what's so ridiculous about Vishnu, Brahma, and the rest of that pantheon besides Hanuman just throwing in the towel," blurted Lucifer. "They honestly believe that fate is sealed and we are all doomed. All they're basing that belief on is an answer they got from an oracle hyper-computer that's supposed to be able to give you an infallible answer if you give it enough data to compute. That's called a self-fulfilling prophecy."

"The three of us—you, me, and Odin—all swore an oath to save the world from Armageddon, even if it costs us our existence. If Vishnu-Brahma-Hanuman's brand of fate gets in the way we'll rip it in half," brandishes Lucifer.

"There's always a chance if you try," Odin replies. "Besides Hanuman isn't giving up because there is no Hanuman. Hanuman's just another name for our very own Chinese Trickster God, Sun Wukong, or Monkey as we know him. After the events chronicled in Journey to the West happened, the Indian gods made him an honorary member of their assemblage. Monkey uses the Hanuman persona whenever he needs to point the finger at someone else. He should be here pretty soon so you can ask him about it, yourself," adds Odin.

Lucifer snaps, "Did you really need to invite him? Last time he came, the monkey stole everything on me but my wings. You never can prove anything either."

Atlas chimes in, "Monkey might be a thief and trickster, but you got to give it to him, he always comes through in a jam. Anyway, I've been wondering how much of that Yahweh stuff in that Bible of theirs is true?"

Lucifer spits, "Well I guess I'll start from the beginning." He sighs, "The first part I'm only basing off information reports Odin has received from his operatives. Apparently before Yahweh came to Earth, he was a servant to a minor deity of a distant world in this dimension. As an underling in a company of hundreds of gods he knew he'd never be a real Power. He wanted out, and he wanted power. He devised a scheme whereby he could temporarily leech away the power of his entire pantheon. And he knew the power he took could not renew itself. He'd be like a battery. Any of the power spent would not be recoverable but it would be enough to establish himself in a new world, obtaining his own power by means I'll explain later. The problem was the pantheon would recover almost instantly. He knew he'd be lucky if all they did was kill him for such an affront. Knowing that, he knew he'd need a way to escape that couldn't be tracked. But, he could not figure out a way to evade pursuit from a throng of angry gods.

"So he waited for the perfect opportunity. It finally came one day when a wormhole opened up relatively close to his world. He initiated his plan. For a brief instant, he sapped the pantheon's power. Instilled with it he escaped. He made it to the wormhole seconds before the gods did and using some of his stolen power, he closed up the hole.

Lucifer continues, "That's how he met our sorry lot. He was drunk with power he previously couldn't even dream of. He still had nearly all the power he'd stolen and was experimenting with his enhanced powers of perception when he sensed us. We, were soldiers that had fallen into a trap imprisoning us in a dimensional bubble. We were members of a people that had been at war with another race for millennia.

"By the way, that's why there are no female angels in our midst. Our military did not have women in it. Too bad, eh?

"We have no idea how long we were in the bubble, but it felt like thousands of years had passed by the time Yahweh came. Time doesn't quite have the same meaning when you're trapped in the barren void of a dimensional bubble. Then we all heard a voice offering to free us. We'd tried every possible avenue of escape and failed, so we readily accepted his agreement.

Finally, we soldiers became Yahweh's Angelic Host after he agreed to free us from the dimensional bubble in exchange for our eternal service to him. Besides, we had no idea where our home was or even if it existed any more. I still wonder whether the war rages on. As I said, I don't know where home is relative to us, even now. To our command we may have only been gone for minutes. On the other hand, millions of years may have passed and the world I knew is either dead or so altered that it would be unrecognizable to me. Of course, if it has only been a few minutes I'm so altered I'd hardly be recognizable to them.

"After Yahweh freed us, we waited in a kind of swirling suspension. We all had our environmental armor on so no matter what we were going through or where we would end up, exposure wasn't an issue. Finally the wormhole spat us out. Since there's no way to predict where a wormhole will send you, we were amazed when we discovered a world with relatively sentient life near us.

"Yahweh reached out with his mind to survey the world. When he realized there were already gods in the world he was somewhat dismayed. But there wasn't any other world with life close by and he didn't want to waste his stolen power looking. He decided on a sparsely populated but beautiful place near what is now called the Middle East. It had the lowest concentration of gods; the ones that were there, had grown bored, and were planning their departure. They really cared less about his arrival, so when he arrived, the first being he met was a human being named Adam.

"For awhile this world wasn't such a bad deal for us. When we first set foot in the Middle East, we were so alien we couldn't even survive without our environmental armor. That's when Yahweh saw that it was necessary to alter us.

"It was his idea to transform us into his ideal of the perfect human being, but with wings. We had to have wings! Walking was just too tedious, and, well, human. Yahweh also infused us with some modicum of power. Fortunately, our race is naturally endowed with a few esoteric powers. So Yahweh enhanced our native powers and expanded upon them using the essence of a local god he'd slain.

"Actually, Yahweh's design was quite ingenious. He made it so our commingled essence with the slain god's would continually grow more powerful, independent of any outside help. Why he didn't use the power himself, I don't know. But that's when we became the Angelic Host. We were immortal and had the power of minor gods in our own right. For eight of us something happened in the process that exponentially increased the affect. Eventually we became as powerful as many of the native gods, and Yahweh called us 'Archangels'.

"The native gods of this world spent much of their time squabbling and weren't concerned about the mortal humans for reasons I'll explain later. But Yahweh knew there was a chance for him to take over rule of all the mortals. In order to continue with his plan for domination of the world, he needed to find his own place away from the native gods and their pettiness. An adjacent, unoccupied dimension seemed a perfect place and he named it 'Heaven'."

Convergence III

"All of this effort was taking its toll on Yahweh's stolen power. He had misjudged how much power was needed to change us into Archangels and then to make his Heaven. It was interesting to find out that his natural powers would increase with the worship of human mortals. And of course their souls were rich in energy once he managed to grab them. The more worshippers he controlled, combined with their level of daily devotion determined his level of power and overall strength as a god. Without worshippers he'd be no more than a simple spirit. He'd barely be able to burn a bush let alone rule the world. Yahweh wanted more. He was siphoning off some of our power as we gained worshippers, but he was having a problem getting the worshippers he needed to achieve his goal of domination. His message, intended to recruit mortal souls, was not spreading quickly enough through humanity for his needs. He knew that if he became weaker than any of the ancient gods such as, Buddha, Odin, or Atlas, or the Angelic Host (with which he had an agreement of freedom for servitude) there might be a problem.

"Yahweh realized that a massive flood was coming to the Middle East and decided to use this as an opportunity for recruiting more worshippers. So he sent a message through his faithful human beings that the God of Gods, Yahweh, was about to punish humanity for not praising his name. His faithful followers spread the word, but were laughed at and ridiculed. You probably remember how the flood came about, but in case you were imprisoned during that period, I'll tell you how it happened. What is now called the Suez Canal used to be a gigantic land bridge. It was only a matter of time before the bridge broke due to slow erosion processes brought on by climatic change. The trick Yahweh used was to predict when it would happen, and to capitalize on the horrible outcome. The prediction of the devastation drew masses of people to worship him. So his powers were multiplied thousands of times over. Not only was he saved from extinction, he was becoming one of the earth's most powerful deities.

"Seeing the foothold this gave him in the relatively unpopulated Middle East, he realized that scaring people into worshiping him was working. And his lust for power grew along with his powers. All the vengeful killing, turning people to salt, devastating plagues, were only a small example of his greed for power. Soon he was becoming bored and he also came to realize that depicting himself as a murderous bastard who kills people just because they won't get on their knees, only worked on certain humans. The other humans were becoming resentful of the madness. Yahweh kept an eye on us and saw that the Buddha was attracting worshippers through gentle means. Now that Yahweh had expanded his powers, he could try something new, more challenging, like a softer touch on the other humans to see if he could attract more followers.

"Also the other deities associated with this world were beginning to notice his activities in the Middle East. Yahweh, though not ready to take on any major gods, became a master at telling stories, rewriting history to suit his needs. Gradually, he's been using this story telling as one of his methods for influencing the masses, slowly whittling away at the truth of his murderous nature. A lot of us found it distasteful but we had an agreement with Yahweh for our freedom. But, finally he crossed the line.

"This is the bit about me and the rest of the 'fallen angels'. I don't know if you guys ever read Yahweh's version in his bible, but the party line is found in Ezekiel 28:17; roughly stated, 'You (that's me, Lucifer) were lifted up because of thy beauty; thou hast corrupted thy wisdom by reason of thy brightness.' Do you guys know what that really means? I overheard a conversation Yahweh was having with Michael discussing his end game which as you know is obliterating anyone that will not follow him. Since I wasn't about to be part of mass genocide, my wisdom was corrupted. The part about my pride was that I used my own judgment instead of following him like a sheep and decided I wanted nothing to do with him. After informing the rest of the host, a third of them agreed with me and joined my side. As for the archangels that stayed, part of it was the deal, but the truth is I think they were starting to believe him. The Michael I remember would never have been a part of this genocide idea. That's where the Christened one, came in. Yahweh knew he had to redo his image if he was going to increase his worshipper base. He also realized he needed to make the story believable as to why he changed into a compassionate god, so he made up the Christ to be the fall guy." Lucifer continued.

"Is he really the son of Yahweh," asks Atlas?

"According to Yahweh, we're all his sons; that's how much of a megalomaniac he is." Lucifer shook his head. "Beyond that, the Christ was just a regular kid that got picked out to change Yahweh's image. I tried to warn him. That story about me tempting Christ on the mountain; I got him up there to show him the beauty of the world. I was trying to show him what Yahweh was planning; to destroy humanity. Two thousand years later it's me, good ol' Lucifer, trying to tempt the Christ with the 'worldly' evils. But by the time I got to the Christ, he was already too brainwashed, believing he alone could save the world. He really believed he was the one and only Son of Yahweh, and he wouldn't believe me. I really wished I had realized Yahweh's plan earlier; maybe I could have convinced the Christ not to go along with Yahweh. That's why you don't hear about the first 30 years of Christ's life. He spent most of it not believing the notion of him being the Son of Yahweh. But when you have a god whispering in your ear every day, giving you power to work miracles, anybody is going to get brainwashed," Lucifer paused.

"Of course there was Judas in the mix. He was the Christ's best friend, and he never really betrayed him. For Yahweh's plan to work Christ had to be the sacrificial lamb; he had to die. Gabriel, who was Yahweh's go to guy, went to Judas offering him power, fame, and anything else that he thought might tempt Judas in exchange for his betrayal of his friend. Judas adamantly refused. So, Gabriel took over his body and all of you know what happened next. Before Gabriel left Judas' body, he wiped away any memories Judas had of Gabriel's intervention. Then thinking that somehow he had betrayed his best friend, Judas hanged himself.

"Christ never found out the truth. You know those two grew up together. Judas was always trying to convince Christ he could live his own life. He didn't need to listen to some voice in his head telling him what to do. That's why he was chosen to betray Christ. He needed to be put out of the picture, silenced. They couldn't just kill him or Christ might have renounced Yahweh for the death of his best friend. So the plan had to have Judas do something Christ would feel was unforgiveable. Since bribing Judas didn't work, possessing him was the only option. The other Apostles came along later following like the sheep Yahweh wants everyone to be. Yahweh won't let the Christ remember any it of course. He's warped his memories. Now that he's in Yahweh's realm it's a whole lot easier to control him. In the Christ's recollection, I, Lucifer, conned Judas, who supposedly delighted in the idea of betraying the Christ willingly. That's all lies, of course, so when the time comes, Judas gets Gabriel, and I'll enjoy watching."

"All of the other angels that left heaven with me helped instill Judas with power and he's had millennia to prepare. So, when we all meet again, Gabriel will be in for a surprise; and before Judas is done Gabriel will be begging him for death," gloats Lucifer.

Odin replies, "I know the dwarves promise they'll have something special for Judas when he needs it."

Lucifer sighed, "The worst part is the Revelations chapter of Yahweh's bible. In the first place, I'm not trying to destroy the world. Second, how does anyone actually believe that even if I were trying to destroy the world I would let him find out? And third, if Yahweh did find out, why wouldn't I change tactics? If people would just use their heads for something other than a hairpiece, they'd see all the logical gaps in the Bible. Do you think Robert E. Lee and Ulysses S. Grant exchanged battle plans before Gettysburg?"

Atlas chimed in, "You know if humanity could just get a little formal logic as part of their early education, they'd be a lot better off."

Odin agreed, "True, so true."

Lucifer nodded and went on, "The really ingenious part of Yahweh's overall plan was to create another major belief system in Islam. He knew Christianity could only appeal to a certain segment of humanity, and an even smaller group in Judaism, so he designed another religion with different tenants in order to get the people that found Christianity unappealing. So with the three religions of Judaism, Christianity, and Islam, it really doesn't matter to Yahweh, which one they choose, they're all worshipping him, and empowering him. For him and only him, sentient worship brings him power and that's what he's after.

"And if he's successful in destroying everyone that doesn't worship him that takes away power going to the other deities. That's his endgame as to this planet, control of all worshippers, death to all non-worshippers. He'll leave some of the angels. He'll leave one of the archangels, I charge. Then he'll move to another world to gather more followers. That's why he's more aggressive in actively attracting followers than Odin, Atlas, Zeus, and most of the other gods. Their power stems from themselves and it doesn't matter whether they have no followers or a trillion, their power is still the same." Sighed Lucifer.

"Enough of the history lesson!" complains Odin. "How is it that our players got dumped in a carnivorous forest being attacked by armed guards? We paid that charlatan more than enough to keep them alive at least so that they could try to get in and not be in life and death peril within minutes of arrival," exclaims Odin.

"Well that's what we get for having Monkey find us the transporter. Relying on the Chinese Trickster might not have been the best idea," replies Lucifer. "We're lucky we managed to get them close at all. Sending someone that far is an inherently risky transmittance. Besides if we'd done it ourselves we could have only sent them so far. This way, if the Christ's hordes do figure out what we're up to they won't be able to reach them."

Chapter 2

> Presaging, since with sorrow and hearts distress
> Wearied I fell asleep: but now lead on;
> In mee is no delay; with thee to goe, [615]
> Is to stay here; without thee here to stay,
> Is to go hence unwilling; thou to mee
> Art all things under Heav'n, all places thou,
> Who for my wilful crime art banisht hence.
> This further consolation yet secure [620]
> I carry hence; though all by mee is lost,
> Such favour I unworthie am voutsaft
> —John Milton Paradise Lost Book 12

I wake up to a face that belongs to Michelle now. "What the hell happened? I thought we all died." I shake my head in disbelief. "How the hell did I survive that? Hell, how did you survive getting most of your torso blown away?"

"The forest saved me, saved us. When I was alert enough to think, I had asked the flora to heal our entire group. So everybody's fine. I'd just like to know where we are, right now," asked Michelle.

I gaze at the sky: it is still the colors of fox fire and the forest is still the same carnivorous lavender. I am having a really hard time believing this. But who cares whether it's real or not. It's not like I was having the time of my life back in, back where, reality? So, I say to myself as I get up, "Let's see where we go from here."

Harvey Bivens wanders over looking healthy and refreshed. He takes me aside, "Good you're awake. Michelle probably didn't want to tell you but the plants initially didn't want to work on you. They told her you were already dead. They could sense vital functions but no life force, no soul. The forest told her even if they healed you, you'd be basically a vegetable. She had to beg them to try. They still say you have no soul or life force aura. But you look OK to me. Hell, who knows! They are sentient trees that eat people, so I don't think they have room to talk about your aura," scoffed Bivins. "Look," he continued, "I looted what I could from those horse creatures and the remaining bodies. I got a few coins which I'll assume is money around here and some food," he spreads a wide palm with some shiny silver-like discs. Then looking away, he says, "We had to get rid of the horses and all of the other evidence. If those guys were guardians, like they said, then we just killed 22 of this world's cops." Harvey looks at me rather displeased, "I've got 20 years on the force. I know how cops think, even if they're from some weird place. So that's the first thing I did after I got up . . . get rid of the evidence. I told Michelle to command the trees to eat the mounts, the remaining bodies, and then bury all the evidence as deep as they could. Ecogirl had a fit over the mounts, but after explaining to her we were all dead if she didn't, she finally agreed." Bivens shrugged.

I look around at our group, "Where are Rodney, Linh, and Bobby?" I ask.

Bivens reports, "I sent Linh off to go scouting. Rodney and Bobby are both trying out their new skills."

"Alright," I nod, "By the way what's the head count?

"We've got thirteen people, if that's the right word, including you and me. Everybody says they're from Leah's party. I guess I believe them, but they've changed one way or another. You're actually the odd one. Outside of looking quite a bit younger and fitter you're the only one that hasn't been transformed." Then Harvey tells me, "You don't look different but you seem, I don't know, actually a little off."

"You know, Harvey, that I do know a little about martial arts," I nudge, "Anyway I don't know what's going on, but I want to get out of this forest and find a road or something leading to whatever civilization this place has. We need to figure out where we are and more importantly what areas get you killed on sight around here."

Harvey agrees, "This is worse than the jungle in Nam."

"What abilities have the others demonstrated?" I ask.

"Well, for one thing, there is one guy that the plants insisted leave. Everywhere he went the plants started wilting, so they kicked him out! Other than the ones who fought the guards, no one else has really displayed anything remarkable. They look weird but that's about it." Harvey noted.

I look at the square build of Harvey and say, "It kind of makes sense. Only when one of us was in peril did someone transform to help save him. So I guess fear or adrenaline triggers the changes."

"We're all back to some sort of normal," Harvey says, "Bobby is big but not gigantic like he was. I'm sort of the same: A little stronger maybe. But, I'm wondering about you. Those beams from those guards blew a hole in everybody else, but bounced off you like a flashlight beam."

"I have no idea what that was all about," I shake my head. "All I know is that I can see and feel everything around me without even looking. Maybe it has something to do with this no aura business." I look away, "Anyway I want to get out of here the minute Linh gets back. We can all get acquainted with everyone else on the road."

The small group begins walking.

Rodney says, "I'm detecting a large group of beings towards the south. They're basically stationary. It might be an encampment or a town."

"I feel like Alice in Wonderland," I spout. "This place is just too weird with the energies in the plants and rocks and earth; there are all kinds of lights flying through the sky." I say.

"And all of them are alive," Rodney confirms. "I can't really make out individual life signs but large groups glow, like a bright light, in my head."

I stare at Rodney noticing he has grown a third eye on his forehead. "Damn, Rodney, what the hell is that thing?" I see that it is opaque white like his other ones were. His regular eyes have returned to normal. "Maybe it has something to do with the Tibetan third eye. Can you see out of it?"

"Not in the traditional sense." He says. "It's almost like seeing heat glowing in the air above some living things."

We wander on out of the woods. Even the plants and the animals seem to be out of a bad acid trip. Thousands of little things are weird and look wrong. I think I see sprites and fairies dancing in a mushroom forest. There are lavender blossoms growing out of mushroom stalks a hundred feet tall. Seemingly ordinary plants transform into animal-like beings and run off; or grow jaws and try to bite you if you get too close. Other barely corporeal beings walk around us. The place is teeming with all kinds of life. In the sky I see what appears to be a flying pack of winged boar.

I notice the guy the forest kicked out. It looks like my friend, Martin Korematsu, but I barely recognize him. He normally plays in a death metal band that does local shows around town. Last time I saw him was at Leah's party where he filled in for the band's guitarist. Martin must be hard up for cash to agree to play with a pop band. I met Martin a couple of years ago at a bar in which he was performing. After the show he put on a Manowar track which led to Martin commenting on how Therion would have been a better option. He and I had a debate lasting for over an hour before we agreed to call it a draw.

Martin is an interesting character. He's half white, half Asian, and all strange. While his face expresses primarily his Anglo blood his eyes give away his Oriental heritage. His parents met while his mother was working as a molecular biologist in Tokyo. For as long as I've known Martin, he always wears the same basic attire; some metal band's shirt and worn jeans. From the look of him he's just another metal head in his late twenties. But in reality he is a genius. By day, he actually is a physicist. He got his PhD from M.I.T. at age twenty-one. However, a childhood of tutors, private schools, and forced study had done a number on him. In his youth he found a cassette of Iron Maiden's "The Number of the Beast" album. He was absorbed by it, listening to it every night. It was the only real act of rebellion against his classical music lessons. The one time he mentioned a desire to learn to play contemporary style music, he received a beating that left him bruised for weeks. When he finally was free of the classical shackles, he taught himself how to play the bass and guitar.

Now, he works as a theoretical physicist for a research group studying neutrinos. Despite being well compensated, he's always broke due to a drug habit that would make Timothy Leary shudder. I've seen Martin take every drug I've ever heard of and quite a few I haven't. Martin's favorite is unfortunately methamphetamine. This drug has turned him into a thin, almost emaciated, toothless addict. His employers are well aware of his proclivities; you can't miss them. And anybody else would have been fired ages ago. But he makes breakthroughs in just weeks that normally would take a team of researchers months. Sometimes he doesn't even show up for work. He's either getting high, playing his music, or both. However, these "vacations" from work do something to his brain and when he comes back in he'll have devised a solution to some problem his colleagues haven't even begun to figure out. So at the end of the day, his employers just let him be.

Over the years Martin and I have become good friends. While he's embraced more than his share of excesses over the years, there are times when even he voices his concerns. A self-proclaimed nihilist Martin would always quote a random Heidegger passage in response and pass me the glass pipe.

I finally take a good look at Martin. I should have been shocked but in light of recent events I wasn't the least surprised. Martin has always looked gaunt and depressingly gothic but it was nothing compared to what I saw before me. He exuded a preternatural macabre visage. Martin's skin had turned blue as death. His fingernails were ebony. His eyes were hollow and sunken. The whites of his eyes had turned a twilight crepuscular color. Even now as he walked everything around him wilted from whatever consumptive quality had a grip on him.

Martin finally notices me and I ask, "What's up brother?"

Martin spouts, "Dude this is some serious brain damage, man. Either I'm on the best trip of my life or something seriously fucked up's going on."

"Quit fucking around and give me your best take on this, Martin. What do you think's going on? Do you even remember coming here? I mean after the fire do you remember anything before you woke up here?" I ask.

Martin replies, "I've got some theories but you are going to think I'm crazy."

"Crazy?" I mutter, "Did you see the pack of flying boars? And did you notice the fact that everybody has been transformed into something out of a Role Playing Game? I'm open to pretty much anything you can think of right now."

"If I had to guess, I'd say we're all hooked up to some sort of machine and this is some sort of government mind control experiment," he smiled.

I laughed, "That's possible but why would they pick a bunch of people that are going to be missed? I mean me and you sure. Everybody would just think we overdosed in an alley. But the big dudes and the straight laced lawyers are bound to be missed unless they're all part of an hallucination."

"The logical extreme of that line of thought is that you're not real either. Let's accept, just for fun, the premise that what we see is real and go from there," he suggests.

"Okay," I agree, "but you're not going to like what I've got to say. You know all the theories in quantum mechanics are based on assertions. Basically we guess at what a good starting place is and go from there. Remember Edward Witten, in 1995 he proposed what's been called the Second Superstring Revolution by introducing M-theory."

Martin chimes in, "Yeah, I know, he basically theorized there are eleven dimensions and a near infinite number of worlds completely independent of each other. But unlike most parallel world theories where the laws of physics are all the same, he claims each world is completely separate from each other and has its own laws of physics."

"Even with my basic, no offense understanding of physics I know the things we've seen defy a hundred different natural laws," I admit.

Martin continues, "Well, my best bet is we got caught in some sort of wormhole and got sent here. During that process we absorbed something of this universe and that's why we changed. How or why this happened is beyond me. But you don't seem that surprised."

"You're right, Martin," I comment, "I thought of the same thing. I can't do the math like you but I read the literature. I just wanted someone else to be the first one to say it."

I pause then hushed I say, "I felt myself burn to death. Something other than the plants healed us and then transformed us, Martin."

"Yeah, but what? There is one thing," he added, "you don't seem weak. The others, especially the elf-types, say they feel weak and lethargic around me. Are you just being polite or are you not really feeling anything."

"Honestly," I say, "I can't feel a thing, bad or good. I didn't realize that you were affecting everyone, not just the plants. Maybe my not feeling anything is related to the fact that no one can focus or sense me with magic. I really need to figure out what this no aura business is about."

"I've been curious about that myself," he says, "It also may be why you didn't get physically transformed like everyone else. What if part of you didn't make it all the way or ended up somewhere slightly different than everybody else. I've got a theory that your essence/soul/aura, whatever, is out of phase with everything else. Let's say it's still connected to you but is in a slightly different dimension. Let's just guess for a moment. Think of an 11 dimensional array. We stayed on the same line for most of them. But maybe the rest of us got sent across, say six dimensions and your essence is in a seventh. It's just a guess but it explains why you got burned by the spear but no other magic has worked on you; intangible magic that requires detecting or focusing on your mind or soul does not work on you. However, if the energy has been turned into something tangible already it can hurt you. I'm sure there's a lot more to all this but it's a start," Martin finishes.

"Everyone else I've talked to has said the same thing but I remember falling forever through something," I look away and say quietly, "I also remember a figure. I know you're going to think I'm really wacked, but I swear it looked like Odin. The silhouette was of a man with a spear on a six legged horse with a raven on each shoulder." Shuffling my feet I then say, "There is something else; it seems that the transformations of everyone are based on their personalities and nature.

"Bobby's a bounty hunter and he turns into some sort of lycanthrope. He says even when not in that form his senses are heightened especially his nose. He says he can track scent like a dog now, whereas most of the lawyer types turned into elf-like personas. Elves in Nordic mythology are the jaded aristocracy of the culture. What is more fitting for a bunch of high level corporate lawyers?" I smirk.

Martin says, "Give me a breakdown of the rest of the group? I kind of know Bobby and Linh but only casually. The rest I have no clue about."

"Well," I start, "since most of them are out hunting and right now, there's plenty of time for a rundown of everyone. About six of them are out with Bobby. The rest are searching for a spot to make camp."

I surveyed the group for him. "I know most of them. The most successful is Magnus McCullough. He is the senior partner of the biggest firm in town. And he's a legend. Between golden gloves champion and Harvard Law honors he started a meteoric rise that has made him one of the most influential people in the country. Senators and Fortune 500 CEOs literally have him on their speed dial. He's won several Supreme Court cases. He speaks a number of different languages so fluently that native speakers cannot tell he's self taught."

I spotted him a few yards away and gestured in his direction. "That's him over there, the large elf-like man in his late sixties, though he looks younger and stronger than I've ever seen him. I guess he could be considered one of the elf-types, but he looks more like himself than the others, heavier and just bigger."

Martin commented, "Man, talk about an aura of confidence, you could take a shower in it."

"Yeah," I said, "he's not a man you'd want to cross, either. Nine years ago his wife of many years was killed by a gang during a carjacking. Literally every member of that gang disappeared over the course of six months. And a dozen people went missing without a single body showing up. I sometimes wonder if Harvey Bivens was in on it. The D.A. wasn't even close to being stupid enough to consider charges. Besides, there wasn't an iota of evidence. As far as the police were concerned, they must have felt he'd done the public a service," I snorted.

Martin shrugged, "I hope I never show up on his radar screen."

I continued, "Then there was the shooting five years ago at his firm. One of the associates had a breakdown and went to the top level and started shooting the partners. While everyone hid, including security, Magnus walked right up to him and grabbed the gun. The official story is the associate fell out a window during the scuffle. In reality, everyone knows Magnus slammed the gun out of his hand, grabbed the man by the throat, and threw him out of the most convenient window. Mind you, Magnus was sixty at that point and the associate couldn't have been more than thirty."

"Next up, is Cory. I don't know much about him personally other than he is the reason that Leah's firm had the party. He was their client in a huge class action suit against the fishing industry. Having grown up in Alaska he worked on crab ships doing the most dangerous type of fishing known. In that industry it was common to lose at least a man a season. He'd been a Navy S.E.A.L. and when he got out he went right back to the ocean. He'd fished every ocean and sea in the world. Finally, he'd come back to Alaska, back to the crab fishing he'd grown up on. The lawsuit had something to do with the fishing refineries unfair trade practices but all anyone cared about was they'd just made the law firm a ton of money. I'm not sure exactly what Cory's transformed into but I am sure it had something to do with the sea. Besides his fishing background, I noticed that he had what looked like gills on each side of his torso. Plus his hands are webbed and his eyes seemed to have a film like a fish so most likely he can clearly see underwater. While for the most part he looks human, I'm waiting to see what happens if he gets into a fight on water.

"Then there's Eric. He's become an elf too. He is probably the most charismatic trial attorney in town. He's won cases where every single fact was against him. He specializes in personal injury and occasionally does criminal trials. Magnus wins through thoughtful arguments based on well researched facts and analysis. Eric basically knows how to con a jury. He was a junior partner at Magnus's firm and told everyone he was a partner. He never takes cases where the judge was the adjudicator of fact. If he pulled his stunts on a judge he'd get thrown out of a courtroom on his head. However, when it comes down to twelve regular people that don't know anything about the law, he can have them thinking this is their chance to stick up for the little guy, even when the little guy is a billion dollar corporation and DNA is no more than a myth. He's a good looking and incredibly charming showman that knows how to tell a story. He donates to charities and is considered a pillar of the community, but it is all for show, and is just a lie. I don't have much else to say about him other than that he is garbage. The man is fake and shallow, and treats his wife like shit.

"I like Evelyn, his wife. She's a microbiologist that came from a prominent wealthy family. She was the youngest of the litter and probably the smartest. Eric married her because he had political aspirations and she had a huge trust. Plus her family had connections. She married him because her family thought it would be a useful alliance with one of the most powerful firms in the country, one worth sacrificing a daughter for. Evelyn is brilliant in her own way but she's a bit overtly naïve. She pretends that Eric really is working every single one of those late hours, instead of facing the fact Eric has cheated on her with dozens of women. Her family put so much pressure on her to marry him that she finally gave in. Once I saw her after Eric had lost a case. She had a bruised lip and black eye that she blamed on a lab accident. It had taken two tasers and six security guards to stop me from killing him. The only reason I hadn't found him later was she begged me not to. She's got classic battered women's syndrome. She's told me more than once that she just needs to change. She thinks it is her fault. She generally believes that she's a bad wife and is bringing it on herself. While he's mostly verbally abusive, in the end it's not right. To be honest I'm tempted to kill him if we find ourselves alone. I don't understand how an otherwise intelligent, rational woman can't see she deserves better.

"Evelyn has been transformed into something different from the others. She is a pretty women but in a very ordinary way, and she's normally too busy with her research to care about make-up or her hair. Now she looks dramatically sleek in shiny black skin-tight clothes, long straight blue-black hair, tiny demon-like horns and tail, and beautiful gossamer bat wings. She exudes an unearthly gothic beauty that saturates her being, and mine.

"Next up is Ace. He's a good guy. I met him competing at a Renaissance festival a few years back. He was competing at a sword fighting competition. He's the defending champ at the melee. Apparently he went to the Olympics for fencing. We didn't see each other for a few years until I ran into him in court as opposing counsel. He made me swear never to tell anyone from the firm about his hobby. Again, aside from being an elf, I don't know of any powers.

"Then there are my boys, Linh and Bobby.

"I first got to know Bobby when he showed up at my gym six or so years ago and we've grown to be good friends. Bobby is a one stop shopping mall for people with problems. He does detective work, retrieval, bounty hunting, and bail bonds. He is a bounty hunter in the literal sense of the word. If the government has a price on your head he'll track you down. He likes his work. He's tracked drug lords down for the Mexican Government; Colombian dealers for both the Colombian and US government. Anybody with a price tag over 50K, he's after you. He'll track down just about anything for you. Other than Bivens who is a police detective, Bobby's the best in town. And he's a good guy too; he also does rescue work, mostly when kids get kidnapped and you don't want to go to the cops. As long as you don't ask questions he'll do it. He retrieved one of the local crime family's daughter a couple years ago so he's fairly well protected. Prior to bounty work, he spent eight years as a Green Beret until he was discharged for assaulting his CO. His CO nearly got Bobby's men killed by sending them needlessly into harm's way. The position could easily have been taken out without any friendly casualties by calling in an air strike. Yet even after knowing his order would get more men killed, the CO wouldn't rescind it. So Bobby decked him and said the CO was incapacitated. He gave the order to fall back and called in the air strike. The court martial considered the facts surrounding the assault and only gave him a couple years at Leavenworth. Ever since he got out, he's been a bounty hunter.

"Linh is technically a computer programmer for a software company. The company is owned by a Hong Kong triad that decided to tryout the U.S. market. He's one of their top hackers. It started in college when one his friend's was flunking out of college. Linh spent every night for months getting the guys grades up. When he graduated he found out his friend from Hong Kong was the son of a prominent triad member. Like a lot of Vietnamese youths he'd been in a street gang growing up so he wasn't averse to working for a non-US company and doing some under-the-table hacking. So whenever a company's getting a competitive advantage they send him in to upload a virus or hack their trade secrets. If that doesn't work they tend to just burn the place down, so he says. Bobby gets Linh to help him when there's a software component to his work. Sometimes the three us go hunting for bad guys just for fun. I guess Linh is like a shadow in a way. He's going through the holes and backdoors of supposedly impenetrable systems. He also has been doing Muay Thai since he was a kid ever since his family escaped from the jungles of Vietnam east of Da Nang in the Hue province. He's one of the best strikers I've ever met and we've taught him some grappling to go with it. Although he thinks of himself as fully American, he still honors our Vietnamese culture. I strayed away from our faith for years until I met him. Now I too study the ways of Lord Buddha as does he."

Martin asks, "I take it you haven't got disbarred yet. I mean you've been up for ethics violations two dozen times and every time they apologize for the mistake."

I smile, "Well, you'd be amazed at what you can find on people with a little help from your friends. Take my little assault on Eric, for example. Linh found evidence on two of Eric's colleagues stealing from clients and one case of insider trading. Bobby got pictures of Eric cheating on his wife and another of his colleague snorting coke at a gay bar. The last one was running for a judgeship on a conservative platform mind you. Every time they've found some way to get me off. Worst comes to worst, why I just bribe them", I say with a laugh.

Martin mentions, "You've already told me about Bivens so there's one last one. It's that girl isn't it!"

"Fuck off Marty!" and I get up and walk away.

After talking with Martin, I decided to get in some training. Even though more subtle than everyone else, I realized that I was continuing to transform as well. Although definitely still human I felt I was stronger and faster than I'd ever been. So I experimented with some moves, testing my balance which has always been my weakest part. So I could hardly believe it when I was able to do flips and tumbles like an acrobat. I accidentally scrape myself. The wound took only moments to heal. I'm sure I'm not a superhuman be any means but at the very least I probably had the attributes of a world class triathlon competitor.

The group decides on a cave they found to spend the night. As they start to step up camp they hear the sound of something thunderous charging out of the cave. It is a giant lizard that resembles a komodo dragon; a komodo dragon that is fifty feet long and appears to be roughly 12,000 lbs, that is. We must be trespassing on in its territory. The lizard spits a ball of mucous. Bivens instinctively calls up his power, and without even realizing it, a wall of earth appears in front of the lizard. The spittle is a very caustic acid and when it splatters off the wall, it hits a couple trees melting them like butter. Roaring ferociously, the lizard charges the wall. Bivens tries to reinforce it as much as he can but the lizard breaks through. However, it was visibly shaken by the effort and appears dazed. That gives everyone ample time to scatter.

I shout to Michelle to use the plants to get the group to safety. She immediately obliges, and the vines pull the wiggling bodies safely away from the combat zone. Leah tries to hit the lizard with her bow but the arrows bounce right off. Michelle then commands the plants to attack the lizard but the acid just melts the plants. She then uses long snake-like vines to bind the lizard legs but it rips right through them like nothing.

Bobby's adrenalin kicks in and he transforms into his lycanthrope beast, charging the lizard head on. His razor sharp horns barely pierce the beasts hide. Linh activates his power over shadows. He feels his control grow, and catalyzed by fear of imminent death, his powers transform him like the last time. But now he can make the shadows do his bidding. He reaches out to all of the shadows in the area and wills them to go after the lizard. The molten shadows wrap around the lizard and bind it in place. Bivens and Bobby attack at the same time. Bobby hits the same spot he had cut with his poisoned tail. As Linh's shadows hold it in place, Bobby injects his entire reserve of poison into the lizard. Bivens sprouts spears of stone from each of his hands. He keeps pounding on the lizard, but the hide is so tough and the lizard is just too big; he does little damage.

It is short of a minute but Linh is approaching his limit holding the lizard down. I feel impotent as I see my friends fight while I stand by, seemingly helpless against this monster. There really wasn't anything I could do with my bare hands, and then I notice a number of boulders on a rock face above that look like they can be loosened. I climb up the cliff wall faster than I should have been able to, and yell down my plan. Just as the lizard breaks free of Linh's shadows, I thrust a branch under the largest boulder and leverage it loose unlatching a landslide of rocks. Linh grabs everyone close by and uses the shadows to transport them to safety. Tons of rocks and debris hit the lizard. I think I've killed it but then it struggles out of the pile. It is hurt it but it still has some life. Rodney barely dodges a wad of acid when the Lizard hurls at him again. Unable to move out of the way, Rodney somehow raises his arms forming a shield of bright white energy. The acid bounces off, harmlessly. Then Rodney shoots back at the Lizard with energy like the elves used in the forest. Shearing through two trees and a rock like butter, the rays strike the lizard dead on; but they only cause minor damage to the lizard. Rodney fires again and again each time scoring. After a dozen blasts the huge monster starts to weaken dramatically. The lizard spits again and this time Rodney's energy shield only half defends. While it diverts the acid it does not stop the force and he is flung back 20 feet slamming into a tree, unconscious.

Bivens comes up with a new strategy and using his power over earth he begins to create a sinkhole to try and suck the lizard in. It was slowing down the monster but it was obvious that the lizard was too massive to be sucked in. Bivens kept up the effort as long as he could, but after ten or so seconds, blood began to run from his mouth. In a few more moments, Bivens was forced to let go. Finally, the lizard hits Bivens with its tail sending him flying through the air. He lands on his head and stays down. The lizard starts to come after Bivens, but Bobby attacks again head on. He gets knocked back fifty feet but charges again. The lizard rears back and we know he's about to spit when suddenly out from Bobby's mouth comes a burst of flames.

"Well that's new," I thought.

The flames seared the lizard badly. Between the poison, rockslide, and now flames, the beast was weakening. Bobby gasps finally and runs out of fire. The lizard slams Bobby with his tail again, knocking him on his back.

It then comes down with its teeth and bites Bobby gnawing on his shoulder. Bobby's a goner if I don't do something, anything. I leap down from the rocks concentrating a kick at the Lizard with all my might. I bounce off like rubber. At least I have its attention. Everyone was out of the fight and now the lizard was on me. At the every last instant I hear the whizzing of arrows flying by from above. One strikes the lizard right in the eye. Magnus was the only one still standing and he manages to shoot the lizard right through the eye from a hundred yards. He keeps shooting with incredible aim. An arrow precisely hits its other eye, and they keep hitting it over and over again through the eyes. The huge tail swings back. Blinded, it misses everyone and hits the ground next to him with an earth-jarring thump. That is enough to wrench the bow from Magnus hands and send him flying back against a tree, unable to move. The lizard charges. Blinding it was not enough; its other senses took over. Magnus looks like he's a goner but then a fireball hits the lizard between the eyes. Evelyn's taut body was soaring and hovering over the monster throwing little fireballs. Apparently, those wings aren't just for show. As good as she looks; her fireballs are just not inflicting enough damage. She keeps firing but the lizard is aware of her now. He spits a blast that she barely dodges dropping her to within range of its tail. It strikes her and sends her flying. I think I am the last one left to fight, and this time I know I am really dead. But, as the lizard turns toward me, Martin jumps up a good fifty feet onto its back and latches on. Martin begins to realize more of his potency, and he focuses his consumptive aura on the beast. He feels its power and begins to drink in its essence, consuming its life force. The lizard feels itself weakening and tries to buck him off. Martin, already possessing supernatural strength, is getting stronger moment by moment as he absorbs the lizard's essence. Then, when he feels the beast wriggling beneath him, he rams his fist through the beast's hide. He grabs on to the screaming monster's muscles and continues to suck from the beast-trough. He attaches with his other arm. He is giddy with strength as his vampiric power saps the lizard's strength. After a few minutes the lizard was empty of life and fell dead. Its body withers like a dead flower and turns gray. While some of the others look away, as scared of Martin as they were the lizard, I walk over to him and congratulate him.

"You stole his soul man, how metal was that?" I ask.

Bivens, Bobby, and Linh are healing miraculously fast with Michele's help. They all go over to him.

"Did you know you could do that," asked Bobby?

Martin replied, "Hell No, man, I just felt a change and then for the first time since we got here I could actually sense a life force and focus my power on it."

The others chime in divulging similar new experiences.

I move away from the group, feeling again like I am the only one without powers.

We travel for two more days in the direction Rodney tells us to go, and finally we come to a road. It is made out of an organic crystal material and undulates ever so minutely under foot. Harvey gives it a couple of whacks. He actually makes a dent but the road immediately fixes itself. I suggest that he might refrain from doing that again; no telling what it will do to us. The road is well developed to say the least. I notice that as you walk, the road actually helps you along. It appears to be covered with tiny filaments that move you along dependent on the direction you apply pressure. Pretty amazing.

My senses become alerted again and I freeze. I perceive a group of people ahead of us. A dozen of what appear to be bandits confront us on the road. The bandits are a hodgepodge of different races. Some of them are human. These are the first "normal" humanoids we've seen since arriving here. There are a couple of troll-like beings, a bipedal lizard, plus an elf who appears to be their leader. We ready ourselves for an attack. I think to myself, "Is getting into this many fights common here or are we just that unlucky?" The bandits demand the usual that being our money and the girls, like that's going to happen.

Bivens says, "Make sure to keep the elf alive. I want to get some answers about where we are."

Magnus signals us back; it is obvious that his power is about to manifest. "His voice bellowed full of confidence, "How dare you attack us? All of you kneel. Except for you elf, everyone take out your weapon and kill yourself." Magnus's extraordinary voice; the unique power given to Magnus was a voice that could compel a troop of bandits to kill themselves.

The bandits actually obey. Each one of them guts himself in one way or another. No one really knows what to say: this raw display of power is staggering. I believe it must only work on sentient creatures with language capabilities since this talent had not been manifested during the fight with the lizard.

Bivens grabs the elf from behind, "I'm going to get some answers from this guy about where we are. Please don't follow me and ignore the screams." Bivens took the elf off into the woods and commenced an interrogation.

While waiting, I decide it is time to talk to Magnus. "Mr. McCullough, could we have a word?" I ask.

"It's Magnus here," he says casually.

I confront him face to face, "What are you? I don't mean what you've become since you came here. I mean what did you start off as? You aren't just a lawyer. According to Bobby, you move and track through the woods better than a Beret. You make traps and bows like it is second nature. Furthermore, you seem to know some spells unlike the others. They have powers that come unbidden. You seem to know actual rituals and incantations. Martin's the only other one that knows incantations like that, but he grew up attending a Theravada Buddhist temple. He got taught that by the monks. What you do is different but it seems familiar to me, a lot like Celtic magic. Where did you learn your craft?" I looked him straight in the eye, "Don't lie to me! At night you've tried to be subtle but I see you patrolling the grounds."

Magnus smiles and shoots back, "Hold on there, one thing at a time. I'll tell you the whole story, but I can't have anyone else know. You'll have to be the only person outside of West Virginia who knows what I am. Not even my children know." He sighed and pointed to a couple of boulders. "It's a long story." They sat down and he began, "I was born in the Southern Appalachian Mountains of West Virginia. Our clan still keeps the old ways from Ireland. I grew up speaking more Gaelic than English, and spent the first twenty years of my life living off the land like anybody from our area. I saw a recruiter going into town one day and joined the infantry, traipsing from one battlefield to another until my four years were up. On my way home I got sent to Boston instead of Virginia by mistake. I had maybe twenty bucks in my pocket and no idea what to do or where to go. I have a natural gift for languages that is bolstered by the gift of sight (he could see the supernatural and moments into the future among other things.) While stationed overseas, I learned two dialects of Arabic, some German and a fair bit of Spanish during my enlistment without really trying. Just being around it, I pick it up. My ear has always been especially perceptive. I didn't know what to do so I ended up getting a job doing construction. I took some classes at a local junior college to collect my G.I.Bill, but I assumed I'd head back home when I had the money. Then one day I pushed a man out of the way of a speeding car saving his life. He happened to be the assistant dean at Harvard. You know what happened afterwards. What you've seen me do has mostly been simple warding spells but I am capable of more. Especially in this place, it's like gravity is lighter when it comes to lifting magic. My family taught me the craft from the day I could speak. My clan has been practicing Appalachian

Magic since before they came here from Ireland. I wasn't the most adept by far but I can pull off a few glamours, the more sophisticated spells. Our world might not be full of magic like this one but magic still exists. I haven't forgotten the old ways or the old gods. Many of the fae folk came with us to the America's, you know. My annual hunting trip is really an excuse to go back home, even though people are always speculating about some secret deal or other. I couldn't imagine how strong some of them would be if they were here. Why grandmother can make it rain and most of my family can turn into at least one animal of their choice. Here I probably could do the same but I haven't tried." Magnus smiled and stretched his limbs. "So now you know all the stories, about me coming from a wealthy confidential family, are a lie. I spent the first twenty years of my life living in a dirt-floor room. I grew up around more fairies than humans. I can track a man or animal across a hundred miles if need be but I didn't learn to read until I was sixteen. When I was supposedly partying in my family's villa in Europe, I was getting shot at for some cause I didn't understand." He looked at me straight on, "So now you know, but please keep it to yourself."

After an hour of screaming and cries from the captured elf, a muffled screech ended the affair. Harvey Bivens came back with some answers. "Apparently we are on the outskirts of an Empire ruled by elves, who depend on the power of The Imperial Source for their dominance. The Source is the stolen energy from the powers of all the gods the elven gods have slain.

Harvey continues, "This world consisted of hundreds of different sentient races. Many of whom had been brought in through dimensional travel. But once, this part of this world's surface was occupied predominantly by humans. About 15,000 years ago a group of elves showed up fleeing from their own dying world. Since then, these alien elves have slowly taken over. With them have come experiments horrible and beyond belief. Many of the plants and animals one sees are the product of some elf experiments. Practically everything elves use is organic and normally alive as well. This includes everything from their ships to their weapons. Right now we are near a fringe city," Harvey paused for a moment pointing in the direction of the city.

Harvey continued, "The elves do not occupy the entire world. They own the choicest continent out of a total of nine continents. Besides the main continent, the elves have substantial populations on two more. This is one of them. To the North is frigid tundra where the strongest contingents of free humans live. They are barbarians and berserkers that worship gods named Odin, Vili, and Ve. Apparently, after they arrived, the elven gods made a nonaggression pact with the gods of the humans that once were worshipped here.

"Most of the human gods ran when ambushed, the few that stayed were killed. Except for Vili, his story is a bit different. He slew three quarters of the elven gods. He is a berserker god without any fear of death. He fought mindlessly, feeling no pain or fear. The elves knew that they could not beat him or face him head on even though they outnumbered him hundreds to one even after the losses in the ranks of the elven gods. The elven gods used a strategy where Vili could not attack the elven gods or the elves because Vili's own troops were placed in his line of attack. Now Vili could not attack without killing his own people. This resulted in many of the elves dying because of Vili's warriors killing them. But it bought them enough time so that they could use the life force of all the gods Vili had already killed in order to imprison him.

But the sacrifice was worth it in the elves' opinion. Faced with the option of killing hundreds of thousands of his followers, Vili stopped his attack. Before he could change strategies, the elves had used the life forces of the 1000 elf gods he himself had slain to create Vili's dimensional prison. He has been trapped there ever since.

The elves can't wipe out the remaining humans, however. There is still a fraction of Vili's energy that can release itself and connect with the humans. Vili uses that energy to make his most loyal human followers into blood thirsty berserkers who have super human strength and stamina in battle. The most devout of his followers he makes even tougher. Besides, where these berserkers are located is in the Northlands, and who wants a continent of frozen tundra anyway? The elven gods didn't use all the energy from the slain gods, however. They had enough to create a hole between this realm and one that is solely comprised of magical energy. It constantly replenishes a vessel that has been designed to store that energy. That is what it means to be a Noble Elf. Nobles can access that power which is called The Imperial Source. It enhances their magical strength and keeps them from aging. Basically, most other races and species are second class citizens here. At best they can get on good standing in society but the rank of Noble is for elves alone." Harvey sighed.

I replied, "Well gosh I guess we're just going to find the one who's stupid enough to fight me and show them their place, because from what I've seen their nothing special."

Magnus suggested, "Let's go talk to these elves. Eric you do the talking. If elves are the ruling class, one of us elves should talk and you're the one with the silver tongue."

Chapter 3

> "There is no better way to die than in the midst of battle . . . fighting to the very end . . . like a man." I hope this answers your question. No I will never tap. It may sound stupid but I would rather die than tap.
>
> —Enson Inoue

Our small group enters the city. I see a place that looks like a main guard office. I tell everyone I'll get directions since I am the most normal looking human of us. I decide to walk in. I open a door to a corridor and walk towards another door. I notice a number of statues that look very detailed. I finally open a door to a room. Inside I see guards dressed similarly to the ones who attacked us in the woods. With a stunned look, most of them don't move. One of them stands up and before I can open my mouth he pulls out his sword to attack. I grab the wielding wrist and disarm him with a joint lock designed not to injure. His friends pull out their weapons. As before, I am unarmed, but they notice how easily I defeated their compatriot.

I back off and put my hands up. "I'm sorry. I'm not from around here. I didn't realize that this was a restricted area. I'm just looking for directions or a map of your city."

The guard replies, "It's not that. This is a heavily protected area with a dozen different magic security wards and you just walk right in like the magic was gone. No one is immune to every magic spell. Opening either door should have incinerated you. Each ward engages a different type of attack designed to kill you in a unique way. Even if you are protected by magic, at the very least, they would have alerted us to your presence. The golems, the statues, are designed to come to life and attack trespassers. It's like they didn't even sense you. How did you get in here without setting off all those security wards of magic?"

"I honestly don't know," I respond. "It's as if spells ignore me, but I have no idea why. I really am just looking for a map or directions to lodging for me and my friends."

One of the alarmed guards quickly tosses me a map and gives me some directions to a cheap inn. I thank him and leave. I realize I need to figure out what I can and can't get away with because of my immunity. So far it is working out pretty nice, though.

With the map and directions we easily find a tavern. The coins they got from the guards in the woods were enough to rent rooms for everyone. We decide to check out the city, so I get Bobby, Rodney, Linh, and Martin and off we go. We pass a sign advertising gladiator matches. Underneath it was another sign asking for participants.

"Well I guess some things don't change; I think I know how we're taking care of the cash flow problem," I suggest.

We follow the instructions and show up at an arena. Other than being some sort of sentient insect, the Hector was no different from a typical promoter from home. That being, you'd take the word of a snake oil salesman over him and a serial killer would have more concern for your well being. Likely, when the Hector looks at us all he sees are ticket sales. It doesn't matter one bit to him if that involves you going home in small chunks. I take charge of the rules and purse negotiations. Since I'm not sure what the going rates are I just use a figure I'd heard and quadruple it. The rules are pretty basic. A field is set up so that no arcane magic can be used. And weapons are not allowed, but anything else is ok. They agree to fight any one of the fighters that has assembled for half what I offer or they can fight in the main event for twenty times that amount. That is just to show up and fight.

"What's the catch? Don't fuck with me. You just don't give a fish a title shot." I say.

Hector replies, "Honestly, he's undefeated in over 1000 bouts. The rough average is you've got 40/60 chance of making it out alive. He's killed his last three opponents. No one will fight him nowadays. Just getting him on the card will guarantee me a full house."

Bobby stepped up. "I'll fight whatever you got. I'll show your boys what tough really is."

I shake my head. Bobby's a good fighter but he always was a bit too cocky for his own good.

Hector gives him a grin and says, "Remember, I warned you."

I had to give Hector credit; that was more than what any promoter back home would have done. We descend down the narrow stairs into the staging area. There is an array of beings ranging from a troll-like giant to an apparently sentient walking thorn plant. I notice again that I'm the only normal looking human out of the lot.

"This is going to be fun," I whisper under my breath. I look around for a suitable opponent to challenge, and it turns out to not be a very difficult pick. I see what could best be described as a scorpion human hybrid approaching me. Part of it resembles a scorpion. Its torso was humanoid but that's where the similarity ended. It had a pair of giant pincers; below it were a pair of arms that ended in claws. Its whole body was red and armored in chitin. Its hairless head had no outer ears or a nose and its mouth had rows of teeth much like a sharks.

"Human, what is your business down here?" asks the scorpion beast?

I reply, "I'm looking for an opponent."

The creature snorts, "You're only a human. Without your magic or weapons, you won't last a second against the weakest one of us."

I smile, "So I take it you'll be my opponent then."

In reply, the scorpion says, "I'm Kali, of the Jzarith and I take it you came here to die. I'll be happy to oblige."

I nod with a wry smile, "We shall see," and I turn to find a place to stretch.

I ignore the other matches while I warm up with some light shadow boxing and stretches. Shadow boxing has a whole new meaning to me now that Linh is hooked up to shadows in this strange world. Finally my match is called.

A plant-like being grabs my shoulder from behind. I whisk about and am about to hit the thing when it speaks.

"I don't know what you came here to prove, but all your going to do is die. Kali is a Jzarith. You can't beat him."

I ask, "What is that exactly?"

The plant pauses, his vine extremities knotting and unknotting for a second before he replies, "I take it you've lived a very parochial life. That's the name of his race. They live far to the south in a desert portion of this world. More importantly his tail has one of the most deadly poisons known. If you're scratched, you're dead in seconds. The betting odds are 1800-1 against you. Walk away while you still can, human."

I nod to the plant, "I appreciate the concern, but I'll take my chances." With odds like that I couldn't turn down a bet. I locate a runner and have him place my entire purse on the fight. I'll either win big or die, so why not bet it all?

I walk out onto a large circular arena. It is surrounded with tall stone walls. There are thousands of spectators from hundreds of different species attending. This is the sort of fight I always wanted. I feel like a gladiator in ancient Rome.

Kali is already in the ring and comes at me quick and hard. It strikes at me with his tail, and I roll to the right in order to dodge it. I spring up to my feet with the precision that only comes with decades of practice, and throw a hard kick to Kali's front leg. As I kick I rotate my hip with just the right torque to create a whipping action that maximizes power, and make sure I strike with the shin bone. Without landing with the shin bone, the kick would have virtually no affect against Kali's chitin legs and would badly bruise my leg as well. Kali repeats his attack, but again with the result is the same.

I could hear the voice and replay a scene from one of the many instructors of my youth:

"Rotate your fucking hip right. Kicking like that; If he checks your kick right, you're done. You know what, fuck this! You're wasting my time. You know what I think of when you kick like that? I think of the great deals I could be getting at the health food market down the road. How about I drive down there and checkout the great deals I could be getting if I wasn't wasting time with you. Maybe, when I come back you'll quit wasting my time and kick right."

I never forgot to rotate my hip correctly after that. Kali keeps attacking with his tail and pincers but I am especially adept at evading. I land kick after kick to the same leg. Eventually Kali begins to slow. Finally, I hear the right leg cracking, like the shell of a lobster. It's oozing gray ichors. Two more kicks and the leg finally gives way. The scorpion roars with pain, but with five remaining legs Kali isn't impaired much. If Kali keeps attacking with his poisonous tail he'll probably land a strike eventually. The poison would do the rest. But Kali is too enraged by pain to fight intelligently. Kali charges mindlessly with his guard wide open.

"Just another street fighter that thinks he can take me," I thought.

Kali raises his talons and pincers ready to pierce right through me. But I see that to do this Kali's body has to be low, open to attack. At just the last second I charge at him and leap in the air. Caught off guard the scorpion is defenseless. My shin bone lands precisely on Kali's temple. I hear a satisfying crack as Kali falls unconscious. The shocked crowd stares in disbelief at my victory then jumps up roaring in satisfaction at what they have just seen.

I take a moment then realize it's time to go pick up my winnings.

Hector, the promoter, is in disbelief at how much he owes me now. "I won't even make a profit if I have to pay you that much!" he whimpers.

"That's what you get for setting 1800 to 1 odds," I offer. "Maybe you should have had a little faith in my abilities," I say.

"Look, I can't pay you the full amount until I get the concession sales in," Hector says.

I reply, "Alright give me what you've got and I'll collect the rest afterwards."

I walk over to where Bobby is warming up. Bobby begins to change into his beast form. Bobby's opponent, Plagon, the arena champion, is a bipedal fiend with horns. It is 8 feet tall, black, with scales over its whole body and an obvious pair of horns. The two beasts square off with one another. They ram into each other; Bobby, his two sets of arms getting double under hooks. He goes for a takedown. He is in perfect position but the fiend just stands there as Bobby tries to throw him. Plagon doesn't even try to resist; he simply is possessed with such superior strength that he can't be moved. The fiend grabs Bobby by the throat with unbelievable strength that dwarfs Bobby's massive transformation. Plagon throws Bobby using just one arm nearly 100 feet. As Bobby gets up the fiend charges again with amazing speed. He impales Bobby through the chest, but Bobby keeps hitting the fiend a dozen times, with absolutely no impact. Bobby's spiked tail cannot even pierce the thick hide. Bobby breathes a jet of fire. The flames char the stone wall on the opposite side of the arena. But the fire has no effect on the fiend.

Bobby is dying. There has to be something I can do other than helplessly watch this horrifying scene.

I run over to the Hector and yell, "Stop the fight! If you let me fight Plagon, and he wins, I'll give you what I won in my first fight. That's two fights for the price of one."

The Hector quickly realizes how much money he'll save. He calls out to the fiend, "Plagon, stop!"

Then he uses some sort of control word. Immediately Plagon lets go of Bobby who makes his way to the side of the arena. Thankfully, Bobby's regenerative powers start to take effect and his wounds begin to mend before our eyes.

I jump down into the arena for what is likely my last roll of the dice.

Seeing the Duke of the City in his royal box, I salute the Duke. "Hail, Duke! I who is about to die salute you!"

Then I turn to face the fiend and my fight to the death. Plagon immediately charges and I drop to my back, preparing for the collision. When it hits me, I plant my feet at the bottom of its hips. I'm driven back by the force of the beast, but luckily suffer no damage. It comes at me again and again but each time it hits me I use its own strength to push off on its thigh, hip, or ankle.

And then the beast gets in too close for me to push off on him so I turn my back to it, and roll into a turtle-like position pushing with one leg, then using the fiend's momentum to help me roll back into my original position. As I repeat these moves, I realize that the only way I'm going to have any chance at all is to tire it out. I just don't know whether that's possible or not. If I lose my composure once I'm dead. A single mistake would likely mean the end. So over and over I change the angle of my backward motion just enough so I never encounter a wall. Rolling around like a monkey I'm keeping the fiend away with my legs using the beasts own power to propel me away. The crowd begins to boo. They want blood not technique.

One of the elves shouts, "What is he doing?"

Linh replies, "He's using a defensive technique called an open guard. Since he's mostly using the beasts momentum to propel himself, he is expending very little of his own energy. He has one of the best open guards I've ever seen and can carry it out almost indefinitely. Since I haven't seen a single offensive attack, Linh continued, "I imagine he's waiting to get the beast tired before he makes a move."

Just then I notice the slightest bit of sweat and panting coming from the fiend. That's it; I know I can take it. All I need is precision and patience. Another hour goes by with the same result, and then another. The fiend is getting visibly tired. It is panting hard and sweat drips down its hide. Although this strange defensive technique is not the most exciting to watch, it is keeping me alive. While many in the crowd leave, the true fans are intrigued. Plagon has fought the best in the capitol and won every time. Now it is having problems with a puny human that just keeps rolling around in the dirt. The fiend fumes with anger as it has never encountered anything as exasperating as this before. It knew it was being played with and that made it even more angry. But the anger it'd relied on before in the thousands of bouts it had won before was working against it. And no one had lasted a tenth as long as this bout. The fiend had fought demons, dragons, monsters of all sorts. Now all its attacks are being parried by an ordinary, mundane, puny, little human. The fiend finally loses its composure. The enraged fiend jumps in the air. As it comes down it tries to impale me with one of its arms. I move just in time to dodge the attack. The fiend is in between my legs now, closing enough distance to strike. It keeps trying to hit me. Finally as it comes in for a blow I seize the moment and trap the fiend in between my legs. I wrap my legs around the fiend's neck together with one of its arms. I make a triangle with his legs and begin to squeeze my thighs together. The fiend slashes with his free arm ripping chunks of flesh from the side of my torso. Ignoring the pain,

I grab its head and force it down in order to choke it with its own arm and legs. When properly applied on a human, the maneuver which is known as a triangle choke, cuts off oxygen to the brain by restricting blood flow through the carotid arteries. A human passes out in seconds. I know that this beast has to breathe; I just hope it delivers oxygen to its brain in a similar enough fashion that the move will work on it. Plagon rises up lifting me into the air and slams me to the ground. I make sure to keep my neck up in order to minimize damage to my head. It repeats the effort again and again. Minutes go by; a human would have long ago asphyxiated but I knew the triangle was having an effect because the slams were getting weaker. I could feel my ribs break and blood pouring out from puncture wounds. At this point, I don't care. Maintaining my composure I keep the triangle tight and keep pulling its head down with a viselike grip. I can tell it is beginning to suffocate. It is now filled with the energy that comes from desperation. With one last effort, it slams me into the ground with its remaining strength. Just before my own consciousness begins to fade, I notice my legs are still locked then, as it seems to be happening a lot to me recently, everything goes black.

Convergence IV

Another figure comes in. It's Monkey. "You know I'd like a little appreciation here. Who freed Sisyphus from Zeus? Do you know what it took for me, Sandy, and Pigsy to get rid of that boulder? You know how hard it is to find a being that controls transport over ten dimensions? And who got the Jade Emperor to join up with you?" Monkey says.

Odin replies, "That was Buddha, Monkey."

"Well I was with him for moral support. Besides I'm an icon. Having me around gives you guy's street credibility." Monkey insists. "Journey to the West is still a best seller you know. Everyone thinks it's a work of fiction but the truth is Wu Trang-en was doing a biography on me when both of us realized it would sell better as fiction. When's the last time Prose Edda made the best seller list Odin? And as to you Lucifer you might be in a best seller but being that your depicted in it as being the incarnation of evil and the cause of all suffering, it doesn't really count."

Odin adds, "Well since you're still alive, I take it you pulled off the job."

Atlas asks, "Who did you find and how did you send them?"

Monkey leans in, "Have you ever heard of the Wizard of Yendor? No? Well he's one of the most powerful beings alive. They say he was alive before this cycle of creation," intones Monkey. "Well anyway, he lives in a dungeon he built outside of normal reality. Most frames of reality are constantly shifting in ways that should not be possible. At shifting spots in space are a few entrances to it. The popular view is he allows these openings to exist so he can watch those that are stupid enough to travel there. The few that actually make it out alive tend to come back with strange powers and wealth. Major Gods aren't allowed in. Those that have tried, get one warning and if they try to enter again they're blasted out of existence. That's how powerful he is," boasts Monkey.

Atlas asks, "Well if the spots keep shifting, how did you find out about it?"

Monkey chatters, "Well the Wizard thought it would be a nice joke if he put the idea in a few human programmers' heads to make a game where you have to get to the bottom of the dungeon. All of them still have a weak connection with it, so I found one of them and followed the trail. It led me to an entrance. I might be a minor god but I'm still a god. I fought off more creatures, traps, curses, and even weirder things than I have in my whole life. I've been to most of the heavens and most of the hells," Monkey pauses, then laughs, "normally to steal things. How mortals have managed to survive I have no idea. I found the Wizard of Yendor at the bottom level waiting for me. He knew without me telling him what I wanted. He was the one who agreed to transport our little group from earth to here if I agreed to retrieve something for him. Some mortal had actually pulled off the impossible and stole an amulet from him. For some reason he couldn't or wouldn't retrieve it himself. I just got back from returning it to him. You know the original Oracle of Delphi resides in that place. She did the Wizard a favor once so when she asked to live there he obliged. I asked her why she'd want to stay in a place like that and she told me something, some entity is coming; she doesn't know exactly when or what but it's something that's coming for all of existence. She told me, 'From a place beyond any reality I can comprehend I sensed the afterimage of the death cries of a countless multitude of souls. Mortals, gods, Powers even greater than the mightiest of gods, even the multiverses they existed in, all killed in an instant. But they weren't really dead; their souls had been absorb into an entity, a being so vast and horrible even its reflection attenuated trillion upon trillions of times almost shattering my mind. They're in it with an infinity of others, screaming. I heard voices, 'It's so cold here, it won't let me die, I try and go insane but it just brings me back, it's feeding on our souls, it won't let me die.' She told me this entity is coming, it might not be in this or the next thousand cycles of the universe but one day it will come. She's hiding there, outside reality and time, in the only place she thinks will be safe. I didn't really want to hear anymore about it, so I changed topics and asked for her help to locate the amulet. Compared to the Dungeon retrieving the amulet was a walk in the park."

Atlas responded, "I'm the oldest out of all of us here. I know what the Oracle has seen and done so if you ever hear anymore along those lines, keep it to yourself. Anyway, the Wizard actually took your word that you'd retrieve the amulet for him, Monkey."

Odin joins in, "No, he just knows that even Monkey wouldn't be stupid enough to cross the Wizard of Yendor. The reason the Wizard didn't personally collect it is properties of that amulet are such that you have to physically transport it. The truth is for all his power the Wizard has a severe case of agoraphobia which means there's almost no reason for which he will leave his dungeon. He's made it so that he could have his own universe to hide in. Also I'd like to second the Atlas's motion; anything that scares the greatest seer of this or any other time is not really anything I want to hear about. Atlas and I were both there when one of the Ancients escaped its bounds a million years ago. A trillion gods went insane just by being in its presence before we could finally rebind it. Those that didn't kill themselves we gave the coup de grace. If you'd seen them you'd understand that killing them was the most merciful option. The Oracle on the other hand never even blinked so I'd rather not even contemplate something that would concern her. She's more than just a seer she can control causality and space. There are other Powers that can do that with more energy even, but all of us that can, even me, are a berserker's axe compared to a surgeon's scalpel as to the preciseness and subtlety she possesses. Most of the Powers are from millions of dimensions and we still would have lost if not for her intervention. For a moment, so brief no one but she could detect it, the entity got distracted during the battle. Seeing her opening she was able to line up causality just enough so that Atlas, the only one strong enough to hold the entity in place even for a nanosecond, held it while I and countless others combined our wills to rebind it. Anyway, we have more immediate concerns. Good work Monkey! Well, let's check up on our little group."

Chapter 4

> . . . Next came one
> Who mourned in earnest, when the captive ark
> Maimed his brute image, head and hands lopt off,
> In his own temple, on the grunsel-edge,
> Where he fell flat and shamed his worshippers:
> Dagon his name, sea-monster, upward man
> And downward fish; yet had his temple high
> Reared in Azotus, dreaded through the coast
> Of Palestine, in Gath and Ascalon,
> And Accaron and Gaza's frontier bounds.
> —John Milton *Paradise Lost Book 1*

I wake up to see my group and the Hector leaning over a very large chest of coins.

"What happened?" I ask.

Linh replies, "The quintessential fighting moment is what. The fiend blacked out just as it slammed you to the mat. You were completely out. Neither of you were moving. None of the staff knew what to do. Your triangle was still locked in, choking it even though you were unconscious. After a few minutes they decided to check on the status of both of you. By the time they got to you, the fiend had suffocated to death. You almost died from blood loss, but hey, you won. We found Michelle and got her over here. She used a bed of flowers to heal you," Linh acknowledges.

I gave half my share to my friends to use as they liked. To the rest of our group, I gave enough to buy anything they needed. I estimated that a gold piece was worth 250 dollars of purchasing power in this world. I had won a little over 100,000 gold pieces.

Magnus wanted to go to the Capital which would be a lengthy ride. We booked tickets on a ship that was to leave in eleven days. There was something I wanted to get custom made for Magnus now that I knew where he was from and what he really was. I went shopping not really sure what to buy. Since I can't use magic items, those are out of the picture, and I don't know how to use a weapon for the life of me.

We asked the Hector where to buy the best weapons in town. He gave us a couple of names and directions. There are specialists in many different fields of weaponry residing in this city on the frontier. We split up into different groups depending on what we were looking for. Linh and Martin went with me. First place I went to was a music shop to place a custom order. Linh ordered a bamboo flute. He wanted one that resembled a traditional Buddhist bamboo flute. They cast away evil, protected against magic amongst other things. Surprisingly, they had several in stock since the barbarian human shamans to the north used them frequently. Bobby had asked me to order a harmonica and Martin orders a bass made that would play like an electric one.

We went to a shop that dealt in a variety of magical goods next. Not surprisingly, I couldn't use a single one. The shopkeeper used every divining trick he had to try and make them work on me but to no avail. Since I couldn't use magic I was somewhat limited in my options. The others made some purchases ranging from talismans to cloaks. I didn't really pay attention. I was thinking about how screwed I'd be if I got into a fight where magic worked on me. I did note Martin found a ring that helped him diminish the effects of his energy zapping field on the others. Linh said he felt the field lessen in strength considerably once Martin activated it.

Hector had mentioned an armor shop that made unique things, unavailable even in the capital. It was run by an elf who specialized in plant armor or environmental suits as he called them. All of his suits were alive. They were made from the same life form but had their genes (we assumed they had DNA) tailored to meet the needs of the user. I told the armor maker that I wanted the most durable armor he could make and to give me some options as to what properties the armor could have.

He looked at my pretty ragged outfit and demeanor and in as polite a tone as he could said, "My cheapest suits cost more than most people make in a lifetime."

To which I took out my bag of gold, and even after giving the bulk of it to the others, weighed a good bit. I asked if he'd heard about the fight I had been in. Apparently the entire town knew because every patron had mentioned it since it had happened.

"The rumors said you were an ordinary human but I thought it was an exaggeration. I'm going to make something special for you as long as you promise to tell anyone that asks who made it. I have a feeling you're going to be making some ripples and I want people to know it is my armor you are wearing."

I had the same problem as I had earlier, no magic. As before he said he'd never seen anything like it but he had an idea that didn't involve magic. We had Linh go first since he was least likely to have problems getting fitted. Martin tried to get fitted but the armor died within two minutes of his donning it. Apparently the ring he'd bought could only weaken his energy-zapping field so much.

Making the armor, especially mine, was going to take time. I gave him extra money so that he could work solely on our suits. We spent the next couple of days learning about this city and this world. For some reason, I felt compelled to learn as much about the North as I could. I had a suspicion I should go there but that would split up the group.

While Martin's childhood was deprived of many things, his father was a karate and kubudo expert. He had insisted that Martin follow suit. Kubodo is an ancient form of Okinawan weapons fighting. Martin has always excelled at the kusari-gama. Kusari-gama is a traditional Japanese weapon that consists of kama (the Japanese equivalent of a sickle) on a metal chain with a heavy iron weight at the end. Attacking with the weapon usually entailed swinging the weighted chain in a large circle over one's head, and then whipping it forward to entangle an opponent's spear, sword, or other weapon, or immobilizing his arms or legs. This allows the kusari-gama user to easily rush forward and strike with the sickle. A kusari-gama wielder might also strike with the spinning weighted end of the chain directly, causing serious or deadly injury to his opponent while still outside the range of the opponent's sword or spear Martin got a kusari-gama that created a field of energy around each piece. A single blow would be lethal. Apparently they didn't have them on this world so he had to give the weapons maker the design specs. The weapons maker chose from some enchanted scrolls that automatically imprinted the enchantment onto the weapon. After blowing up a boulder with just a tap Martin was pretty happy about his purchase.

Bobby got an extremely large axe that after the first blow would determine the correct vibrational resonance to cut through an item. I just picked up a pure iron sword and daggers plus identical silver ones. You never knew when the legends might be true. I trained for the next couple days while I waited. I also bought the closest thing I could to Buddhist prayer beads. Linh and I both agreed we needed some help from Lord Buddha.

Finally it was time to get our suits. Both Linh's and my suits had chameleon properties to them. Whenever activated the suit would adjust to the color of the environment perfectly camouflaged. More impressively the suits also adjusted to the smell and temperature of the atmosphere. The suits did the latter by taking in or exhausting out heat from itself. It also could mask your magical presence to the surroundings. The weapons maker had gotten rid of my difficulty with magic by changing the approach the suit used to communicate with me. Normally the suit uses magic to interact with its owner. In my case it was done by reading my brain wave output similar to a biofeedback machine. This made the interaction process necessarily more difficult, so my suit would take at least a week of practice before it would get used to me. I found it amazing that there was no magic involved in the actual suit. Although magic was used to make it, my suit was simply an organic being. It made its properties even more amazing. It normally would reside in my chest cavity until called upon to activate. Both our suits were able to grow functional wings, withstand extreme heat and cold. When willed to do so it could cover your face and let you breathe atmosphere that had components that could be turned into air. Outside of that, it kept several hours of air in it as a reserve. It also augmented strength, speed, and healing. Normally it stayed alive through a combination of photosynthesis and feeding off a person's ambient magical energy. In my case I would have to eat a lot more because it would be feeding off my fat cells. It also would take in any ambient particles in the air. However, when it was dormant in my chest it would not require sustenance.

Both suits could make blades and vines extend from any part of our body. Both suits could grow poison arrows that could be propelled with a thought. The poison was supposed to kill a man in seconds or simply tranquilize depending on the suit owner's desire. My suit was made of a much tougher material than Linh's. Apparently the material used to make my suit inhibited magic so it would negate Linh's power. We had paid enough for a small barony but as I tried out my suit it was well worth it.

I noticed that the range on all the elven energy weapons was less than 75 meters. An M-16 service rifle could hit an area target from 800 meters away. If we need to take on any of these characters, that would work a lot better than these elven weapons.

Magnus is the first person we see. He looks stronger and fitter, though still elf-like, and he's carrying a composite longbow, a sword, and a specially made bowie knife. He'd done his research a bit better than us. Apparently there is a procedure available for body modification. After having the body modification procedure, he says he is roughly five times faster and stronger than he was before. Since elves were the only ones that tended to have enough money to pay for such a procedure, the technique had been designed and was only available to elves in this town. However, in the Capital city, it apparently is a different story. Anything can be had there for the right price. Magnus tells us that he isn't completely an elf according to the doctors that preformed the procedure. They thought he was a hybrid of sorts. They said his physiology resembles a human's in many ways. They were barely able to do the procedure. Magnus had loaned money to Ace so that he could have the same work done. He is still being worked on so he wouldn't be by until later. Magnus's bow is a thing of beauty. It's an enchanted composite long bow made out of polymers and fibers. It's not alive. Magnus didn't want exposure to Martin to kill it. It is custom made for Magnus. With it he can hit targets from several thousand yards out. It does come with a living quiver. It grows arrows and creates a resin made out of living bacteria for use in repair of any damage to the bow.

    I bring out the present I had made for Magnus. It is an enchanted fiddle. Magnus's people are famous for their fiddle playing and it is a huge part of their magic as well.

    "Geez," smiled Magnus, "I haven't played one of these for years!"

    "I'm sure you still have it," I wink. "Let's hear a tune."

    Magnus began to play. He played a haunting Celtic tune that turned into a fast-paced song from Dixie. His skill lived up to his reputation. Magnus bowed the fiddle like he was playing the Devil for his soul.

    Harvey wandered by next. He's dressed like a tank. Not surprising since he is sort of a tank, more dwarf than human. He's wearing a custom-made armor suit made by a dwarf craftsman. It is made out of some alloy hundreds of times harder than steel and enchanted with hundreds of charms. He could convert any part of the armor to whatever shape he desired. He showed us that he could make thousands of spikes all over his suit, grown from all angles. Then he turned his gauntlets into any weapons he chose. The armor including the helmet could become air tight with a thought and yet still keep him mobile and breathing. It enhanced his strength and speed exponentially and could sustain him indefinitely. The suit recycles oxygen and has plant microbes inside so you don't go without oxygen. It can convert any organic material into food, and can extract water from anything that has it and then purifies it for the wearer. It protects him against spells as well. The armor can shoot blasts of energy from its arms and helmet. To top it off, it can create a heat up to several thousand degrees Fahrenheit without him breaking a sweat. So if Harvey touched anybody they'd turn to ash immediately.

I had provided the others with fewer resources so they weren't as well equipped but Cory seems to have barely made an effort at all to equip himself. All he had bought was a pair of shoes that would not let you slip, magic daggers, and an enchanted net and harpoon. The net was designed to constrict and bind anything. It also could send waves of energy into a trapped body to kill it. The harpoon was the only really powerful magic item. Once it hit you, it latched on and sent paralyzing waves down your body. It could paralyze a whale without a problem. And if you missed your target, it simply returned to you. If you hit your intended victim, it returned to you with the victim while at the same time killing it. The harpoon would start off with electricity and moved through a gambit of attacks including microwaves and sound until it found something that would harm you. Regardless the harpoon was designed to always bring back an edible carcass. I noticed that Cory had branded the mark of his god, Ngord on himself and "Hail the Aesir. Hail the Vanir."

I asked, "Is that for show or do you follow the old ways as well, Cory?"

Cory replied, "My parents both lived off the sea. I grew up in Norway. Ngord has smiled over me my entire life. So you follow him as well?" he asked.

I replied, "No, Odin and the Theravada path of the truly Enlightened One have taken me through my life. I do follow the old rites as does Magnus and Bobby, to a lesser extent, however."

Ace came back from his body modification procedure looking rather happy, looking less elf than gymnast. He performed a triple back flip followed by a one armed hand spring to demonstrate his new abilities. He also brought back a dozen different edged weapons. Mostly swords and knives that were enchanted simply to be extra sharp and make the user faster, not fatigue, stronger, and more agile. The procedure had gone much smoother on him than it had on Magnus. While they still could tell he was a hybrid of sorts he didn't have as many human parts as Magnus. I wasn't sure what to say about that. His only armor was enchanted chain mail he'd purchased from a human armor maker.

I inquired if he needed more money for better armor, but he replied, "I really don't want a living organism as part of me. Thanks for the offer but you and Linh can be Spiderman's Venom and Carnage. I think I'm okay."

I was beginning to like him quite a bit better. The others came back with assorted spell books, talismans, and wands for the most part. No one else had anything that particularly piqued my interest.

For our voyage to the Capital City, we boarded the elven ship. It was a giant plant the size of a Navy destroyer. It was loaded with an assortment of weapons to handle the daily incidents and threats along the trip. Sundry life forms were involved with the attacks but they were mostly taken care of by the crew. The crew was comprised of a diverse mixture of different races, and included several dozen magic users. Surprisingly enough, the Captain of this elven ship was a dwarf. He always carried an axe with him and smoked a pipe. The smokers in our group rejoiced when we found out this world had tobacco.

In the first incident where we help out the crew, the ship is surrounded by thousands of spirits. There are too many for Rodney or anyone else to control directly. All of a sudden I hear a fiddle start playing, and then a flute. I look over to see Magnus and Linh sitting together on a small bench using the incantations they'd learned in our world and playing Appalachian music that had been past down for generations. After awhile, the music changes to an old Celtic melody. I was amazed that Linh knew these tunes. But the music repelled the spirits as we traveled through their midst. After hours of travel through the horde of spirits, the soothing music from Linh and Magnus kept them at bay the entire time.

Several uneventful months go by. I train with Linh and Bobby everyday for six to eight hours. Martin, Ace, and Harvey often join us. Magnus, Cory, and Rodney join us occasionally. Cory's more interested in learning about this new sea. Magnus and Rodney spend a predominant amount of time working with each other to expand their powers. Martin and I are continuing to research this world. If Martin is right this world's twenty times bigger than Earth's. He's using a method similar to the classical mathematician Eratosthenes' method of calculating and comparing distances by measuring the sun's angles when this world is at high noon along the journey.

I spend much of my time reading from the crew's library. The prevailing scientists believe this world is mostly hollow. That might be why gravity seems about normal but who knows? Physicists on earth are still trying to figure out what this means with respect to our Earth.

Other than reading and working out, we spend the nights getting blasted. I've tried to get Leah to come out and join us but she's still shell shocked by this whole experience. She spends all her time locked in the Captain's library reading treatises on magic. I'm still hoping this voyage will give me some time with her, but it looks like that's not going to be the case.

Eric is aware that I'm watching him and so he's keeping himself and Evelyn away from me. Michelle spends a lot of time studying the flora of this world but she comes out for a drink most nights. This world definitely has some killer drugs. If we make it home I hope this stuff will grow on Earth.

There's a psychotropic that gives you visuals better than the best peyote acid mix available.

The Captain tells me we are less than a week away from the main continent. I'm daydreaming when Rodney yells that a creature is attacking the ship. Tentacles start creeping up over the side of the ship. It's trying to pull the ship down. The crews are all experienced seamen. They man their posts.

Someone yells out, "It's a Kraken."

"Great," I mutter under my breath, "this world has every monster man's ever dreamed of and then some." As I recall, a Kraken is a giant intelligent squid of myth; from the looks of the hundred foot tentacles they are not myths here.

Suddenly there's a huge crash against the side of the ship. I see hundreds of giant sea monster's being ridden by humanoid shaped beings. Magnus uses his vast knowledge and talents to compel the sea creatures to attack each other. The humanoids command their mounts to attack one another. Magnus is literally controlling close to a thousand beings. I can feel the Kraken calling out with his mind to stop the carnage. And I perceive a change in Cory. It was time to see what he could do. Martin, Cory, and I jump over the side of the ship into the churning waters below. Cory is using some sort of echolocation weapon. He sends out the beam through the water killing dozens. My suit grows a fish tail as does Martin's. Cory is becoming half human half fish like a merman. At the same time my perceptions start to expand as well. I can tell Magnus is in a mental war with the Kraken. Rodney's powers too have grown considerably, evidenced by the lightning bolts he is conjuring from the sky. The sailors have all manned positions and are firing on the sea monsters. I finally see the Kraken. It was a mile long and half a mile wide. Meanwhile Bobby has sprouted wings and takes off into the air.

Harvey, with his new armor, is rather annoyed that he can't join in. But since Michelle can control the boat since it is basically a giant plant, she commands it to create a giant tentacle attached to Harvey's legs. Now he can attack the creatures while on board, remaining out of the water. His armor is practically impenetrable, and from his armor he creates giant spikes and starts impaling the creatures. He's so successful a number of them dive back into the water. One of the sea monsters finally jumps up on Harvey's tentacle and bites Harvey's connection to the ship. The vine gets ripped in half and before Michelle can bring another one out to grab him Harvey plummets into the sea. Harvey's armor gives him an indefinite amount of oxygen; but at the rate he is sinking deeper below the surface, he's going to reach a pressure level before too long that will kill him. We all go after him but he's sinking too fast. Then

Cory starts convulsing like Bobby did the first time he changed. Cory turns into a majestic white horse. His speed triples and he is able to catch up with Harvey's descending body. As I suspected Cory had been transformed into an ocean nix, a water dwelling creature described by a hundred mythologies. He scoops up Harvey from the depths and carries him to the surface where Bobby collects him and flies him onto the ship's deck.

I return to the ship's deck knowing that even though the sea creatures are taking hundreds of casualties, they are eventually going to win. There are thousands of the creatures and hundreds of the sea monsters still remaining. Some have already boarded and even if we kill another thousand eventually they are going to win. The only way is to take out their leader. Kraken must be killed. My senses tell me he is the one controlling all the other creatures. With luck they will all be demoralized and retreat if we take him out. I come up with a plan to destroy the Kraken. Harvey's armor has unique heat generating properties. I quickly explain my plan to the others. Harvey is not exactly pleased but he agrees to comply. I am pretty certain not one of us, despite our armor, is sufficient to survive passing through the Kraken's hundreds of lines of razor sharp fangs besides Harvey. I tell Cory and Linh to keep the Kraken busy. Bobby, Harvey, and I slip over the side again and start swimming towards the Kraken. We hold Harvey by the arms, and Cory comes up behind him. I feed as much adrenalin from my suit as I can into my system without causing me to have a heart attack. Then, on the count of three, we throw Harvey with all our strength. Cory uses his control over water to increase Harvey's speed until he his traveling in excess of two hundred miles per hour. As he reaches the Kraken's mouth, thankfully, Harvey's armor protects him from the endless rows of needle sharp teeth. The kraken's teeth shatter as they try to bite down on Harvey. Finally Harvey is swallowed by the Kraken. The Kraken disengages from the ship's hull and begins to convulse. Harvey is using the heat generating properties of his armor to produce a field of five thousand degrees Fahrenheit. He's burning the Kraken from the inside. The thrashing tentacles kill some of the other creatures near the Kraken. We all keep our distance, and hope that Harvey will survive. After a couple of minutes the Kraken is in its death throes. Its entire insides must be burning to ash. Harvey chars through the monsters body and is released into the sea. Harvey has not turned off his armor and he starts boiling all the water around him heating a wide swath of the sea. My armor and the other's respective abilities are the only things that save us from being boiled alive. But Harvey is sinking far too fast for even Cory to catch up with him. Cory commands the water once again. He closes his eyes and creates a whirlwind that begins to pull Harvey towards the surface. Bobby flies towards Harvey grabbing him and extending his wings flying onto the ship's deck.

Magnus is too drained from his mental battle with the Kraken to compel the sea creatures to fight each other again. But he and Rodney combine their energies to compel sea creatures to flee. Distraught and demoralized they all swim away. Michelle compels the boat to create vines to help the rest of us on board. Cory declines the offer and creates another white pillar of water to lift him up to the ship. The crewmen look at us in awe. They ask us if we want anything. We're too drained to even consider anything other than sleep. I spend the next few days in bed. When I finally awake we have arrived at the main continent.

Chapter 5

> "Suppose nothing else were 'given' as real except our world of desires and passions, and we could not get down, or up, to any other 'reality' besides the reality of our drives—for thinking is merely a relation of these drives to each other."
>
> —Frederick Nietzsche

We enter into the main continent. I see that everything is noticeably more civilized. The city is a giant expanse. Constructed out of crystal spires as before, however the magnitude of this city made the former look like a shire in comparison. I notice there are a lot more elves here than in the last city. Everyone is getting along pretty well. We still have a lot of money from before so we are in good shape for the time being.

Ever since our encounter with the Kraken, Linh has been mentioning he can see magic. Apparently, Martin, Magnus, and Rodney can see magic to a lesser degree as well so they are all trying to figure out this new tool. Being the only real human left in our group, I notice, probably more than anyone else, the human population really is a second class here. My first experience of it, while traveling with Ace to make some housing arrangements, we come across an elf dressed gaudier than most. As I walk by him, he strikes me from behind.

"How dare you not bow to a Noble, human?" Presumably addressing Ace, "Don't you know to handle your servants better?"

"Boy, I don't know who you think you are but I've killed a lot tougher things than you in less time than you've been speaking," I spouted.

Flabbergasted at my apparent insolence he begins to summon what I assume is this Imperial Power, The Source, I've heard so much about. I'm not sure whether I should don my armor or wait. It currently is inside my chest cavity. The gaudy elf begins to create a visible energy around him. He strikes at me with it and nothing happens. He looks rather confused.

"Your spells are too paltry to work on me, elf!" I say.

Trying to maintain some of his dignity he accuses Ace. "You are liable for the trespasses of those in your employ. You will pay me compensation," he demands.

Ace replies, "I believe I am entitled to a duel if I desire." This is the first time I've seen Ace in action. I am curious to see how Olympic level fencing translates to swordplay here.

"You're a commoner," the elf retorts. "You should know better than to challenge a Noble. You do not have the power of The Source nor do you have our training. I can see by your garments that you are from the frontier. I will give you one more chance to compensate me for your servant's trespass."

Ace pulls out his sword, "I challenge you to a duel of swords, to the death."

The elf shakes his head, "I warned you."

Ace attacks first. He really is everything he claims to be. His guard is perfect. He lashes out with a dozen small strokes that all draw blood before the other elf can react. The Noble lunges forward in frustration. I can tell he is an experienced swordsman. He thrusts again and again with expert precision. But he simply isn't anywhere near Ace's level of skill or speed. A crowd is forming around us. We are in a wealthy part of town so the crowd consists of mostly elves. I can tell a few of them are in awe of Aces swordplay. The elf is bleeding from a dozen small wounds now. He is covered in green blood. Ace isn't even sweating yet. The Noble makes a desperate charge. Ace skewers him through the stomach. At that moment I can tell the Noble elf is humiliated and ready to break whatever rules of dueling he is required to abide by.

Someone in the crowd yells, "He's about to use his Noble power!"

I see visible energy about to discharge, and shove Ace out of the way. The bolt of energy hits me and disperses harmlessly. I have had about enough of this. I jump up in the air and I strike his head with the point of my elbow. It fractures his skull killing him. Dozens of guards assemble at our position. I'm pretty sure even if I manage to kill these, dozens more will take their place.

"Ace, I suggest we both put up our hands and surrender. We'll have to figure out another way out of this." Ace and I comply and are taken into custody.

Once taken to the jailhouse we wait for whatever judicial proceedings this world offers. When we finally go before the magistrate, I again see the disparity between how elves and humans are treated in this land. The magistrate hears the accounts of what happened from the witnesses. For Ace, it is a fair proceeding that results in him being exonerated as the laws of this land allows for consensual dueling. But for me, the law governing humans is more like the rules governing pet dogs and the like back home. Even though I acted in third person self defense, the magistrate says I'm a danger to society since I killed a noble and interfered in a duel between elves. Ace is given two options for dealing with me; I can either spend the next ten years in hard labor or I can play in the Wild Hunt. Not exactly overly thrilled about ten years of labor I inquire what the Wild Hunt consists of. Apparently it is not much different from the Wild Hunt from European mythology. It is a rite of passage for the youths of the Nobles. On their fiftieth birthday they are given access to The Imperial Source. Promptly afterwards they are expected to engage in the Wild Hunt which consists of a host of unarmed beings running for their lives. If the prey can make it to the other end of the grounds, they are set free. Moreover, if one survives until the dawn then you survive as well. On the other hand you are completely unarmed and the elves are armed as well as one could possibly be. They all have packs of magical hunting hounds. So while it is not unheard of for a hunted being to survive it is incredibly rare for a Noble to be even wounded while hunting. It is really more of a caged hunt than anything else. But it sounds better to me than ten years labor.

So far apparently The Imperial Source doesn't affect me and the elves have not noticed my suit of armor stored within my chest cavity. I find out that while my actions were perceived as those of an untamed wild animal, a number of the Nobles that had watched the duel were so impressed with Ace's swordplay that they want to sponsor him for a swordsmanship competition. Apparently thousands of common elves come every year to compete. The winner is made a low level noble. The event isn't for six months, so I promise Ace I'll be there to see him compete.

I am touched but not overly surprised when Bobby, Linh, Harvey, Rodney, and Martin show up unannounced to my prison cell. Rodney has been teaching Linh and Martin to harness their powers. Linh has excelled at this. He has learned to control his ability to see enchantments. He's also discovered that spells are much like computer programs in their logic; they basically are binary codes. Ever the hacker, Linh has started to break into the villas of the Nobles. Using those same skills Linh manages to break through all the wards within the prison and using his shadow teleportation he transported all of them into my cell. They have come with an escape plan; but, because their magic doesn't work on me, I can't be transported out with Linh's technique.

Harvey is sure he can build a tunnel that will lead me to safety. I ask them then where will we be going to? We don't know that much yet about this world other than this is the most civilized part we've found so far. If it were a death sentence I'd be out of here in a heartbeat but from my understanding I just have to survive one night against a bunch of adolescent punks that are going to rely on their magic to try and take me out. Maybe I'm nuts, but I think this is going to be fun. I give my money to Magnus so you guys will be taken care of. Wait for me in the Capital when this is done I'll find you there. We all hug and Linh prepares a Buddhist cleansing ritual. Everyone takes part out of respect for me more than anything else. We spend the next hour chanting the sutras. When finished they leave like they came in, and bid me good luck.

The next day, Evelyn, Michelle, and Leah come by to talk me out of joining the Wild Hunt. Evelyn pleads for me to take the labor sentence. They are sure they can figure out some way to bribe someone to commute my sentence. I touch Evelyn on the shoulder and tell her not to worry. I didn't mention that I had told Bobby and Linh to kill Eric, if they found out he is beating her again. The following day I'm transported to a facility that is to hold the prisoners for the Wild Hunt. I am not fed at all during the several days' travels over to the area. My symbiote armor provides me with some strength but I don't want to draw on its strength too much as I have a feeling I'll need it in the near future. By the time I get to the site of the Wild Hunt, I am extremely famished. There is a whole assortment of beings almost as varied as in the arena pits. I notice there is one considerable difference. Most of the beings here have a sickly look likely attributable to malnutrition. Furthermore, the more powerful beings I had seen in the arena were not present here. It seemed this hunt is even more weighted than I had first thought. Looking for a place to sit down I notice that the center of the facility serves as a latrine so only the edges of this prison were clean enough to sit down. But it looks like all the spots along the walls are taken. A couple of the weaker beings are forced to stand in the filth in the middle. Then there are some that actually like the filth. I see a couple of what presumably are sentient dung beetles having a rather good time in there. They seem to be the only ones not malnourished.

A creature beckons me over. He looks like a giant bipedal mole with hands. "I'm Caspian," he sticks out his hand. It is lined with claws and besides an opposable thumb the Caspian resembles a giant vole like what we might find back home. A little bit reluctantly I shake his extended mitt. He offers me a seat. He apparently has carved a small cavern in the prison wall. He says any deeper and the security wards would go off. He's apparently from an underground race of voles that are a bipedal, intelligent race that is related to moles in looks only. He is in here for accosting a Noble that was shoplifting his wares. I tell him not to worry. Stick with me and you'll be fine. Over the next weeks we become friends.

Finally the day of the hunt arrives. I begin my preparations. Hundreds of us lesser unarmed beings are lined up at the edge of a forest. There are a little over a hundred young elves awaiting the hunt in anticipation.

The hunt master gives us the instructions. "You will have an hour head start. Your objective is either to make it to the finish line or to survive until sunrise. Once the Wild Hunt begins all sides of the forest will be sealed and guarded except for the finish line."

All of a sudden, a loud gong is struck and the order to run is sounded. We all take off. Unlike the other prey, Caspian and I only run about a mile into the forest to begin our preparations. Caspian has a power similar to Harvey's. He can move earth and tunnel through solid stone. I tell him to tunnel but not too deep. He's going to be bait. If I'm right, the elves' hounds will be able to track our scent. They'll think we are both hiding in the overtly visible hole. I unleash my symbiotic armor from my chest. Now I'm undetectable to both magic and ordinary forms of sensing. I climb to the top of a nearby tree and wait. Soon the horn sounds indicating the elves are on the move. Before too long, a group of five elves show up at our location. They are riding everything from flying carpets to what appear to be clouds. Beneath them are packs of plants that have a doglike appearance. They are sniffing at the tunnel.

Laughing, one of the youths dismounts and says, "Looks like we got our first kill, boys."

The others follow suit, dismounting and jostling each other. The minute they are all beside the tunnel I drop from the tree. Willing my suit to transform, I extend my armor into dozens of spikes that impale the lot of them. Then the hounds attack. Just before they strike, the ground gives way beneath them. The hounds are being buried alive in what has turned into a pit of quicksand. Caspian pulls himself out, obviously controlling this phenomenon. Before the elves die, Caspian draws out their magical power and absorbs it. His blotchy gray fur is gone. Now he appears as the warrior he claims to be.

The rest of the night continues in much the same manner. We ambush elf after elf. Every time they rely on The Imperial Source for power. After that doesn't work they panic. Regardless, they die either under blade or through Caspian's spells and fangs. When dawn arrives, 117 are dead by our hands;

every time we kill an elf we cut off his ears. We show up at the finish line on a moving mound of dirt controlled by Caspian. Beyond the finish line are throngs of Nobles; parents, relatives, and friends assembled to greet their sons completing this rite of passage. For the first time in memory not a single family has a son to greet.

I walk towards the hunt master and ask, "Does this mean we are free to go?"

He stutters, "Ye . . . es it does. Any and all crimes have been paid in full."

Then I walk over to the Nobles and dump my bag. 117 pairs of ears fall to the ground. I announce, "You thought that just because we were unarmed and malnourished you could beat us so easily?" The shocked crowd's gasps and crying is answer enough. Out of the corner of my eye I notice a few other prisoners had made it out, also.

I am confronted by a particularly well dressed Noble.

"I'm the Earl of Daloch and you have killed my son. If you think you're going to get away with this, you are mistaken!"

"Should I feel sorry for your son who, against an unarmed human, is well fed and well trained while he is commanding a pack of hounds and equipped with the best Imperial weapons money can buy?" I ask. "I am sorry you lost a son. I am not sorry I killed an adversary."

The hunt master cautions the Earl that the surviving prisoners are now free to go. Angry, the Earl with his magic, flings the hunt master twenty feet. He lashes out with his magic against me and as usual nothing happens.

I sneer, "That stuff doesn't work on me. Your son is dead. Accept it and move on."

I get into the vehicle provided for those that survived. The dozen of us are allowed transport anywhere we wish.

Caspian gives me a talisman he's forged out of the ground. "Use this if you ever need to contact me or my people. Its signal will give you safe passage." I embrace him and we part ways.

As I am delivered to the Capital City, I realize I've made it back in time for Ace's tournament. There are banners advertising the competition in a dozen languages. The Capital is even more amazing than the previous city. It's the size of ten New York Cities with sky scrapers that are on average triple the height of the Empire State Building.

When the wagon drops me off, throngs of people greet me, the human that slew 117 Nobles in one night. It seems I have become a celebrity. I hope I won't be too much of a disappointment. From the looks and sounds of the crowd, apparently I am not. There are women of all races screaming for me.

Then I see my group; everyone is there safe and sound. After five months in a tiny prison cell full of all kinds of strange prisoners, my crew is a sight for sore eyes.

Evelyn is crying. She hugs me like I'm family in all ways but blood. She is the most obviously jubilant member of the group and wraps her tail around my waist; we fly off.

"Don't ever scare me like that. I thought for sure we lost you," Evelyn scolds.

I tell her about what happened, watered down quite a bit, while we are flying. "So what do you think about my new look?" I take a real long look at her for the first time in a very long while. Dressed in black leather, looking every part a temptress from legend I had to admit, the look really worked.

"So do you trust me not to let you fall," she smiled mischievously.

I realized she might be flirting with me which isn't the worst thing in the world. However, with the realization I'd just spent five months in a dungeon so my wits were not at their sharpest, and that she still wore her wedding band, sobered me up from that idea. I finally get her to stop crying and we land. Everyone seems to be doing fairly well. Most of them seem to be stronger than before. Rodney says his powers have tripled and he has a whole new batch of tricks. Magnus informs me that he's running circles around this world's brokers. I've told him he can keep ten percent of the net profit so he has some incentive in the matter. Regardless he says a conservative estimate is quintupling my money within three years. I personally don't really care right now. I'm sore, tired, and haven't had a woman in god knows how long and I've just killed a hundred and seventeen elves. It's time to party.

I grab some money from Magnus and I spend the next couple weeks prior to Ace's tournament with Martin, Linh, and Bobby. Since none of us are sword fighters there's nothing we really can do to help Ace train. Magnus, Harvey, and Corey have at least some experience with melee weapons. Magnus has fenced for a number of years so he's the best equipped to practice with Ace. Ace's training taken care of, we decide to go on a drug binge that probably would have killed any of our previous bodies. Martin is a little disappointed because due to the changes to his body he has a resistance to most drugs. On the other hand, I don't get to try out any of the magical delights the others are experimenting with. Having plenty of money we try every vice this world has to offer. We go through everything from psychotropic drugs that make an LSD trip seem like a bong hit to speed that makes you feel like a god. Between the brothels and the loose women impressed with our money, we collectively go through women from dozens of different races; elves, humans, and demon-like women. You name it, we did it.

Our excesses draw the attention of more than a few would-be muggers as well. The first bunch is only a dozen poorly armed bandits that confront us. While Linh and I go into a corner to puke, Bobby and Martin wait out front. The troupe of bandits demands our money, but we just laugh at them.

Martin says he's going to show me a new trick and waves the rest of us off. "If the twelve of you can beat me my friends will give you everything they have."

The bandits charge. I'm about done puking so I light a cigarette and watch the show. One of the bandits slams a sword right into Martin's stomach; the blade snaps as the bandit stares in disbelief. Martin has disappeared. He reforms in the middle of them as a body of mist that solidifies into Martins body. Apparently since I've last seen Martin he has developed the power to turn into mist. Then Martin turns up his consumptive aura. Instead of running as they should have, the admittedly brave or truly stupid bandits charge. Martin entangles several of them with his kusari-gama while the rest attack him. Before they know it they are too weak to move. All twelve bandits fall to the ground. Their bodies are turning an ashy gray as they lay dying. After a half dozen more attempts that result in the deaths of other would-be bandits and gangs, the word gets out to stay away from us.

We have a week left before Ace's tournament and we continue with our exploits. One night while roaming the streets, I notice figures tailing us out of the corner of my eye. From the professional nature of their stealth I know what it has to be. I tell the group in English that assassins have probably been hired to kill me by one of the elves' parents. I knew I'm not going to get away scot-free after killing that many Nobles' sons. I might be free by law but I expect the families of the dead Nobles to eventually come after me.

We all take a chemical that's supposed to sober us up and then we devise a plan. Bobby and I are going to split up from Martin and Linh. While they hide we'll lead the assassins into an alley. Then when they attack us, Martin and Linh will ambush them from the back. We proceed according to the plan and lure the assassins toward us. As they approach Bobby begins to transform. I notice that in addition to his normal fox-faced, winged-form, he now has several new tails that have the same stingers at the end as his original tail. In most Asian cultures, especially Japan, the fox is a symbol of the mystical. The similarities are too much to not notice. The more tails a fox has the more powerful it is. The most the mystical fox could have is nine and I would not be surprised if that's how many my friend ends up having before this journey is over.

    Martin seems to have become a dragur, an undead from the Norse tales. It is blue as death and has many powers such as being immune to normal weapons and being able to turn into mist. Only iron and silver weapons can hurt it. Other than that its opponents normally have to fight it barehanded to defeat it. Now it's time to fight, not to think. I summon my suit and prepare. There are over a hundred fifty assassins; all elves and all obviously well trained. They are armed with a variety of weapons ranging from swords to wands and they all obviously know what they're doing. Bobby takes to the air. Instantly, Bobby incinerates two with his fiery breath. He strikes with his various tails killing one with each blow but the assassins retaliate with magic. From a dozen positions they bombard him and eventually he crashes to the ground. Knowing that their magic will not affect me I engage them head-to-head. I'm fighting a dozen of them. For everyone I kill I get hit a dozen times. My armor is the only thing keeping me alive. Then Linh and Martin come streaking into the fight. They use their respective powers to aid me. Linh strangles several with his shadows. Martin wields his kusari-gama, swinging the weighted chain in a large circle over his head, and then whipping it forward to entangle an assassin's weapons. Martin rushes forward and strikes with the sickle; then he uses his power in a fashion I'd never seen before. Apparently he can rapidly consume a person even if his contact is solely through his weaponry. Everyone he entangles dies in moments. Bobby's regenerative power has saved him again and he's back in the fight. He gores one assassin through the heart with his horns and then breathes a blaze of fire that kills several more. However, there are too many; we are losing. Martin is being pelted and takes dozens of little wounds. Unlike the arms of the bandits, the assassins' weapons have magic that cause injury to him. Linh and Bobby are no better off. There are simply too many. We've killed forty-five but there are still over a hundred and we are all dead tired. Too many nights of partying and too many opponents have slowed us down. The assassins aren't focused on finishing off anybody but me, so I tell the guys to retreat and save themselves. All of my guys refuse to leave me. Then I notice a sewer grate. I tell Linh to command the shadows to pry it open. I see Linh carry Martin and Bobby off into the shadows just as I dive in. I hear some of the braver or stupider assassins dive in with me. Either from exhaustion or injury I black out.

Convergence V

"Well, isn't John a little handful. He's still alive though," says Monkey.

Lucifer asks the others, "I've told you my reason for concentrating on this world, for committing to its deliverance from Yahweh and his hordes; why are the rest of you remaining when we most likely cannot stop the Armageddon? Oh, and Odin, please leave out the 'honor in death' language, too. I'd like to know the real reasons," Lucifer scans their expressions.

Atlas replies, "It is true that I and the rest of us known as Titans have spent very little time on this world compared to the other powers. However, I've grown fond of this planet as has my sister, Hecate, and a few of the Titans. Moreover, I have a friend, Ern, who was born on this world and refuses to leave. He's currently doing recon but he'll be leading the second retrieval mission.

"Second retrieval mission; what do you mean?" Monkey asks.

Odin interjects, "I need my brothers, Vili and Ve, to complete the summoning circle against Yahweh. We will be useless without them, and I'm depending on our little cluster of mortals to find Vili and then to retrieve each of them from their concealment places. It's definitely a huge challenge; that's why our mortals need so long to develop and prepare."

Atlas clears his throat, "Ahem, if you're finished, I believe I was talking. My friend, Ern is invested in this world and is busy searching for Vili and Ve. When he locates where they are and has made his plans, he'll lead the mission to retrieve Ve." Atlas paused in thought and then continued, "I am millions of years older than any other being worshipped by the mortals. Only a handful of beings mentioned in the world's myths are of my age. One of those is Odin's grandfather Búri. If things go as planned, I will see my old friend again. Including Búri, the original Buddha, and a few of the primordial gods and me, we are the oldest. The creation story of the Olympian gods incorporated me and the other Titans simply because they had to account for our presence, somehow. We Titans have no direct relationship to the Olympians. Besides, the Olympians needed to save face for losing control to us so swiftly. I'll tell you about that another time, Monkey. So why does the Trickster wish to remain?" asks Atlas.

Monkey replies, "I'm not like the rest of you, I was born mortal. I'm neither as powerful nor as old. You count time by epochs. Ten thousand years is like a day to you, while I've barely been alive that long. This world is my home and I'll do everything I can not to let the terrorist Yahweh take it from me. How about you, Odin," Monkey asks?

Odin responds, "I've been part of this world's progression as much as any supremacy has. While my relations and I are worshipped on many worlds and throughout unseen dimensions, the truth is, I personally have never failed to protect any other world like I have failed here. I ignored Yahweh, and in doing so, allowed him to gain the power that puts us in this untenable position. It is all due to my own hubris.

"My failure began during a party hosted by Dionysus. Our Aesir brother Thor was drunk, as was the Olympian, Heracles. They bumped into one another and being the hot headed fools they are, started to fight. Instead of stopping them, I ignored them," Odin said. "After a few minutes Thor got the better of Heracles and was so drunk he was ready to finish him off. Zeus stepped in to protect Heracles, his son, by throwing a lightning bolt that nearly killed Thor. And that was the beginning of the war between our two races, my Aesir brethren, and the Olympians, which has lasted millennia.

"During this time, my attention was so focused on the war, that I did not realize the stealthy plan taking place in the World's Middle East. And then there was the human war. While we Aesir were fighting the Olympians, the humans had their own parallel war going on between the Romans and the peoples of Northern Europe and Britannia, called the Vandals. At first the Olympians were winning the war against us. We were rusty warriors having refrained from a true war for eons, so we were as disorganized as the berserkers who worshipped us. And in parallel to our situation, the Romans were conquering all of what's now known of as the European continent. Finally our resolve began to change the tide.

"Meantime Yahweh's control of humanity was seeping out over the rest of the world, particularly throughout the European continent. I noticed Yahweh briefly, but I ignored him as just another god who would soon run out of power. By the time I realized how much influence he'd gained, how many worshippers were feeding his power, I was too embroiled with Zeus to make any clear moves. Not one of us was aware of the degree of Yahweh's influence over the world including his taking the whole of the Roman Empire as his own. When we finally beat the Olympians in the fourth century of this first post-Christ millennium, this victory was paralleled by my followers and the barbarous Vandals in the sacking of Rome. We had slaughtered dozens of the Olympian gods and Zeus was forced to formally surrender. Our victory weakened the Olympians to the point that they were forced to retire to Olympus.

Odin continued, "Then there was Camelot. The real story of Camelot occurred around the same time that we had beaten the Olympians and Rome had been taken by the Vandals. The Vanir were part of the world. They were helping us in our fight with the Olympians so they were not minding their lands. Merlin, the son of a debauched god, probably Loki, and a mortal woman, met Arthur and saw that the man possessed a special quality. Arthur was a rare breed, educated, charismatic, yet with the sort of directness the people would accept. Well, Merlin, a brilliant magician, could tell the story better but Arthur was a good man. It was Arthur who planned to create a civilization that had Rome's disciplined advancements in technology and government, but at the same time honoring the ways of the Aesir and the Celtic old ways. Within a few years Arthur had founded the Kingdom of Camelot and appeared to be succeeding in carrying out his plan for the idyllic state. He married Morgan le Fay, who bore him a son.

Yahweh's desires for more power drew him to view Camelot and Arthur as enemies of his own plan to strip all the power from this world. Yahweh knew that if Arthur succeeded, it would impede his immediate plans for taking all of Europe. He knew that as with Adam of millennia earlier, temptation was the best way to attack Arthur's moral foundation and to sway the populace against Arthur. Yahweh found Guinevere, and with Arthur in mind, gifted her with the power to charm him. Seduction of Arthur was simple for the temptress and fabricating evidence against Arthur's wife, Morgan le Fay, was even simpler with Yahweh's help. Morgan le Fay was banished from Camelot. Guinevere was thorough, making sure her rival and the son were penniless and broken. But Morgan le Fay was no submissive. She had one last trick; she called for help from the old gods and Lady Mabb appeared. Morgan le Fay's son by Arthur, Mordred, grew up under Mabb's tutelage and ultimately sought revenge for his mother's expulsion from Camelot. And, when Arthur died, going to his afterlife of service, Merlin released the charm placed on him by Guinevere. Arthur spent years trying to win back Morgan le Fay and make amends to Mordred. Mordred could not forgive Arthur who had hurt his mother so badly, failed him as father, and ultimately failed mankind. If not for Arthur's weakness in the temptress, Guinevere, Armageddon would have been stopped before it even began. The sad thing is, Arthur could have single-handedly derailed the efforts of Yahweh, and Arthur knew it. That's why Arthur takes so many missions for me now. It lets him drown out the guilt. Morgan le Fay has forgiven Arthur, however. She's tried to bring Arthur and Mordred together again but to no avail.

Odin continued, "If we hadn't been so caught up in our petty warring with the Olympians, we would have been able to thwart Camelot's fall; the Dark Ages would have never happened; Christianity would have been rebuked in all of Europe. All this could have been averted but for our struggle with the Olympians, and Yahweh would be only a memory. This was enough to make me want to stay and stop Yahweh's great scheme for annihilation after sucking out all the power this world has.

"Tragically, ignoring the power struggles occurring in this world was not my worst blunder." Odin continued, "I inspired one of my greatest followers, Adam Alfred Rudolf Glauer, to form the Study Group for Germanic Antiquity, which was a German occultist and Völkisch group in Munich. It was later renamed the Thule Society after the north-most region of Europe which is believed by many to actually be Asgard. He went by the alias Rudolf Freiherr von Sebottendorff. Our plan was to have the Thule Society inspire Germanic peoples to re-embrace my teachings of the old ways and rebut Christianity, creating a new government in the process. Germany was in a major depression after its loss in World War I, and was ripe for political upheaval. The Germans sought a leader who could reestablish the country as a world power and return its financial and social health. Based on the Thule Society's plan, the leadership was supposed to begin to disseminate my message of self improvement. The leader would secure the people's freedom with a competent military force. I intended for us to take Scandinavia and all of my other old territories. I could feel the Northern European people's desire for renewal. That is why when World War II finally did come about, Scandinavia did not overtly resist joining with the Thule's, later known as the Nazi Party. The plan was to start rebuilding society; it was going to be a second chance at Camelot.

Odin shook his head and closing his eyes as if to block the memory said, "All was going according to plan until the Christian year 1916. In that year, however, Adam Alfred Rudolf Glauer, aka. Rudolf Freiherr von Sebottendorff, came into contact with another organization called Germanenorden. It had a similar agenda and he felt he could use them. He was subsequently appointed the Ordensmeister (local group leader) for the Bavaria division of the schismatic Germanenorden Walvater of the Holy Grail. Settling in Munich, he established the Thule Society, which became increasingly political, and by 1918 was established as a political party known as the German Workers' Party. This was exactly as we had planned.

"But due to Yahweh's success with subversion, I again didn't notice that Yahweh's influence was infiltrating the party in 1919. The infiltrator was one of the most charismatic speakers in the history of humankind, and next to the Christ, was Yahweh's greatest pawn, Adolf Hitler. Hitler had been gifted by Yahweh with the power to sway people through his speeches. He changed the name from the German Worker's Party to the Nazi party. Knowing he had failed, Sebottendorff left his now irreparably changed Thule Society. Later, after realizing the tragedy unfolding at the hands of Hitler, Sebottendorf tried to correct the mistake and turned over evidence to the Bavarian government about the Nazi Party. He managed to get seven members executed after the attack on the Munich government in April 1919 but it wasn't enough to stop them.

"Sebottendorff fled Germany for Switzerland and then to Turkey. He resides with me in Asgard now, and is planning his revenge. His magical powers have become phenomenal since his death. He's with the others we selected to plan the mortal's part of the fight.

World War II was the biggest fuck up in my existence. All along I have underestimated Yahweh's treacherous intent. I didn't think he would take it so far; he was able to subvert things so that madman Hitler could take over. Six billion lives have been sacrificed, most of them were his followers. It was through Hitler that Yahweh made people blame everything on the Thule's. And thereby the finger of blame is pointed at me. And I am to blame for misreading Yahweh.

That megalomaniac Yahweh protected Hitler during every one of the assassination attempts. When they called on me, it was his voice they heard. I knew no peace could be had with a man like that. It was Yahweh that told Hitler to invade Russia. He wanted everyone to have my name attached to the biggest genocide in history. Then his men could come in after all that and save the day. The truth is I wanted Erwin Rommel to eventually take power. He understood war and reason is as true as I am the God of War and Knowledge. For these reasons I am honor bound to stop Yahweh or die in the attempt.

Odin sighed heavily, "I'd rather stop thinking about my failures. Let's check on our group."

Chapter 6

> "In all social systems there must be a class to do the menial duties, to perform the drudgery of life. That is, a class requiring but a low order of intellect and but little skill. Its requisites are vigor, docility, fidelity. Such a class you must have, or you would not have that other class which leads progress, civilization, and refinement. It constitutes the very mud-sill of society and of political government; and you might as well attempt to build a house in the air, as to build either the one or the other, except on this mud-sill.
> —"The 'Mudsill' Theory," by Senator James Henry Hammond
> Speech to the U.S. Senate, March 4, 1858
> With the purpose of attempting to validate slavery.

I wake up, presumably a few minutes later. I slide through the sewer for what must be miles until I hit a main refuse river where I am buffeted by the mixture of garbage and feces. Thankfully I'm wearing my suit of environmental armor or else I would have assuredly drowned by now. I extend a tail from my suit so I can swim with the current. I hear some of the assassins that are following me floundering in the sewage as well. In the water my suit makes me more than their match. One of them has the ability to fly as he is in the air above the river trying to find me. The river is so tainted it is totally opaque; I have the advantage. I first take on the assassins in the river with me. The current is extremely strong but my suit let's me maneuver enough to get to each of them. While they apparently have spells that let them swim underwater without air they still are awkward compared to me. My senses have heightened again so I'm able to sense the slight rippling of their bodies. I swim up to each one. The water's muddiness lets me approach and they don't even know I'm there. I impale each one through the torso. Now it is time to take on the flier. I extend my suit like a lasso and rope his legs. I engulf him in the suit choking him until he is unconscious but alive. I need him alive to answer questions. Nearly an hour goes by until we get dropped over a thousand foot fall into a huge pool of debris.

I see land and swim towards it with the assassin in tow. I shake him and slap his face to wake him up. I can tell he's not only an elf, but a Noble from the looks of things.

I give him a very simple proposition. "You can tell me who sent you and where we are and you can live. If not I'll torture you until you tell me something and then I'll kill you."

The assassin agrees that living is the better option. He tells me his name is Regansi. We are in the bottom habitable level of the Capitol. Here all the refuse from the Capitol and the surrounding areas is used as fertilizer for the organic factories. Nearly all of the elves' property, possessions, and machines are organic-based in some fashion or another. The sewage is processed and used to feed the factories. The workers are all human and an elven commoner normally runs each factory. The elves that had been sent to kill me are the assassins from a major house. The Noble I had captured was put in charge of the whole operation and was the sole Noble of the group. Regansi is a minor cousin related to several of the houses but quite distant from any position of any real import. He is just barely a Noble.

He tells me, "This was nothing personal. You killed the heir to the House of Talus and they were willing to give me a real title if I managed to kill you. It's no different than people I'm sure you've killed. Even if you kill me, they'll just send more until you are dead."

"If that's the case, I've got a proposition for you. If you get me access to that house I'll kill off everybody there. That would get you your title and more importantly stop any more assassination attempts. All you have to do is distract some guards and tell me when the shift changes are. Trust me, I've got more companions, and we can get the job done." I tell him where to find me if he agrees.

Regansi leaves. I decide I'll explore this place where all the finery up top is created. The sight I see is sickening. Millions of humans live down here. Most are pale and malnourished. I find an inn and discover that the people down here are indentured servants for the most part. Most people down here are illiterate. They receive no schooling except how to operate the factories. Most only leave if the elves need conscripts for their wars. Then they are the cannon fodder. Unless they have special connections, even for those that don't work in the factories, this is one of the few places where a human can own land. Therefore, even some of those who work on the higher levels own property and live down here. The streets are littered with cripples injured from working in the factories. I spend a couple days viewing the area and give what coin I have to the local children. There is nothing I can do right now but I promise to myself I'll try to make it right at some point.

It's nearly time for Ace's fight so I hurry back up the levels to join him. I meet up with the rest of the group and after some healing by Michelle they seem to be no worse for wear.

Well, for once I get to be the fan watching someone else fight it out for my enjoyment. Ace is looking fit and trim. He's the dark horse in this tournament. No one knows who he is except for rumors about his fight with that Noble. Since there are thousands of applicants from all around the Empire there had been a preliminary event beforehand. That involved a skills test against one of the Imperial sword masters. The point wasn't to win, merely prove your skill. The matches were held in private so we were not allowed to attend those. Unbeknownst to everyone but us, Ace had nearly beaten a sword master with hundreds of years of practice.

The rules are fairly simple and quite a bit more civilized than in the arena. All applicants are given identical swords. They duel for a five minute round. The winner is decided afterwards either by who scored the most blows, balanced by the severity of the blows. If an applicant scores a mortal wound on his opponent he is immediately declared the winner. The wounds are never truly mortal because there is a team of wizards who specialize in healing-in-wait during each match. They heal both opponents promptly afterwards.

Ace's first match is against a lanky elf with a number of scars he likely has kept like tattoos for looks. They touch swords and begin. Ace drops his guard slightly, in an attempt to bait his opponent. It works. Looking for a quick win the elf commits to a thrust to Ace's heart. Ace skillfully sidesteps then sidesteps while spinning. With his back to the elf he skewers him through the side ending the match. The rest of Ace's matches go pretty much the same. Ace has had time to adapt to the Empire's style of fighting while no one has seen his particular style of fencing. It is a trend I've noticed among the elves. Despite their superior magic and intellect the elves seem to have difficulty adapting to new variables. After the final match the Emperor himself comes out to congratulate Ace. During some formalities, Ace is made a member of the Nobility. The procedure is not what I expected. Energy starts coursing into him. At first he starts going into spasms. After a few minutes he is aroused looking invigorated.

He now has at his command the power of The Imperial Source.

I spend the next few weeks training with Linh and Bobby. Bobby and Harvey have gone back to their jobs and are leaving soon for a bounty hunt. I find Corey is leaving for a fishing expedition fairly soon. Rodney and Magnus have been working closely with each other in my absence, to learn to control their magic better. They want to catch the monsters these seas posses. Linh and Martin have taken a different approach to spending their time. While not experimenting with the plethora of drugs this land provides, they both have been studying how to disarm magic security wards or spells. They are able to detect and read enchantments. Linh tells me it's not that different from a computer code, i.e., he can hack into a system without much difficulty whether it's a computer or an enchantment. So far, they have broken into several villas of the Nobles and are having a great time. I go on jobs with them when I'm bored. My special immunity to magic is a great asset to them. Michelle is on a journey studying the botany of the area, so I haven't seen much of her. Leah is studying magic at a school so she's been busy. When she has time we grab a drink. I see a lot of Evelyn. She comes by everyday to have lunch. Eric has found some work with a Noble magistrate so she's by herself much of the time.

 Regansi, the assassin I contracted in the debris river, comes by the inn where I'm staying and agrees to my plan. He tells me that he'll be in charge of the watch in three nights. He gives me the times of the watch changes, and tells me he'll try and delay any reinforcements. He also gives me a map of the interior of the mansion owned by the Noble who ordered our assassinations.

 As is usual, Martin and Linh "hack" the magic code first. Martin turns into mist just like a true dragur from legend and enters the mansion from the top while Linh uses the shadows to transport himself into the villa. I have my envirosuit on so it's not much of a matter to sneak in. Linh takes out the guards we encounter with poison darts shot from his suit. Following the map, we find the bedchambers of the family. Regansi is standing right in front of us with a sword in his hand. Thinking that it's an ambush, we get ready to fight.

 Regansi waves his hand to silence us and whispers, "I've been kicked around for a century, human. Did you think I was going to let you have all the fun?"

 We smile and head for each bed chamber. We cut off the Nobles' heads. Once Regansi says we've killed everyone in line for the title he wants, Regansi along with us start grabbing anything of value. Linh transports it out of the mansion.

 I shake Regansi's hand saying, "Good doing business with you."

 "Likewise," he says. "My plan tomorrow is to 'discover' the remains and tearfully take over."

"Hopefully that's the end to my assassin problem," I suggest, and we take our leave.

Leah and I are having lunch. She's been studying magic fairly intensely recently, and has just completed a rudimentary course on magic. She wants to go to an intermediate level magic school. It's a three year live-in program. She is short on money, however. For a Noble it's straightforward to enter into this program, but for a commoner it is extremely expensive requiring a Noble's introduction. Later that day, I contact Magnus and ask about the funds I left to him. He quite thoroughly explains the investments he's made. Unfortunately most of the funds are legitimately tied up. Therefore, there are not enough funds to pay for the school.

I want to help Leah and outside of breaking into places with Linh, I really have only one option, the arena. I contact the management there. Having heard of my Wild Hunt slaughter in the forest they are eager to sign me up. There are a whole lot of elves that would love to see me ripped to shreds on the arena hard packed sands.

I have my first match in the Capitol today. I'm told I'm supposed to fight a Noble. I come out into the pits. It has recently become fashionable for the Noble youths to compete in the Arena. Steps are made to ensure they don't die. Apparently this fellow is among the finest duelists in the Capitol. Sporting light chain mail and wielding two swords he's apparently won sixty-seven bouts in the arena and well over a thousand duels. He's called "Kid Death." I'm looking to make a statement and he seems to be the right man for my job.

Kid Death flings a bolt of magic at me and it bounces off. "So it is true a mere human somehow has a defense from The Source itself. Very well, you'll be easy enough to deal with using my swords," he sneers.

"I don't even know what The Source is," I mock the Kid, "let alone be afraid of it."

Kid Death retorts, "You should be afraid for The Source imparts all the energy from this conquered world's dead gods united into one powerful channel that gives us our strength and protects us from scum like you."

"The power of The Source cannot compete with one human's strength. Prepare to be annihilated," I yell.

I'm shirtless and wearing only a pair of shorts and carrying no armaments. I am hoping not to need my suit this match. No one outside of my group knows about it or can detect it for that matter, so I'm trying to keep it as a trump card.

I cry out like a gladiator to the crowd, "Hail! We who are about to die salute you," and we begin.

The Kid comes out with prefect technique. He thrusts at me and I narrowly dodge. He does this again and again until I time a push kick through his guard. He backs off a few feet. I jump in the air, and through a karate style jumping crane kick, I smack him in the face. But it does almost no damage. However that's not my purpose. I merely want to distract him. It works, now his attention is on protecting his face. Expecting to receive another blow to his face, he never sees what is coming; and it's likely the first time this world has witnessed this maneuver performed. I leap into the air and on my way down I do a corkscrew baseball slide towards his legs. I grab his left leg and use my momentum to spin underneath that leg. I trap his leg in between my two legs, like pincers. I wrap my left arm underneath his ankle, and grab my left hand with my right, cranking on his ankle. The pressure forces him to fall over but before he does, he has the good sense to stab me with his sword. As he falls the sword stays inside of me. Once on the ground I switch the ankle from the left side of my body to the right. The maneuver is called an inverted heel hook. I crank and all the ligaments in his knee and ankle rip. I pull the sword out of my body, ignoring the calls to stop the fight and I cut his head off. I grab the severed head and hold it out high. The crowd is stunned. Their Kid Death has been killed in less than a minute.

My next fight is with a huge female demon that the Noble families have hired for the sole purpose of killing me, spending a tremendous amount of money to bring her from another dimension. She stands roughly thirty-five feet tall and has five tentacles on each side of her torso that she uses like arms. Her humanoid face is studded with a forked tongue and large jagged teeth. Except for her tremendous bosom, there is nothing feminine about her. Her tentacles are flexible yet tactile to the point that she can clutch and operate weapons with them. In her tentacles, she carries a menagerie of weaponry ranging from swords to morning stars, those deadly metal balls attached to a chain on a handle. She's sprouted a pair of bat-like wings and two claw-like feet that allow her to perch, much like a bird. Oddly the rest of her lower body is shaped more like that of a serpent.

I can tell that I'm going to need my suit for this match. The morning stars are the worst for me; I just can't get my distance. They have a range of twenty feet and she manipulates four of them nearly simultaneously. I was going to use the suit as a surprise weapon but even one strike would do me in. I pull on my suit from my chest and engage. I throw dozens of poison darts at her she parries nearly all of them. Those that do hit have virtually no effect. She seems immune to the poison. I am getting pummeled from multiple directions. The morning stars are just too much for me to handle. I know even with my suit on I'm going to die. Every dodge I try just gets me hit by another morning star. I know I'm beat and am probably going to die so I make one last desperate charge at her. I wasn't even close but just like that fight with the elves I got the curious feeling reality was bending. I should have been twenty feet away and right in front of a morning star. Instead I've driven both of my speared hands through her neck. While in her death throes she flings me hard against the arena wall. As I lay there stunned, I watch as she bleeds out. The crowd doesn't know what is happening. Neither do I. I do know: I'm alive. I spend the rest of the show recovering in the back while Martin and Linh guard me.

Bobby fights that night as well. He wins but due to my condition I am in no shape to watch. After the show we collect our pay and leave. The others want to celebrate but I'm too beat to do anything but buy a bottle of the strongest liquor I can and head home. I guarantee them that I'm not hurt which is more or less true and I bid them ado. I've made enough money to pay for the initial payment of Leah's schooling so I hire a carriage to take me to that part of town. The school opens in the early hours of the morning so I go to the school and pay for Leah's enrollment.

I'm a little drunk and in the mood for a walk so I tell the carriage to leave. I'm drinking my whiskey-like libation when I see some flashes of energy emanating from an alley. Curious, I go investigate. I see a hooded figure being accosted by six elves. It looks like an entertaining show so I light a cigarette and enjoy. There are two dozen similarly dressed elf remains surrounding the figure. Obviously this fellow has some skill. However, he's fading. I'm guessing he's a wizard by the looks of things because he finished off one of the six with a lightning bolt of magic. His opponents are wizards as well; they keep bombarding him with spells that he blocks by a shield around him. His shield begins to fail and lets some magic through, albeit attenuated. The hooded figure falls to one knee. Finally the hooded figure is thrown violently into a wall by the force of the elves' arcane energies. Barely able to move he pulls out a knife. I think that out of desperation the hooded figure is going to try to engage them in hand to hand, though I don't think it is his forte. I am wrong. The hooded figure still has a spell or two up his sleeve. He slashes open his palm while chanting; a demon appears with horns, a barbed tail, claws, the whole bit. It slashes down on the first elf ripping it apart. The other wizards concentrate on the demon while the hooded figure tries to scramble off; but he is too weak to do anything other than crawl. The demon slams his tail into the back of one of the elves. The remaining three elves blast the demon with magical energy. They blow holes through it. The demon turns around and charges, slamming into them, driving two aside and biting off one elf's face. The remaining two elves blast the demon to dust. They approach the hooded figure, ready to finish him off.

The hooded figure has nothing left. He grabs his knife ready to die fighting. I admire his spirit so I decide to help him out. I toss my cigarette and empty my bottle, then engage. The first elf sees me just in time to catch a flying knee to the face. The other elf casts some sort of spell that falls impotently off me as those things do. I throw a spinning back fist at the other elf, knocking him unconscious. I stomp on the other elf lying on the ground, shattering his shoulder. By this time the hooded figure has managed to crawl over to the unconscious elf and slit his throat. I help the figure up. After taking off its hood I see that he's a male elf but different than any I've yet seen. He's even gaunter than the average elf. His eyes are a bold ebony color. Unlike the vibrant energy that emanate from all the elves I've met, his skin is a deathly white color. And unlike the fair haired elves, his hair was raven black. Moreover, where his fingertips should have ended with nails there were claws instead. Overall he had a bit of a ghastly countenance. I already could tell Martin and he were going to get along well.

"My name is Archmage Earl Neriss. You saved my life. Name your reward. Please, would you accompany me to my home? Just call me Neriss." I agree to go with him and we get a carriage. Neriss is hurt pretty badly so I carry his stick-like body into the carriage.

We go to his house which is a rather large mansion in the wealthiest area of the Capitol. He goes to what is presumably a healing chamber. When he returns his wounds have healed. He tells me that he is the head of a prominent family. However he leaves the day to day work to a relative, in part, so that he can pursue his magic. The other reason is that while he is the head of the family he is still perceived as a pariah since he is a mixed breed. When he was conceived his father commingled his essence with that of a powerful demon. The mixing was only partially successful, however. Neriss should have been given both the strength and the magical power of a demon with the intelligence and status of a Noble. Instead, his physical strength and bulk have always paled compared even to pure elves. The worst part of this bad idea was that his mother died during childbirth, something his father never got over. His father died when he was a child and since that day assassins have come for him, coveting his powerful position. The assassins could very easily be hired by his own family; they view him as a horribly failed experiment. He himself is embarrassed at having High Noble status, but with the essence and overt characteristics of a demon.

"I've killed hundreds of assassins," he said, "I have great magical power but am extremely weak, physically." He pointed to the staff he needs to walk any distance.

I've heard this line before, and suggest, "That, my friend, is a self-fulfilling prophecy. Where I come from, centuries ago the founder of one of the greatest martial arts systems was the weakest of his brothers. He learned to use leverage and cunning to beat his opponents. In the process he became healthy and strong." I said. Touching his arm, I suggest, "Neriss, you can do the same. You said that I could have anything I want. This is what I want. You are going to train with me a minimum of five times a week for the next year in exchange for me saving your life," I bargained. "After that year, if you still think you are too weak, then by all means whine to me about being physically inept," I smirked.

We were quickly forming a bond and so I feel it's acceptable to use this level of honesty. "That's the whole point of martial arts, Neriss. If one was already stronger and faster than everyone else there would be no point in training. Martial arts let's you overcome your shortcomings and become stronger. What about it, Neriss?" I put out my hand. He extends his pale, thin, claw-tipped hand and we shake. I know I have a convert.

The next three years go by fairly smoothly. Neriss keeps his word and comes by regularly. The first few months are extremely hard on him but he slowly begins to make gains. Within a year he is becoming proficient at hand to hand and is visibly more fit. Instead of a staff for support just to walk, he is now running each morning. I am pleased to see that he is meshing well with our group. Since his birth he has been surrounded by people either jealous or scared enough to kill him. This is the first time in his life he's ever had real friends. Linh and Martin train with me daily for the arena. Magnus and Rodney come by several times a week as well. Magnus has hired a private sword trainer and is training daily in both swordsmanship and the arcane magic arts. Apparently, he is quickly becoming a master at both. Rodney's power is growing rapidly, too. On occasion I see Cory when he's in port but he spends most of his time on the high seas. Ace has been recruited as an officer in the Imperial Guard so I don't get to see him as much as the others. Michelle's dedicated herself to learning about this world's ecology but she comes by quite often. I have noticed that Linh and she are growing quite close; when we don't go out as a group, they often go out together. I see Evelyn every day. Martin helps her with her magic while I train her in the martial arts every day. She's quite the asset; since Bobby and Harvey are out bounty hunting, quite often we don't have anyone else to prepare me for winged opponents.

I'm glad to see that Eric ignores her as he is trying his best to brown nose his way up the elfs' social ladder; having a demon wife doesn't help, apparently. Linh and Martin have decided to take stealing to another level. They rob a Nobles villa at least once a month. Neriss hires them to steal from his rivals. I come along occasionally, especially for a large job. We have become infamous for our thefts. No one can figure out how we pull off our jobs. However I spend much of my time with Evelyn at Neriss's home studying the lore of this land. Neriss also has taken an interest in my apparent immunity to magic. I'm honored to let him study me. I mention the instances when I felt reality bend as well. I really want to know how I do it or if it's even me that's doing it. He tells me it's already making his head hurt figuring out about how and of what I am capable.

As the years go by I become a crowd favorite in the arena. The fights aren't normally supposed to be to the death but that is often the result. I fight monsters ranging from acid spewing amoebas that sprout caustic tentacles to flying plants brandishing vines covered in thorns dripping with poison. I normally win even when I don't put on a good show. I've actually become a favorite of the Emperor's. He appears at most of my fights. Whenever I fight and he's there I begin my fight with a salute and like a gladiator proclaim, "Hail to the Emperor! We who are about to die, salute you." He seems to get a kick out of it because he salutes back. Michelle patches me up after each match.

Although Neriss offers to pay for Leah's schooling, we decline. I fight one to two times a month and it makes me happy to fight and to provide for Leah. I still count the days until Leah comes back from her school. I spend the rest of my money on the human inhabitants at the lowest level of society. I also am beginning to be a hero to the people on the bottom level. They actually have built a statue of me. Neriss gives substantial amounts of money to the cause, more for my sake than anything else. Linh donates most of what he steals to the effort as well. We have built over a dozen schools and medical facilities. These years go by well. Our little group engages in all sorts of pranks and debauchery.

After my last fight a courier comes and tells me the Emperor wants an audience. The courier takes me to a flying carriage that delivers me to the palace. I see him up close for the first time. The Living God, Commander of The Imperial Source, he is ancient and regal. I can literally feel the authority that permeates through him. As elegant as an average elf is, the Emperor compares to elves as a diamond compares to charcoal. He carries himself with such elegance that it makes you believe you are in the presence of a god. To his left and right are the three greatest soldiers the Empire has ever known. All three are from the world the elves came from before coming to this world.

First there is the General. The Empire has only one, General Hill. The General is the greatest tactician ever to grace the Empire. An old raw-boned sorrel, he is the embodiment of the lost cause. The soul within his eyes is fearless, exuding a quiet Spartan dignity and confidence. One can gaze on his face and see his honest character as clear as crystal without complications. The years which he has endured have dimmed some of his enthusiasm, but caused no flagging of his pride or vigor. He has served for millennia and it is said that even after countless missions, he has never failed. However, the Empire has failed him. It has become bloated with corruption; leaving behind the honorable, like the General and his troops. Despite that, one cannot see a single kink in his resolve.

Always by his side, Sergeant Major Grimes stands to the General's right. Said to be the oldest elf in the Empire, he is nearly as squat and broad as a dwarf. The quintessential enlisted man, his eyes constantly survey his surroundings for danger. His back is straight in the military habit of being rigidly at attention. Scored with countless scars from the countless battles he has fought for the Empire; he easily could have them removed, but he is not up to such contrivances. Born to the battlefield, Sergeant Major Grimes scoffs at the gaudy parade uniforms so popular among the young now; he wears his field armor even in the Emperor's Court. To look at him is to see a soldier; no more, no less. He is the General's shield and axe and has stood by him for more millennia than the Empire has existed. Together they have saved the Empire dozens of times. While accolades have been bestowed upon others often less deserving, the Sergeant Major's only rewards have been a handful of medals and a wife who has long since left him. He bears it all stoically and has never once questioned his role, being one who would break rather than bend.

To the left of the Emperor, there is Colonel Hague. He is the second highest ranking officer in the Empire. An unassuming elf, one could walk right by him on the street and think he was just another merchant. However, he'd fought in thousands of campaigns for the Empire. In times past, these three leaders controlled all the military forces of the empire. After millennia of political maneuvering by the Nobles, that no longer is the case. Now the bulk of the armed forces of the Empire is controlled by various Noble Houses. The sons of the High Nobles often spend a few years in the High Guard put in place for ceremony and the means for these sons to brag about their service. My understanding is that the High Guard is never put in any real danger and would not know what to do if they were. These three leaders now only have under their direct control a comparatively small contingent of the elite commandos that take on the Empire's most deadly foes in covert wars the rest of the Empire rarely even knows took place.

The Emperor speaks. "So you are the human gladiator that is impervious to magic. I've watched you fight with great heart. You've even managed to befriend our demon spawn Earl Neriss. As long as I've been aware of him, I've never seen him with a friend other than the demons he summons. I'm impressed. I'd like you to come to a gala I'm holding. I can tell you are not the type that enjoys such things, but please consider it."

"Thank you. I am humbled by your audience, Sire." I bow and leave.

Leah is scheduled to graduate. I go to her graduation. She's graduating at the top of her class, and has been invited to move on to the highest level of study. It is a sixty year program that only the best are invited to join. Just my luck, I spend three years getting my brains bashed in to earn her tuition and now she's leaving again. The program starts in three weeks and I want to make the most of it.

Leah and I spend some time together, but while she's thankful for what I've done the most I get are a couple kisses. There is the royal ball coming up. I'd rather not go but after Leah hears about it she begs me to go since I'm allowed a date. She's always been attracted to high society and this is the highest of the high on this world. Neriss is required to go because of his station, so he's hoping for some moral support. Linh and I had thought this would be the perfect opportunity to break into the house of every Noble required to attend. But, I never could say no to Leah.

I decide to go to the ball more because this is the last time I'm going to see Leah than anything else. She's leaving in two days for the master program in magic. Leah and I arrive in our finest at the palace of the Emperor. It truly is a magnificent place. If it hadn't been built with the blood of thousands of so called lesser races I probably would appreciate it more. There are chandeliers tens of feet tall hanging from ceilings a hundred feet high. When the light reflects off them they radiate a kaleidoscope of colors in arrays of light. The walls are draped in the finest silk-like tapestries that move and make stories of the realm. The food and wine are the finest that exist, prepared by chefs from across the realm. Everyone at the gala is dressed in what apparently is in style this season. Variations on a living cloth, tunic for the men and billowing dresses for the women. Leah insisted we go to the Emperor's clothier for our very trendy attire. I had to admit, Leah was stunning, and I wasn't so bad myself.

Personally, I was feeling unarmed and alone. I've grown accustomed to having at least Martin, Linh, or Bobby at my side for much longer than I've resided on this world. I see Neriss and I feel a little better, but I still can't get the sickening feeling that the price of any one of these dresses would feed a whole district of workers for a week. Neriss motions for me to come over.

He's addressing a couple of Nobles and announces, "So here is my gladiator friend. Did I ever tell you the time he saved my life by killing two assassins with his bare hands?"

A Noble who introduces himself as Sadas says, "So you are the famous gladiator that gives his earnings to the poor humans. How quaint. Even though you're human yourself, you are obviously a breed apart from the rest of your species. You could make much better use of those funds than trying to educate the rabble." Sadas smirks and looks around at the others in the circle to catch eyes of agreement.

Just before I hit him, Neriss interjects. "I suppose you haven't met Sadas, yet. You know he's one hundred seventeenth to the throne. At this rate you might be calling him Emperor in say a million years. Anyway there's someone waiting on you and I think you want to see her." Neriss turns us away from the group. Leah grabs me from behind and all other thoughts go away. Tomorrow she goes to the School Arcane to reach the pinnacle of the arcane arts. This will be the last time I see her for at least many, many years. I'm going to make the most of it. I kiss her on the cheek, careful not to disturb her makeup, and we begin to dance, waltz-like, her sparkling, alive gown purring as we dance. It is a wonderful evening. It makes all those nights in the Arena worth it knowing that I'm sending the most wonderful girl I've ever known to a place where she can follow her dreams.

The night goes on for hours; every moment is ecstasy for me. We find the unoccupied Arcane Tower and embrace. Out of the corner of my eye I see a couple of figures. I don't think anything of it until Leah screams. A statue comes shattering towards us.

I block it with my body and tell Leah, "Run, find Magnus."

Once outside my disruptive field she throws something to the ground and vanishes. I finally notice the face of one of the figures. It is Earl Daloch, whose son I slew in the Wild Hunt.

"You may be immune to magic," he says, "but you are not immune to its incidentals. I avenge my son now." At that moment Hundreds of tons of debris crash down as the Arcane Tower I'm in collapses. I know I'm dead, but once again I get that strange sensation that reality is bending right before the debris hits me. I black out.

Convergence VI

"Well these mortals are making some head way but it would seem like it would be better if we had more gods and powers to help us out. So why don't we just get more gods to help us out or at the very least find more mortals for the eventual attack?" asks Monkey.

Lucifer replies, "It is because there are no more gods left who are willing to help. Many things that were worshiped aren't real beings. They are simply manifestations of natural forces like Krounus or pure worship of the sun as opposed to worshipping a being like Apollo or Ra that claims dominion over the Sun. As to the real gods, if you remember, Yahweh killed a god. That god was Baal, also known as Belus or Marduk. Once Yahweh created the Angelic Host, he had expended most of his power as you recall. He was looking for followers. After the Flood Yahweh realized that if he assumed the role of Marduk or Baal, if you prefer, the power of those followers would come to him. Over the years he has engulfed the energies from many of the minor gods into himself, controlling the minions. Most of the Babylonian Gods are his now; they surrendered once they saw they were losing the fight after the Flood. Those that didn't join him such as the Egyptian gods Ra and Isis, long ago fled to other dimensions. The Hindu gods, found a way to remain in this dimension while shielding themselves from Yahweh through thought. The Hindu gods have always been strong, yet passive. And what do you think happened to all those Semitic gods? They're his now. We're not just fighting him we're fighting all the deities that joined him from dozens of belief systems. The Angelic Host, were stronger than the Semetic gods who had little fight left. Those that didn't depart to alternative realities joined him. For example, the South American gods for the most part capitulated when the first European Christians arrived. They realized the strength of Yahweh and his followers. The Incan and Peruvean deities were so war-like yet were over matched; they agreed to be turned into his angels.

Odin adds, "A popular misconception is that all the gods from myth are different; however, many are the same entity but named differently. Take the Aesir and Vanir. You know we fought many thousands of years ago. The Vanir long since made peace with us and are allies with the Aesir. I'm known in the North as Odin, but I'm known in Britain as Dagda. That's because I still pop up once in an awhile. Ishtar is an early edition of Aphrodite, or Venus, if you like. That goes for dozens of gods out there. The Great Spirit of the Americas is joining with us and he's also the tribal god in Mongolia, much of Africa, and Australia. Of course the Islamic god, Allah, is Yahweh by a different name."

Monkey jumps in, "So who's left out there for us to tap into?"

Odin pauses for a moment, "We might be able to find more powers, but it's still going to be hard to do that in time. We are trying to communicate our needs to all the gods that might join us, but we simply are running out of time. As for getting more mortals, you should already know why we can't do that. Most mortals that do not worship a real power or god end up eventually becoming reincarnated, and finding where their souls go afterwards is incredibly hard. A few still stay around because they are strong enough and determined enough to not pass on. However, most of those souls eventually do pass on because their reason for not going was based on fixing some unfinished business from their life. Those who do worship and are found deserving end up in whatever afterlife the god or power has designed. Other than that some gods and powers pick up people that they find interesting."

Lucifer joins in, "That's why the whole notion of a created Hell is so ridiculous. Who would want to waste that much time and effort on gathering up every single soul that didn't follow you and then torture them for all of eternity? It would just be foolish to do so."

Odin remarks, "It is interesting how the notion of Yahweh's hell has changed over the years. I remember before the Renaissance, hell was cold because you were far away from Yahweh's light. After Dante's Inferno, Yahweh really ran with that whole fire and brimstone notion and changed his whole myth on where nonbelievers were going. Don't get me wrong the Lord Buddha is quite correct if you were a piece of shit in this life you are getting reincarnated into something nasty. That's the result of natural forces not any god however. That's not to say some mortals that really pissed off a god don't get tortured. Sisyphus is a perfect example of that. Trying to outsmart the Olympians was not the best of ideas."

"What about the Greek gods?" asks Monkey.

Atlas replies, "The Olympians never cared about humanity. They always thought of them as playthings, nothing else."

Odin continues, "I took my eye off of Yahweh because the war I had with Zeus and the other Greeks. The entire Roman/Gaul fight mimics the fight we had. I finally got Zeus to surrender, but by then I'd screwed up and Yahweh had gotten too much of a head start. Basically every willing and able deity is going to help. It is more my fault than anybody else's." says Odin.

Atlas shrugs, "Odin, let it go. Being so self-flagellating just isn't helpful. What we need to do is start focusing on our plan, not on who did what to whom."

"Still wouldn't it be better to at least send some gods to help out on the retrieval mission?" asks Monkey.

"It would have been impossible for the first group and wouldn't have mattered for the second. The amount of energy used to send the first group that far was already immense. Comparatively, sending a group of mortals is like tossing a grain of salt while sending a god is like tossing a boulder. Remember the Wizard of Yendor? He may be the most powerful entity in all of the universe. Monkey knows him well. Even he wasn't willing to expend that amount of energy. Besides sending a group of gods would have tipped off Yahweh. It wouldn't have mattered for the second group whether they were mortal or gods because in that place all powers are nullified anyway. So a god would be no more powerful than a mortal," says Odin.

"How is Vili going to get back if it takes so much power?" asks Monkey.

"One of the mortals is still coupled to this dimension. The fundamental part of his soul is anchored here. Once Vili sees the connection he'll be able to use it to pull himself back. It's the difference between walking up the face of a mountain and having a rope to climb it. It won't be easy but we can pump power into the tether to help Vili up. That's also why the mortal has been gifted bending space and why he isn't affected by enchantments. Any magic attacking him might as well be attacking thin air if it is targeted at his body. And, since his soul is still tied to this world, a magician would have to know how to find his soul and be able to sling his magic across the distance between these two dimensions in order to attack him. Part of the process of splitting his soul required us to alter his energy signature, and an after affect allows him limited ability to bend space. It is also the reason that he didn't change physically like the other members of his party. We could make him stronger and faster but to bind him to this dimension he obviously couldn't be physically absorbed in the other dimension. The rest of the party is fully tied to that place so we could change them as we see fit," says Odin.

"Okay, but why didn't you even tell them what their mission was? Especially the mortal that is key to its success?" asks Monkey.

"When I cast the runes in advance of their journey the reading was that their chance of success was greatest if I didn't tell them." replied Odin. "Anyway let's see if he's going to survive this one."

Chapter 7

"However many holy words you read,
However many you speak,
What good will they do you
If you do not act upon them?"
                —from Dhammapada: The Sayings of the Buddha

I wake up in total darkness. I'm underground someplace; the smell of lightless earth, rock, and dust fills my senses. I remember studying that the inside of this world is filled with massive caverns all throughout it. I assume this is one of them. The last thing I remember is tons of debris crashing down on me. I move enough earth and rock to pull free of the debris. I feel for the cold, dry walls and try to figure out where I am, whether I'm up or down, how high is the ceiling. I walk through these caves, my eyes aching for light. I am like an invalid without my sight, and I'm thirsty for water I haven't had, or food for that matter, for days. I hear the trickling of water, and search, arms outstretched towards it. I feel around until my fingers find the cool wetness of a trickle of water. I put my mouth to it. Its brackish taste normally would have made me vomit, but right now it tastes like the sweetest nectar. After drinking my fill, I allow my suit to drink its fill.

As I search around, much to my delight, I feel what appears to be a patch of mushrooms. Just as I am about to consume a handful of them, I remember my military survival training from all those years back. These mushrooms could very well by poisonous. I pinch off a small piece of one and press it in between my forearm and bicep. I count off the seconds until half an hour goes by. I feel my arm for any signs of tenderness. Thankfully there is none. If there were any irritation, it would indicate the mushrooms were poisonous. I pinch off another tiny piece from the mushroom. I place it in between my lips and teeth and repeat the timed process. Again there is no tenderness.

Hopefully this means my newly discovered bounty is not poisonous. I gorge on the raw mushrooms. I can feel the mushrooms beneath my feet as I walk; there is a whole grove of them in this space.

I spend the next couple days resting at this spot and recovering my sensitivities. My suit is beginning to regain its strength as well. While in this underground oasis, I meet the first denizens of this subterranean world. I pick one up and feel it. It appears to be some sort of beetle, and I can hear a number of them scramble away as I begin to feel around. I notice that they make almost no sound, just the slightest rustle of their legs on the rocky floor. A survival mechanism I'm sure down in these soundless caves.

I pick the rest the mushrooms and use my suit as a backpack. I also fill it with water. I hear the slightest motion in the background. Before I can run I am overcome by a number of giant worm-like beings. Each one is over six feet long. Unlike normal worms they have maws designed to eat flesh. Most likely the beetles in the grove of mushrooms are among their prey. They wind their slimy bodies around me and begin strangling me. My suit has not yet regained enough of its strength to assist me. I am struggling for air as the worms wrap themselves tighter and tighter. I try to pull them off but it's no use. I am suffocating, so I use the only tactic I have left. I slam my body against the cavern walls, bruising and cutting myself. With death only minutes away, I have no other alternative and gladly pay the price. I repeat the process again and again until the worms are crushed. The tenderized worms are the first protein I have found since arriving in this place. I hungrily pick up each morsel of flesh and consume it. My suit is weak and needs nourishment as well. With a bounty I have not seen since the surface at my disposal I am glad to feel my suit partake in my harvest. Slowly I feel my suit regaining its strength as well. As it does so, it begins to heal my wounds.

I continue searching for light and more water hoping that I am close enough to the surface that I can escape. The air is stagnant and I have yet to feel a draft that would indicate a way to the surface. I keep my hopes up for an escape. After days of meandering blind through this subterranean world, the air is getting warmer and fumy. I follow a vague hint of light. Closing in on the source of the glowing light I finally find it is coming from a pool of magma.

During the months I spent with Caspian he described his underground world. He told me once that the higher caverns were fairly hospitable realms. Some even had luminous moss that would let surface dwellers see in the underworld. However at the deepest levels the world became much more bizarre. There and only there existed free standing pools of magma. If Martin is correct and this world is twenty times the size of Earth then I am thousands of miles below the surface. I remember, from my college years, the radius of the Earth is, on average 3963 miles. Nineteen miles is the depth of the mantle. From my research I know the mantle of this planet is much thinner than Earth's. Even accounting for a core and a mantle I am likely at least ten thousand miles below the surface, further evidence that the laws of physics seem to act differently here. Unlike Earth the subterranean realms have many predators and natural dangers. The plants down here have developed ways to synthesize the ambient radiation that permeates this world in the same way plants synthesize light on the surface.

I realize I may never go home unless I learn to cautiously do whatever it was that allowed me to escape Daloch's attack in the first place. To this day, I have no idea how, when necessity dictates, I have some ability to bend time to survive. I also don't know why I was flung so far away this time when previously I had only traveled short distances. But, I'm beginning to learn how to survive here. I discover that most of the plants are poisonous but my suit has learned to remove the toxins and feed both of us. I fight and feed off of numerous foes ranging from carnivorous centipedes to jellyfish that float on self-produced gases, lashing out with tentacles dozens of feet long.

I travel for what I think are weeks, and learn that I am trapped in these lower levels. I try for a time to travel upwards but in those higher caverns I find there is essentially no life. I assume it is because those caverns are far away from the radiation and heat created on the lowest levels. After awhile the days merge into months and the months into years. I have no idea how long it has been since I fell into these caverns. I fight thousands of battles simply to survive. If it were not for my suit, I would be dead a thousand times over. After a time I have learned to adapt to being blind. My other senses have become acute and I've learned to move without creating any sound. My hearing and sense of smell have become accustomed to being my primary senses. Since there is nearly no air flow in the caverns I have even learned to judge a prey's movement by the changes in the air. I have learned to make a home of sorts down here.

I now can fight nearly as effectively as I once did in sunlight. Light is almost a hindrance to me now. On occasion I will come across a magma pond and I am literally blinded by what once would have been the equivalent of twilight to me. I maintain a cavern where I have built traps to dissuade predators when I sleep. It is between two lakes. There are some kinds of small fish in those ponds, which I harvest. There are larger beings in the ponds as well. Among them are giant crustaceans, insect like beings, and giant amoebas that will engulf you and slowly digest you from within. I learned that lesson the hard way as I nearly died when one of its kind engulfed part of my hand. For the first time since I have been down here I escaped using that bizarre ability to bend space letting me escape. I have been ever vigilant since. My body is changing. I am still becoming faster and stronger. I heal at an almost regenerative rate and I do not feel as if I have aged. On occasion I bring a satchel of water nearby to a magma pond and spill it on the ground so I can see my reflection. Besides my skin having turned nearly albino white and the new scars I have accumulated during my time here, I do not appear much different than before.

One day, while crossing through a large cavern, I feel hundreds of ball-shaped beings on the ground, rolling around my feet. It feels like wading through a room full of balloons. Not only are they rolling but they occasionally bounce up near my face. I lift one of these balls and explore its touch and smell, soothing my hands over its smooth, warm, undulating surface. Suddenly the ball rustles and quivers in my hands, flattening out like a soft, warm clam shell. Its surface seems to be getting warmer and thinner. I can feel its agitation and I imagine that it is changing color from a bluish color to a bright red even though it likely has no color. Then I feel the wafting of a wind current on my cheek—a predator. The balls begin to vibrate rapidly. I can feel them, changing shapes, rippling all in unison. Then I seem to become part of their movement. I feel the rippling of reality. An image appears in my mind, directing me to follow. And I am waffling through some kind of corridor with the ball creatures, all mixed together. I feel as if we are traveling through realities, escaping the predator. Finally we settle down near the sound of some trickling water. My senses tell me we are not in the same cavern but an equally large one with water. The ball creatures have calmed down and at the same time become round again rolling around my legs and bouncing up around me.

I feel very safe with these creatures and begin to see images in my head that I'm guessing are their means of communication. We settle into a pleasant coexistence. My new friends send me images but it takes me what must be weeks or months to learn to communicate with them. Eventually I learn to create images in my mind conforming to what I wish to convey. I learn that they have a power to bend reality. They tell me through their images that I have a similar ability. After decades by myself even these strange creatures are a welcome discovery. I call them Ripplers.

The Ripplers tell me that there is one horrible being they run from that preys on them. I learn to understand they have no concept of self-defense. It is not that they are against it they simply cannot conceive of it. The Ripplers are a curious race. They are vastly more intelligent and sensitive than any I have encountered on this world or back home. Simply, they think differently than anything I've encountered; in many ways they are an introverted philosophical race, thinking in at least four dimensions. They are also able to polymorph themselves into different shapes, like shape shifters.

For millennia on end they have stayed here on the lowest levels of the planet hiding and fleeing from the predators. For some reason, the Ripplers have taken to me and begin to help me harness my own abilities to change the space-time continuum. I slowly and cautiously find I can, at will, bend space. At the same time the Ripplers are teaching me to control my powers, I begin to teach them about a being's right to defend itself and its family. They also do not see time in a linear fashion and have no sense of progress, so I share with them the concepts of discovery and exploration.

After an indeterminate amount of time and practice, our first test of self-defense comes when groups of bat-like predators descend on us. I lead them into battle. Instead of quivering helplessly or escaping through time, for the first time they fight back. They use their vibrational powers to make stalactites fall from the ceiling while I engage the enemy. I will my suit of living armor to grow wings so that I can fly up to engage the bats. Slowly the Ripplers begin to conceive of the necessity and right to defend one's self.

As what I assume are years go by, we continue to enjoy teaching each other. I meet thousands more of them. They learn to fend off attackers by themselves. I teach them the basics of military tactics and martial combat. The Ripplers teach me how to control my mind and how to perceive space as the malleable substance it truly is. My ability is only a small fraction of what they possess but the Ripplers convey to me that there is a power within me that is expanding. However, I am not ready to handle that power yet. I have asked them many times why I possess this ability when other humans do not. They tell me that I have been changed but by whom or why they cannot tell.

The Ripplers have begun to become curious about what exists beyond the recesses of their caverns. I have shown them through images of Earth and the world above the possibilities that await them. I show them the wonders my people observed of the universe. And with their extraordinary power, they can visit what my people could only perceive. Their ability to shift forms is such that they can survive in most environments, such as vacuums and extreme radiation. They can merge with each other into a giant entity while still maintaining their individuality. When in this state as a group the Ripplers are exponentially more powerful.

I also believe the Ripplers can perceive more dimensions than my mind is able to grasp. One day I am daydreaming of the upper world and they sense my longing to return. In truth I had been so enthralled with my studies that I had not realized how much I missed home. They convey to me that they are not sure they can successfully take me fully to the surface as the slightest miscalculation could cause me to be embedded in stone or flung into space. They saw an image of Caspian in my daydreams and they tell me they have observed his kind before. By viewing his kind's minds they know the way to his civilization so they could send me there. They have learned of the concept of money through me. While they of course possess none they give me a bag of gemstones. They think they are valuable because the Voles they encountered came for this type of stone. Knowing that Caspian had mentioned his people lived relatively close to the surface I agree. They bid me farewell and thank me for my teachings. I start to do likewise but before I know it I am flung through space.

Chapter 8

I arrive close to a set of gates guarded by twenty Vole soldiers, the same species as Caspian. They are all wielding halberds, like the witch's guards in the Wizard of Oz, the antiquated weapon made of axe and spear. How they hold themselves and the scars on their faces tell me these Voles are all experienced battle veterans. It makes sense, since danger is more likely to come from the levels farther below from what Caspian used to tell me. This level, Caspian's level, is just below the surface and far above the levels I've spent the last many years.

As I walk up to the Vole who is presumably the sergeant in charge, he loudly asks, "What the hell are you doing coming from the lower levels?"

I tell him, "It's a long strange story. Could you let me inside, please?" I take out the gems from my bag and ask, "Is this worth anything to you? If so, maybe I can buy passage?"

The soldiers immediately go into a fighting stance and the Sergeant says, "Yes those are very precious. Those are among the most valuable gemstones in existence. However, they are only found at the lowest depths of the caverns. Only the best of our explorers can make the journey. No human could. Especially one without any magic as I can sense you have none." He growls, "You have the audacity to try to trade stones to us that you most likely murdered for?"

"I did nothing of the sort!" I retort. Realizing there is no way they will believe my story, I put the stones away. Then I remember the small signet token that Caspian gave me all those years ago after the hunt. I keep it as a memento in the same chest pocket as I keep my armor. I take out the beautiful token and show it to the Sergeant, "I was told by one of your people, that this would give me safe passage into your country."

"Where did you get that"? The Sergeant demands.

I explain to them the details of meeting Caspian during the Wild Hunt. "That's been many, many years ago as you surface dwellers measure time," I realized.

"Guild master Caspian's experience is well known throughout the land. That was more than sixty years ago. The human was supposed to be unable to be affected by magic, however, and without magic your race typically ages twenty times faster than ours. Why would you still be young if you are that human?" He asked.

"Just send for Caspian. Let him be the judge," I suggested.

The Sergeant blustered, "Caspian is a Guild Master. It is not a guard's place to summon one such as he. Besides he is in another city."

"Look," I said, "either I'm his long lost friend or I'm an imposter. If I am his friend and Caspian is so important nowadays that a soldier such as you wouldn't want to keep him waiting to see his friend. If I'm not then he'll want to know and you'll get to cut me to pieces. Regardless," I insisted, "I didn't steal these gems. If they are so valuable can I trade some to you guards for some food? Also, could you at least throw me into a prison cell with a cot and pillow while we're waiting for Caspian?" I plead as I'm close to exasperation. Since I have several hundred, I grab twenty out and toss them at the guard and bargain, "That is one for each of you; is that reasonable?"

"Human, I'm beginning to believe you since you apparently have no idea how much those gems are worth. Even the smallest is worth many years of our pay. Also the stories say that the human was a fool."

"Then, if that's the case, could you relay this as part of the message: 'Caspian you fucking weakling I am standing outside the gates of the city. I don't give a shit what you're doing. Drop it and get the fuck over here.'" I yell.

Now I think the soldiers completely believe me. I can tell. "So do we have a deal gentlemen?" I ask.

The soldiers take me inside the gates and instead of taking me to a prison cell make me a deal. Threesomes of soldiers will take turns guarding me, but they'll let me stay at a local inn.

I ask, "Hey, Sergeant, do Voles drink alcohol and smoke cigarettes and does this inn have them?" When he tells me yes I hug him almost ready to cry, "After living off raw worm flesh and brackish water for so many years, I'd drink beer laced with horse piss." The Sergeant's watch is up and I say, "Take me to where the soldiers and other fighters stay; not some high class joint."

The Sergeant who goes by the name, Barbour, takes me to his favorite pub. I take out one gem and give it to the innkeeper. His eyes bug out.

I ask, "Is this enough to buy everyone here food and drink for the day?"

He says, "For a week!"

I'm drinking and eating and I can feel my suit is digesting the food as fast as I eat and still wants more. The Voles make an especially dark and rich beer made out of some root that grows only on this shallow level beneath the surface. Barbour, the other soldiers, and I start talking. I'm sampling every alcoholic beverage they have. The innkeeper sent one of his sons to buy some tobacco (this world's equivalent anyway). He's just returned. I take my first puff. It feels like heaven.

A rather large vole comes in and the rowdy crowd immediately quiets. I feel the ground shift. Normally I might have dodged it but I'm drunk for the first time in decades. Instantly, I am enveloped in stone up to my neck.

"Are you the one that dared present one of my signets to my soldiers?" It's Caspian and he's decided to have some fun. All of a sudden the soldiers sober up and raise their weapons.

"Nice trick, Caspian," I whisper, unable to breathe in this stone casement. "Good thing I saved your ass so you had time to learn a trick or two," I expel.

Caspian beams and flips a hand to release the stone coffin, "I use my new gift to manipulate stone," he says, "I can even walk through it!"

"Aaahh," I breathe in and out, then, "I've picked up a few new ones myself."

Caspian rushes up towards me forgetting that as a Vole he's ten times as strong as a human; he hugs me with all his might. I think I feel some ribs crack. The guards relax realizing Caspian was joking all the time. "I immediately teleported here the minute I was notified you'd arrived," he gushes. "I heard you were dead, my friend."

Grasping his hand warmly, I say, "Sit down; I'll tell you the whole story."

Caspian sits down with me and tells me he's now the Guild master of the demolitions department for the Guild of Engineering. That basically means he is in charge of blowing things ups. He was a journeyman when I met him and after many years of campaigning on the battlefield he was allowed to come home to head the department. I spend the next few weeks with Caspian. He shows me around his city. It is vast. It is even bigger than the Capitol. I also find out the Voles have their own Republic. Each city elects a Senator and they convene to make any major decisions. Their nation is huge it stretches underneath the Main Continent and shares the Western continent with the Dwarves below ground. The majority of the cities are there. I'd like to go there, but I can't bend space anywhere near that distance and being immune to magic for transporting, that will have to wait. I'm also excited to get back to the Capitol to see my group. So after a few more weeks, I ask Caspian to direct me towards the surface. I want to surprise everyone so I have him take me to the caverns just below the Capitol.

After Caspian takes me to the caverns underneath the Capitol, he and I say our goodbyes. He tells me to contact him if I ever need assistance with anything. I get close enough to the surface, so using my enhanced abilities I can sense where I am. I find the arena. It's been so many years; I want to make a memorable entrance. I'm also hoping everyone is still alive after all this time. I have no idea if any of my friends age, considering what they've become. And even if they do age, I know Magnus would keep true to his word and provide for them. With enough money they could purchase life-extending magic. Magnus for one is definitely alive. He's a survivor by nature. I'm just worried if any of my guys have managed to get themselves killed doing a heist, bounty hunting, whatever. I also am worried about Evelyn. Hopefully my friends have taken care of her and protected her from Eric. My plan is to announce my return, check up on my group, and kill that fucking Earl Daloch who nearly killed me in the collapse of the tower.

I camp out for a couple days until a major show occurs at the arena. I can hear and feel the pounding of the audience cheers as the matches continue. After one of the fights, I close my eyes then using the methods the Ripplers taught me, I will myself to the surface. For a moment I'm blinded. It's been sixty-six years since I last saw the sun. I've grown so accustomed to living with smell, feeling, and hearing that I almost forgot what it is like to use my eyes. I tread down the ramp into the center of the arena. The crowd doesn't recognize me at first. I see the Emperor and bow deeply to him. He immediately recognizes me and stands.

I proclaim, "Hail, to the Emperor! I have returned from the grave and I seek to fight." It's a little corny, but it's been awhile since I did this. Many in the crowd recognize me; I hear a murmur of conversation rumbling through the arena.

"I will take on the next two opponents," I challenge, "unarmed," I raise my hands, "and blindfolded." The crowd thinks it's a stunt but my eyes are so sensitive to the light that it would be to my detriment not to shield my eyes.

The Emperor roars, "The human will use my scarf to cover his eyes!"

Two beings come out from the arena gates. One is a reptile of some sort and the other is a large ogre-like being wielding a mace. I pull my suit of environmental armor from my chest sack.

An aide retrieves the Emperor's brilliant gold, silk-like scarf and delivers it to the manager himself who continues this many years later to manage the arena fights. He walks towards me with a big smile and spins me around with one of his insect feet, placing the scarf over my eyes. He tightens the knot and buzzes in my ear, "We've missed you."

I bait my two opponents to come at me. They charge me from opposite directions. I can hear the reptile coming from behind, about to bite. At the same time I feel the whirring of the ogre's mace in the air. I back flip over the reptile just as the mace comes down. I hear the shattering of bone and smell the blood. The lizard is assuredly dead. I jump on the ogre before he can recover. Grabbing onto his torso, I scramble around to his neck. I wrap my right arm around his enormous neck and grab my right wrist with my left hand. Having successfully sunk in a rear naked choke I squeeze until the ogre goes limp.

The crowd is standing and chanting in unison, "Human! Human!" I remove my blindfold and bow to the crowd. I see a figure flying down from the stands reserved for Nobles. It is Neriss! I had not noticed Neriss in the masses within the arena.

We briefly embrace and he yells over the crowds' noise, "Where the fuck have you been? You must have a good story to tell me."

Neriss and I go to his house. He tells me to make myself comfortable which means dimming the light. He summons a pack of demons to reach those in my group that I want to see and to return with messages telling me where they are and how soon they can make it to Neriss's. Martin is the first one to show. Linh, Bobby, Michelle, everybody starts trickling in one by one except for Ace, Magnus, Cory, Leah, and Eric. Ace and Magnus are away on different assignments. Eric, I didn't want to see and Cory is on the high seas. Leah is just out of school and on business. Magnus also sent a letter back with the demon. With everyone showing up, I decide to open the letter up later. Neriss and Martin fill me in on the group. Martin still helps out Linh but he toggles his time between working with Linh and developing magic with Rodney and Neriss. Rodney and Neriss have been working together. Their magic complements each other well and Martin is a great asset as well. Their raw power is substantially greater than Martin's but Martin's mind is able to do calculations in days that would otherwise take Neriss weeks. Martin has become extremely sensitive to magic so he can see the smallest remnants of enchantments. He's gained some other powers but most importantly to him, he's gotten his aura under control so he can interact with people without draining their energy.

Before Linh and Michelle come the rest of the group all laughingly tell me that the two have been together for decades now. They both think they have kept it a secret from the others but everyone knows. No one's sure why they want to keep it a secret but they just let it be. Linh has become infamous for his heists. His powers have grown tremendously over the years. He's now able to crack the wards of any building in a fraction of the time he used to need. His command over shadows has increased greatly as well. He can transport himself and others to any shadow he's ever visited. Michelle works as a healer in the lower levels. Michelle and Linh show up together soon after, so our snickering over their attempt at concealing their courtship comes to an end. I greet Michelle and Linh with a hug. The rest of the group shows up soon after.

The first thing I notice is that no one looks like they've aged a day since I last saw them. Bobby has become among the most feared bounty hunters in the land and his services are much sought after. Since we last met, Bobby has gained some considerable powers. His ability to track has increased to detecting magical trails as well. If he gets his hands on something the person used or a piece of their body, like a strand of hair, he can track the person's magical signature even if the physical scent is not discernable. He also can become invisible to both physical and magical forms of detection. But, his ability is not absolute like my own. First he has to consciously will it to occur and it is draining for him to maintain it for more than a few hours. And he is not completely undetectable; especially skilled magic users, like several in the room, can sense him. From what I can discern Bobby is using magic to shield himself, so those skilled enough in magic can find him, whereas my ability stems from something else entirely. Bobby also has seven tails now when transformed into his beast-like state. His strength, speed, regenerative powers have become greatly enhanced; and his physical senses have not only been enhanced but he's developed new ones as well. He now has echolocation like a bat. It's not as strong as Cory's where he can sonically injure someone, but it serves its purpose. Bobby sees in the infrared and ultraviolet spectrums now, when he so chooses. The range of his hearing is such that he can hear low and high frequency sounds with ease. Bobby has set limits for his work. He only goes after criminal elves and Nobles. That puts him on a very short list of bounty hunters that are willing to go up against a Noble single-handedly. Bobby took losing me pretty hard. He almost stormed the Noble Court, the meeting place of the aristocratic elves. It took a pack of demons summoned by Neriss and all of Linh's shadows to hold him until he was calm enough to understand that attacking the court would just mean instant death. Bobby finally figured that tracking fugitives was the only way to make the elves pay for my death, without getting himself killed instantly. He's taken down hundreds of fugitive elves since I left. Even though many of the contracts gave extra money if he brought the bounty back alive, he'd yet to give in to that payoff. He generally just brought back the head of the bounty as evidence of the kill. Bobby teams up with Harvey on the more lucrative and by default more difficult cases.

Harvey has become a bounty hunter of some repute himself. He doesn't specialize in any one area; he's worked as a mercenary and hunts whatever will get him paid. He has taken up residency on the Western Continent. There he discovered an entire civilization of dwarves in which he has become kind of a hero. It is just as large as the Elven Empire and if not for the Empire's access to the powers of The Source, probably would be more powerful. Due to slaying a number of rather nasty creatures that had been terrorizing the area, Harvey has become a prominent figure within the Western Continent society. His powers have increased such that he has much greater control and power over earth. He can even meld with the ground and travel through it like a sound wave.

Neriss tells me about Magnus, who has become quite the power as I knew he would. His voice is incredibly powerful and he delves into the arcane arts. By combining his pre-existing knowledge with this world's he has achieved a high level of power sooner than anyone in recent memory. No surprise to me, Magnus achieved Noble status for his more heroic actions. He is actually an Earl of the Elven settlements in the Western Continent, making him a High Noble and giving him greater privileges than most Nobles. He acquired his title by saving a city from a demon and several young dragons. Apparently, the dragons were cubs that had been kidnapped and had been bent to the demon's will. This had transpired on the Western Continent. Magnus was on a business trip to finish a trade deal. Shortly after arriving the dragon cubs attacked. The city's Earl and all of his descendants were attacked first, and killed. Without any leadership the city's guard soon crumbled. Magnus single handedly fought the demon. After a heated battle he decapitated the demon with a mighty blow. Then the dragons who had been pillaging the city attacked after finding their master slain. Magnus used his voice and ordered the dragons to roll over which they did. It was determined the dragons had been brainwashed. By dragon standards they were barely toddlers. So they were returned to one of the far continents that is mostly ruled by dragons. The dragons turned out to be the offspring of a high ranking dragon so returning them solidified the Empire's and the Western continent's relationship with that land. In acknowledgment for his actions and since the Earl and his heirs were dead, Magnus was made the Earl of the Western Continent.

I see Evelyn coming into the room. I stand and cross to greet her. Without saying a word I hug her for an eternity. She looks great. Dressed in a black leather skirt, blouse, and heels she looks like she spent some effort for the occasion.

Neriss quips, "I haven't seen you dress up in decades. What's the reason for the change?" He turns to me, "You know she's been working as my research assistant."

I ask, "What about Eric?"

Neriss responds, "Eric has no problem with it since he thinks that Evelyn working for an Earl might give him an opening into the High Society. Evelyn's become a formidable mage, a sorceress in her own right and in addition, I thought it wise to teach her how to summon and control demons." Neriss smiled at Evelyn, "she has a knack for it. Even when she screws up, demons that normally would shred the summoner to pieces, seem to like and obey her."

I take her hand and gently hold it, "I'm not surprised by your prowess, and I can certainly understand the way that even demons have taken to you." We move to sit again as Neriss continues telling me about my group.

Ace has quickly advanced through the ranks in the Elven military, due to a number of notable exploits, and currently serves as a high ranking officer in the Imperial Guard. Cory has been traveling the high seas all these years. I ask Michelle about how the human settlements are doing. Magnus has donated heavily to the charity work. Michelle has overseen the development of more hospitals, schools, and basic needs. Magnus actually suggested that the workers unionize. Initially the owners of the factories were ready to take some rather drastic measures to stop this movement. Then Neriss sent a demon to every owner and made it clear that any such action would result in a rather grisly death and/or a one way ticket to the worst dimension of hell. That quieted the gentry, and living conditions for the humans and other lower beings have improved markedly.

To my surprise no one thought I was dead, not even Bobby. After removing the rubble there was no evidence of a corpse so everyone assumed that I'd cheated death once again. But where I ended up, no one could guess. Everyone in the room had watched me die or nearly die, and return to the living, so I guess my return again was to be expected. However, what is surprising is I'd become a quasi religious figure to the humans of the Capitol. Neriss and a few others had helped propagate this idea so I actually have a huge following with the human population in the Empire.

Amid the reunion with all of my good friends, and on top of the arena fight, I needed a moment to let it all sink in. I finally read the letter Magnus sent. Amazingly it contains a single sheet of paper with an account number, my name, and an amount. Like the others, he figured I wasn't dead. And he guessed I'd come back someday needing money, so he kept making deposits into the account. I'm richer than most Nobles. I really am touched by all of this. I would not have faulted any of them at all for assuming I was dead after so many years.

Beers in hand, we toast our reunion and my friends ask for the story of what has transpired over the years. Everyone is a surprised to say the least. I give a demonstration of my new ability. It really confounds Neriss because he says what I do isn't magic. He wants to do some experiments with me at a later time. Of course I agree.

Finally, I ask everyone if they are willing to help me get my revenge on Daloch. Almost in lockstep they tell me revenge for my demise is not possible. Less than a day after my "death," Martin, Linh, Bobby, and Neriss nearly had a fight over who got the opportunity to kill Daloch. When Neriss explained he could make Daloch spend millennia tortured by demons before killing him, they all agreed Daloch should be tortured. Neriss, in a fit of rage, killed everyone of Daloch's household before finally sending Daloch to a demon that specialized in torture. To this day Daloch is being tortured. I told Neriss sixty-six years was probably enough and when it was convenient tell the demon to put Daloch out of his misery. We spend the rest of the night partying away.

I hear from Leah the next day. She wants to meet at a restaurant close to the Capitol. I finally get the chance to see Leah after so many years apart. She's wearing a green silken gown. She looks like she could be a princess out of a novel. She's been out of the Academy for a couple years now. Once again she graduated top of her class. Now she works on developing magic for the Empire.

She blushes a little and says, "I just wanted to tell you how much I appreciate what you did for me. I know about how you fought in the arena to pay for my tuition. You should let me pay you back somehow," she offers.

"To see you happy and successful is all the reward I need," I smile. "I'm really happy for you."

Afterwards we have a few drinks at an upscale bar. I see a familiar face there. It is the Noble Sadas I met briefly at the last gala before my little adventure underground.

"Hello, Leah, how do you do?" Sadas bows slightly.

Leah blushes and says, "Quite well, thank you."

I know it's irrational but I'm feeling intensely jealous. I ask her, "How do you know each other? I remember him from the ball," I add.

She tells me, "He's the Noble who owns the development program I work on."

"I see, so he's your boss," I say impetuously as we leave the bar. We take a carriage to her house. I walk her to her door which is on the higher level of a tower in one of the wealthier districts of town. As I get to her door I try to get the nerve to give her a kiss. She beats me to it and asks if I want to come inside. Of course I do.

We spend the next year enjoying our free time together. It's a happy time in my life. The arena calls. They want me back of course. But, between Leah and the money I have now, I decline the offer. A couple months later when Leah was supposed to be at work I see her with Sadas. She tells me they got off early. I'm in a hurry because Neriss wants to run more tests on me. He's been running various tests at least a couple times a week. I don't mind and I often get the chance to see Evelyn.

Finally, Magnus comes to see me. He looks quite regal now, every bit the Noble. He thanks me. He says if not for me, none of this would have happened for him. If I need anything just ask. I see Cory and Ace during this period as well. They both seem quite well. My days are spent training and working on my charity project with Michelle. I train with whomever is available and when Leah is free I spend my nights with her. I've always loved her and I'm thinking I'm going to make it official. I decide to travel to Caspian's Vole tunnels where some of this world's best jewelry smiths are employed for just such a purpose. After a few days, I pick up what they've made for me. It is extraordinary and worth the price I paid.

That night I visit Leah again. But this time I plan on surprising her. I climb up the tower next to her home and plan on swinging down with the bouquet of flowers and the ring made out of a mineral not found on the surface. It is worth the price of a Noble's villa. If it goes right I think I'm going to propose tonight. I scramble up the tower and approach her room. I see Sadas there with Leah. He's undressing her as they embrace. I feel my blood boil. I feel like killing and crying at the same time. I slam my fist into the wall sending my whole arm through the hole. I do it again and again until my hand's a bloody mess. The noise alerts the guards. I see Sadas and Leah looking at me from her room. Leah looks mortified as she dresses and runs to the rear of the house. Sadas just sneers at me. I'm ready to kill him but I'm not about to let him see the tears running down my face. I summon my power and bend space. I don't know where I'm going and I don't care. I spend the better part of three months in the lower levels of the capitol. I'm on the level where any sort of vice can be found. I take more drugs than even Martin would take. I know everyone back in town is looking for me. I hear Magnus traveled back immediately after he heard Sadas bragging about how he had broken the famous gladiator simply by taking his woman. I know if you were to see me right now you'd think I was just a destitute junkie and I don't really give a fuck. But I'm the oxymoronic indigent that is throwing around money left and right. Down here, no one knows who I am so there have been muggers galore trying to take me on. I think I've killed close to fifty people, but to be honest I don't know how many of those fights are hallucinations or are real. I just can't remember due to the drugs. I hear rumors that everyone from Bobby to Neriss are trying to track me down but there is no way I'm going to let them see me like this. I've been staying at the seediest bar I can find. The innkeeper has sent me whore after whore.

I should have known Martin was going to find me. I can barely move, covered in the stench of my own filth when he finds me. He knows the dealers as well as me. So it wasn't that long before he found out where I was hiding. To be honest, even the drug dealers had grown concerned. So it was a relief to everyone except me when Martin shows up as a cloud of mist and cleans me up. This isn't the first time he's seen me like this so he knows what to do. He dumps my head in cold water again and again. He makes me take a plant cocktail that speeds up the body's ability to cleanse impurities. Afterwards he carries me back to Michelle and she spends the next few days getting me detoxified. I spend a few more days at Neriss's. Martin, Evelyn, Neriss, Bobby, and Linh are with me the entire time.

Evelyn finally asks, "Why are you so hung up on her? There are a million women ready to throw themselves at the legendary gladiator. Ever since I've known you it has been this way. Just because we're in a different world doesn't mean she's a different person. She's attracted to power and Sadas is a High Noble. She's shallow and materialistic, but you're blind to that. You're blind to a lot of things. There are girls right next to you who actually give a shit about you."

I look into her eyes, "Who do you mean?"

Evelyn turns her face away, "Never mind, just get some rest, okay? Michelle says your heart was almost ready to stop when Martin called her. So you need some time to heal."

Later on Linh comes by, "You know the only thing that's going to make you feel better is to get back into the ring and forget about that chick."

I concede the point. Bobby, Linh, Martin, and I spend the next few weeks getting me into fighting shape. Neriss summons demons for me to battle after I start feeling myself. Evelyn visits me almost every day. She is truly a special friend to me. I can't think of another woman that has ever stood by me like her. Tomorrow, it is time to get back into the arena.

The crowd is packed. It is my return and I am now the people's champion. My opponent is some sort of subterranean worm that shoots out tentacles from its mouth. It is around six hundred feet long and has thousands of tentacles ready to draw me in. For every tentacle I cut, a dozen more come at me. I'm getting tired and I haven't figured out how to attack the main body which is deep underground. If I try to bend space I might end up lodged in a pile of sand, bonded at the molecular level since I don't know where the worm is exactly. Then I see Sadas sneering at me from the crowd. I'm filled with murderous rage. The tentacles come for me and I dive down its throat. I get taken into its stomach. The acid is eating away at my suit I can feel it scorching my skin and I don't care. I slash at it from the inside. Blow after blow until I rip through its stomach. I'm in a berserk rage and I just keep slashing. I claw my way from one end to another. The worm dies a humiliating death underneath the arena sands. I will myself to the surface of the arena, triumphant. Yet I want more; more blood. I fight again this time against a swarm of giant bats. They claw at me and I claw back within minutes the dozens lay dead. Those that try to flee, I strike down with darts from my suit. I go through a half dozen more combatants before my murderous rage is sated. I walk out of the arena. As I leave I'm handed an official invitation to an Imperial party. Since it is signed by the Emperor personally, I don't have much choice but to go.

I don't want to go to the gala but Neriss advises me that I have to face them at some point or another. I've taken enough anti-anxiety meds to put an elephant to sleep. I'm not going to break in front of them again. At the party, I'm drinking in a corner when I see Leah and Sadas. Leah walks past me without making eye contact. She's doing her best to avoid me without making it too obvious. I'm grateful for that.

I steel myself as I see Sadas approach.

In his arrogant manner he says, "I had the Emperor invite you to this party. I just wanted you to see Leah with a real man for a change. You should stick around; maybe if you're lucky I'll teach you how to satisfy a woman. You know this was the way it was always going to turn out," He sneers. "Did you really think you could keep her? She's an elf and you're just a human. You know the first time I fucked her she told me you couldn't ever make her moan like I could." He starts laughing.

I've had enough. I slam my fist into him. He dodges fast enough to avoid getting hit in the face. Instead I hit his chest. My fist goes bashing right through his breastbone. But before I can strike again, a dozen guards jump on me. I break a dozen of them and again come after him. He uses The Source and teleports away. I have just enough coherent thought to dive through the nearest window to escape. I don my armor and I bend space just enough to cushion the fall. I hit the ground running. The guards are already out looking for me. I make it to a drainage pipe and dive in; then I manage to make it to the lower levels relatively unscathed. I hide out with some humans I know down there. I'm told that within hours the Capital gates are stationed with many guards. Anyone within five miles is checked. This time my immunity to magic is to my detriment. I'm easy to find since all they need to do is determine whether someone has an aura or not. Being the only person, to my knowledge, that doesn't have a discernable aura it narrows the field quite a bit. While I can bend space now, my ability is still fairly limited in range.

The humans down here are willing to hide me indefinitely. They treat me as a Saint that delivered them from squalor, which in a way I suppose I did. That's more of a reason not to stay here for long. There are millions of people down here willing to fight for me. The odds are they will die in the process. It is inevitable that Sadas is going to figure out I'm hiding down here and when he does he'll send an army. While I know Neriss and Magnus will do their best to help, the Imperial law is strict. I've attacked a High Noble and death is the only sentence possible. I have a plan to get out of the city. There are aqueducts that bring in water from outside the Capitol. The problem is each has a series of tremendous filters for the dual purpose of cleansing the water and protecting from intruders. Each aqueduct has dozens of filters. Between the hundred miles an hour current and the massive size of each filter there is no way I can make it by myself even with my special abilities. I simply wouldn't have the strength to swim against the current. However, each filter has a code put into place that can be manually punched in from the inside. It's there for maintenance and it is not magical. The elves use mindless plants to do the work and the plants can't perform magic to unlock wards. Each code is different and is changed weekly. The only person that can get them is Neriss due to his rank but even he will be under surveillance, now. There's no way that he'll be able to deliver the codes. Evelyn is my best bet. Since she works for Neriss it won't draw any suspicion that she's traveling to his abode. After that she'll have to find a runner to deliver them to me. I get one of the youngsters to carry a letter to her detailing my plan.

Upon receiving the message, Evelyn gets the codes from Neriss. The original copy is enchanted by Neriss so that only Evelyn can read it. That way if she gets caught no one will be the wiser. So she makes a copy of the codes for Eric. She thinks that Eric is the best candidate for the job since he's an elf so he has more access to the city and he's not under surveillance. Besides, for all his faults, she believes she can trust him. He is her husband after all.

She tells Eric, "All of us are under surveillance, even me. But since you've never been associated with him, you can bring it to him. He needs to get out of the Capitol otherwise he'll be killed. This is where he'll be."

Eric graciously replies, "Of course I'll do it. I love you, dear. You know you can count on me."

Later that night Eric requests an audience with Sadas. "I know where the fugitive is."

Sadas responds, "If the information you provide me is true, I'll make sure you receive your title as a Noble. Of course it would be a lot easier if you marry into a Noble house. The Baron Corbin's youngest daughter is looking to be wed." Then with a conspirator's tone, Sadas says, "You're already married, aren't you? That could present a problem."

Eric states firmly, "That won't be a problem."

He leaves for home and finds Evelyn, saying coldly, "I married you back home to join your family. Here, you are nothing. You are just an impediment to my ascension. You are just some demon that hinders me now. You're not even human anymore, let alone the stature of an elf like me. By the way, you're little plot is going to make me a Noble. Sadas is going to help me get my title after I dump you and marry a Baroness." Eric grabs her and throws her out onto the street. "Get the hell out of here, imp!" Evelyn picks herself up, crying. She unfurls her diaphanous wings and flies to the rendezvous hoping she's not too late.

I'm waiting at the appointed place. It is right next to the entrance of an aqueduct. But there's something wrong; I see Evelyn flying to me as a patrol of hundreds is marching in my direction.

She hands me the codes and shouts, "Get out of here! I trusted Eric to deliver the codes and he betrayed us. There's still time. I'll hold them off while you enter the code to the first aqueduct."

I'm pretty sure Evelyn has a spell to let her breathe underwater and if not I can just envelop her in my suit. I race over to the aqueduct and punch in the code. Evelyn summons a huge pack of demons. I notice every one of the guards is a member of the elite guard. They are all Nobles and loyal to Sadas. The demons are slowing them down but as Nobles they all have power from

The Source at their disposal so they are whittling them down. Evelyn summons another pack but she doesn't have time to summon anymore. Half of the guards break off to deal with the demons and the other half focuses on us. The guards are already close enough to fire. She raises a protective shield. The guards have been specially briefed on how to fight me. Instead of trying to lock on to me with magic they create natural phenomenon first and direct it at the general area. Most of the guards aren't used to doing that so they are thankfully not particularly proficient. Sadas stays at the back far from danger. He is going to let his men do the dirty work. After a while they realize Evelyn's shield is regular magic so they revert to attacking. I unlock the aqueduct but the mechanism will take minutes to open. I can't use my gift on myself and Evelyn at the same time while she's fighting and shielded. If I do so one of the barrages will hit her right before she is transported. Evelyn is doing her best to hold off the attack with her shield but she is greatly outnumbered. I ask her whether she has a water breathing spell. She says she does. It looks like only one of us is going to make it out alive. There is no way I'm sacrificing her for my sake. I'm getting ready to transport her along with the codes into the aqueduct. Finally the entrance to the aqueduct opens. Sadas sees we are about to escape and summons all of his power as a High Noble and blasts through Evelyn's defenses. The blast of magic goes straight through Evelyn. I already can tell the wound is mortal. I use my gift to make the distance between us and the guards seem like miles.

"Evelyn, are you alright?" I ask knowing otherwise.

Evelyn shivers in my arms, "Would you hold me? I'm so cold. I want you to know that I've always loved you, ever since we were back home. Why I didn't act on it before I don't know. You were always right about Eric. I had hoped that maybe with you back I might finally have something with you but you were so enamored with Leah. Am I really that hideous that you couldn't think of me like that?" She cries.

I feel hot tears running down my cheeks. For all these years I'd been blind. This woman had treated me better than any woman ever had and I'd thought it was just out of friendship. The occasions when the possibility had crossed my mind I'd always figured I could never compete with Eric's smooth tongue and immaculate looks anyway. Right now I just realize that I've wasted decades.

I hold her tightly, "You're beautiful. We'll see each other in the next life," I whisper.

She tilts her head back, "Would you kiss me just this once?" she asks. I pressed my lips to hers and as I feel the life drift out of her I am filled with a guilty melancholy that is only surpassed by my murderous rage.

I could have escaped through the aqueduct but as I see Evelyn's body, all I can think of is vengeance. I surge through the guards like heat lightening. I want Sadas's life in my hands and my last bit of rational thought tells me to bend space to get to him. But, I'm too enraged to use my power. All I want is to kill. For every one that I kill a bit of my armor is struck. Slowly the guard starts to whittle away at me. I killed over three hundred before I am finally brought down. A dozen guards are holding me down. My suit is destroyed and my body is broken. All I have left is my hate.

The last thing I see is Sadas. "You are only human, how did you think you could beat me."

I spit in his face. "Always remember, you were the coward that stood behind your men until I was struck down. Today I slaughtered many more than a hundred Nobles while you at your best are going to kill one human, already beaten to the brink of death. You are weak Sadas."

He pins my neck with his sword and I spit back, "You know why you are weak? You lack hatred. Everything's been given to you so you've had nothing to hate. Even my life is given to you through the sacrifice of your guards. I'm bored and done wasting my time talking to a coward. Finish it."

Sadas drives his sword right through my heart and everything fades to black.

Convergence VII

"Well there go our plans," says Monkey.

"No," Odin replies, "if he were dead, the part of his soul that is over there would have crossed through. There is still a chance and it's our only chance. My older brothers Ve and Vili will help us. My brothers are much stronger than me but they're not nearly strong enough. We've got a plan to summon our grandfather, Búri; we need to get the three of us together in order to summon him."

"Do you even know where he is?" asks Monkey.

"No, that is Ve's role," responds Odin. "Anyway we need to pull a team of our best souls together to track down Ve. We're getting close to finding Vili but it's still going to be a while. We're going to be able to use a bit more high-powered group this time around. Yahweh isn't going to be able to track this group since they will be so close to earth, he won't notice they're gone. We will also be able to transport the individuals personally. Atlas and I have chosen a couple of our own leaders, and are putting together a team. We are trying to keep the group balanced among our various allies for political considerations.

Odin continued, "This is who will be among the team members. We were fortunate to be able to locate them in their various afterlives:

"Vo Nguyen Giap: He was the architect of the three Vietnam Wars. The Vietnamese consider the invasions by Japan, France, and the US as separate conflicts although overlapping. He's one of the best general's in history and helped reunite North and South Vietnam into one country. As of now he is with the other leaders we've chosen to help with strategy.

"Vinh Nqoc Nguyen, is the one Vietnamese enlisted man recommended by Vo Nguyen Giap, who achieved the highest enlisted rank spending the entirety of his career in the jungle. He's the sort of person we need for the mission we are planning. Vinh served from 1941 against the Japanese, then against the French, the U.S., and finally died in 1978 fighting the Chinese. His unit was completely outnumbered. The officers were dead so as the senior enlisted he was in command. When they found his body, he was slumped over a machine gun riddled with rounds. In front of him were roughly 300 dead Chinese troops. Now he is with us and our team.

"The next one is Longinus. He's the roman that pierced the side of Christ. He was tortured by angels as he roamed the earth for centuries until I finally was able to rescue him. The stories about him being immortal are true but that won't matter where they are going. He served Rome honorably and has spent a few hundred years since training for his chance for vengeance against Yahweh.

"Aaron Burr: He was the former Vice President of the United States. He was a hero during the Revolutionary War. While he is remembered for being the only person to kill an American President in a fair fight, the man has many talents. Many of which he has developed since he's been in Hell.

"Red Cloud: The Great Spirit wanted him on this. As you probably already know he was a legend during the Indian American war, leading more raids than anybody else during that period. He is extremely angry at the Christians for destroying his people's way of life, and has a personal grudge against Geronimo for converting to Christianity. He is an excellent bowman and is good at taming mounts, which may come in handy.

"Vlad Tepes is another very angry man; he literally stopped all of Islam and fought for Christ his entire life. Most mortals know him as the inspiration for Dracula but in reality he was just a man defending his country against the invading Turks. His younger brother Radul converted to Islam. After falling out for a few years they agreed to meet. The clergy's knights saw him under a banner of truce. They tried to kill him despite the truce and Vlad telling them he was coming. Then his wife died while he was fighting the Turks. It hasn't been substantiated whether she committed suicide or merely tripped; regardless the clergy deemed her damned. When it came time to bury her, the clergy wouldn't let him bury her in hallowed ground. A Templar started to move the body. Vlad stopped him and said he wanted to bury her personally. At some point the templar referred to her corpse as an unholy piece of trash. By the time it was over nine Templars and four priests had joined her. He's not a vampire but he is pretty damn pissed.

"Ern-Ya: Atlas mentioned him earlier. He's got a club and he's covered in furs but if you guys get into something you can't manage then just let him take care of it. Ern is a cave man in the literal sense. He is a Neanderthal.

Atlas is adamant we send him. Considering where they are going it makes good sense since he will be most accustomed to the environment.

"Kveld-Ulf: He's a berserker who has been with me for a long time. He is the strongest berserker ever to follow me. However he is a tad unstable. For example, when he was alive people thought he was a werewolf because his preference is to bite peoples' throats out. He's been in Valhalla for a long time. The only time he gets put on a mission is when you don't care about the body count.

"St. George, he's mine as well," boasted Odin, "It is kind of amazing how the Christian's have managed to turn St. George into a Saint when he was one of my greatest followers. He really took on a dragon by himself and won. He's been in Valhalla ever since but he's a lot better at being subtle than Kveld so he gets out more.

"Sir Kay, King Arthur's brother. He almost saved Camelot. Out of all the knights of Camelot he was the best fighter in melee or close arms combat by far. There were better horsemen and archers, but when it came to a sword he was unbeatable.

"The real story of Camelot occurred around the 4th century AD, Anglo time. Arthur and his knights, including his brother Sir Kay, were in the process of reuniting all of Briton. Sir Kay is portrayed as a dullard, the result of French writers in the 16th century rewriting Camelot's story into a romance novel. Lancelot, Galahad, and dozens of others are simply products of the French's romantic imagination. Camelot never had knights in shining armor; just some hardened men trying to fight for their freedom from Roman rule. Sir Kay was the hardest of them.

Odin went on, "I've told you about Camelot in general, but to tell Sir Kay's story their needs to be a second telling about his part. Sir Kay was Arthur's older step brother but never once did they love each other any less than had they been related by blood. In fact, it was Sir Kay that taught Arthur how to use a sword and mentored him through his first battles. Sir Kay was raised in the older druidic traditions and unlike Arthur never learned nor cared to learn about Roman advancements in technology. He did see the roman systems of governing as useful in building a kingdom. Sir Kay's younger brother, Arthur, had both the knowledge and charisma to do just that. So with Merlin's special talents, he helped Arthur to form his knights. At first Sir Kay was pleased by his brother's accomplishments and sacrificed for him. Morgan Le Fay was his great love but when politics dictated Arthur solidify his throne by marrying her, Sir Kay gave his blessing. He was the first to suspect something was amiss when Guinevere arrived. Sir Kay kept trying to tell his brother that this was going to lead to his ruin but Arthur was already under her charm. For years he stood by Arthur's side watching the disease of Guinevere's spell spread. By the time Morgan was thrown out of the castle Sir Kay had already left. He couldn't bear to see what was about to happen. Moreover, the Romans were coming to make one last attempt to regain Britannia. Sir Kay went with the best soldiers in the land and met them on open ground. He died surrounded by the dead Romans he had slain. If not for him the Romans would have retaken Britannia. He lives with the Welsh Fae in Avalon now.

"Tom Horn: He's a gunslinger from the Old West. Most of the outlaws never had shoot outs like in the movies. They'd wait and shoot you in the back of the head. Not him, he really did have dozens of movie-like shootouts. He was a hero during the Indian Wars and an excellent detective as well. He worked for the Pinkerton Detective Agency and killed seventeen men for them. He spent his last years working for cattle barons. In the end he killed over two hundred people in his career. He was the greatest killer the Wild West ever saw. The irony is he was hanged in 1902 for a murder he didn't commit. We're just hoping he and Red Cloud can set aside their differences for the time being.

"Quan Li: I don't know much about him other than he's among the best the Shaolin Monks ever produced. Moreover, we need a monk for reasons I'll get into later.

"Tanaka Shimbe—He was one of the four Hitokiri of the Bakumatsu. Hitokiri was a term given to four samurai during the Bakumatsu era in Japanese history. They were against the Tokugawa shogunate which was the ruling party of the time. Hitokiri is a term for his particular level of samurai. It literally means man slayer. These four samurai were among the best samurai ever. They were thought unbeatable by normal people. They were also referred to as 'The Four Butchers' or 'Heaven's Revenge' against the enemies of Imperial restoration. These four men were Kawakami Gensai, Nakamura Hanjiro, Tanaka Shimbe, and Izo Okada. Tanaka Shimbe was a rarity among samurai as he was born a peasant. Despite the normal disdain feudal lords showed towards peasants, such was Shimbe's skill that he was promoted to that rank. All four of them are death on order. The other three are on a different assignment. The Divine Emperor thought we might need Tanaka Shimbe and if he is half what his reputation claims, he'll be up to the task.

Atlas interjects, "So this is the deal, Ve has decided to abandon the warlike ways of his family and seek Enlightenment. He came across the original Buddha in his travels and was deeply touched. From that point on, Ve decided to find emptiness and follow the Buddhist eight fold path. We need to get him out of his place of meditation and back into our reality. Here's the issue. We can't send any gods or powers in. Well we can but they will lose their powers while inside. With the fight approaching so soon we cannot afford to have anyone get injured. By now you can guess where he is in meditation; in the Garden of Eden. If you haven't been there, Eden is Gaia's domain. She is the Ancient Primal Power also referred to as the Earth Mother. Every planet has one. Inside the Garden of Eden is everything that has ever lived on Earth. Every organism that's ever lived on Earth that is now extinct lives there; from the smallest bacteria to the greatest dinosaur. The Garden itself is alive. It normalizes the various areas so that all the different animals have climates that will sustain them. The Garden will let you in but if you die there your essence stays there for good. Controlling the Garden is, of course, Gaia; but in her absence, the Garden itself with the help of the Keeper of the Forest is in control. That also means all items brought their have to be organic and natural elements of nature. No raw or machined metal, magic, or any other items they deem inappropriate, are allowed in. Yes, I have checked, genetically modified plant guns are not allowed either. So we have to get the Asgardian Dwarfs to make the best organic-based weapons they have ever made. If the group makes it to where Ve is staying, hopefully the Shaolin Priest, Quan Li, can talk him into coming out of the Garden and helping us with the summoning. If he will not come out on his own, we assume he'll be powerless in the garden and our team can take him to the edge of the Garden where the gods we have mustered will have enough power to subdue him outside of the Garden. Needless to say, Buddha's not very happy about this. That is why he insisted on Quan Li coming.

"I thought you always made it a point not to have followers? Is Ern an exception?" Monkey asks.

"No Ern is a very good friend of mine." Atlas replied. "He's the reason I was freed from imprisonment," Atlas paused. "Yes, it's true, I was imprisoned. It wasn't by the Olympians, however. They only wish they had the power to do that. I was bound but I was constantly struggling to escape. This caused the prison to keep changing places. Around 120 thousand years ago a portion of my prison came to Earth. Thousands of times I had sensed sentient life forms. I had screamed for help on thousands of occasions.

"I didn't expect anything different, but I still tried. All the members of Ern's tribe and a hundred others ran from the sound of my suffering. Ern was moved by my painful cries and decided to assist me. Originally he thought he was simply going to have to club me to death to end my pain. Ern, as you remember, is half Neanderthal half human. Much stronger and more durable than a human, he could survive in the cold for many times longer than a human. He also had a human's intellect. This was the beginning of Neanderthal being incorporated into the human gene pool. While modern science has the arrival of humans much later, the archeological records are quite inaccurate as you know."

Atlas continued, "Ern combined the strength and the intellect elements of his mixed race to become his tribe's best hunter. He was able to triangulate where my screams were coming from with relative ease. He did not know what the cries meant at the time, however. When he found me I tried to reach out to him with my mind. I connected just barely. He understood, on some primal level, what he needed to do. He reached out with his mind to tighten the connection. We both struggled against the cell. For a full day our combined psyches raged against the field that held me. Then a crack emerged. Slowly I started pouring my strength into him. From his side he was able to widen the crack until eventually, after a hundred thousand years in prison, I broke free. Ern had absorbed some of my power during the struggle, which made him an immortal in his own right. I took him along with me to go see my old comrades. During the next millennia Hecate and Prometheus taught him a great deal. The two clubs he carries were made from the World Tree, Yggdrasill, the same one Odin received his knowledge from. The clubs are virtually indestructible. I made Ern's when I made mine after a journey to, Yggdrasill. We traveled across the cosmos tracking down those that had trapped me. We killed them one by one. Ern was growing discontented, however. He wasn't growing homesick as much as he wanted to bring some of the mysteries of the universe to his people back home.

"Ern asked Prometheus to create a device that would inspire humanity to understand the potential knowledge that lay before them. Prometheus did and gave it to Ern in a box. Now, this is the real story of Pandora's Box," Atlas said. "Ern had the power, at this point, to transport himself without aid. He traveled all over the world using Prometheus' device, teaching humankind to think. There are civilizations that man doesn't even remember, that were started by Ern's teachings. When Ern reached what today is known as Greece he was greeted by Zeus. But, Zeus wanted to keep humanity under his control. He didn't know what effect Ern and the Prometheus' device would have on the Hellenic people, so he attacked Ern. Ern was strong, but he knew when he was out matched. He ran as far as he could until Zeus caught him. With his last act, Ern threw the box containing Prometheus device into the sea. The box eventually washed up on Crete and the device assisted the people to develop the first Hellenic civilization. The Greek myth about Prometheus's brother Epimetheus is actually Ern. Zeus didn't know about the box so he didn't look for it until it was in the hands of the Cretans. This was also part of the war between the Titans and Olympian's where Heracles and Thor got into it.

"Prometheus received a bad omen regarding Ern," Atlas continued. "He approached me and we traveled to Earth looking for Ern. The legends are actually on point regarding this. The Olympians had Ern chained on a mountain with birds feeding on his immortal body. I and my comrade Menoetius stormed Olympus enraged by what we saw. Prometheus being considerably more level headed than us remembered that we were there to free Ern. He and Hecate went to Mount Caucasus where Ern was bound and freed him. By this point we had destroyed half of Olympus. Zeus made a pact with beings he trapped long ago like the Hecatonchires, Gorgons, and Cyclops in order to save himself. The ensuing fight would have destroyed the world Ern loved so much so he begged me to stop. Ironically the Hecatonchires had been imprisoned by trick just as me. They are known as the hundred handed in the Greek myths and the three combined are actually equal to me in strength. We returned from time to time but we signed an accord with Zeus to not usurp his throne. We didn't want it anyway. So with an extra four members we headed home. Ern has been with me ever since. He does go off on his own when he has the urge so there are a number of stories around the cosmos that can be attributed to him. For example, he is Enkidu from the Gilgamesh legends. The story's pretty inaccurate overall but Ern's the inspiration. While its purported that he died he actually just went home.

The irony of the whole thing is Zeus ended up liking having an intelligent civilization to worship him over a bunch of hunters and gathers.

Chapter 9

Of the abode of the god of War:
" . . . Here he saw
Bare barren woods, the sacred haunt of Mars,
(He shuddered at the sight) where his fierce home
On Haemus' further slopes is circled by
A thousand furies. Formed in Iron stand
The walls, in iron the doors grind, the roof
Rests upon iron pillars. Facing it,
The sun's bright beams are blunted, light itself
Dread's that abode, its harsh and steely gleam
Saddens the stars. Fit sentinels it has:
From the first portal mindless Passion leaps,
With red-flushed Rage and pale-cheeked Fear and blind
Wickedness; posted there with sword unseen
Stands Treachery and Strife with two-edged blade.
The court re-echoes countless menaces,
And in the midst stand Courage, deep in gloom,
And Frenzy, glad at heart, and Death sits there
In arms, his face all gory. On the altars
No blood but that of battle and no fire
Not snatched from burning cities. All around
Were spoils of the whole world, the temple's roof
Adorned by captured nations, ships of war,
Fragments of iron-barred gates, and chariots
Empty and faces ground by chariot wheels.
Yes, almost groans! Such woods, such violence
In every form."

—Statius Thebaid ca. 90 CE

My name is Mitais Haldane. My first memory is of my father teaching me how to wield a spear. I was probably three at the time. Although I was born into a human berserker clan, I always felt a little different, like a part of me was somewhere else. And they say I have no aura.

I was an unassuming child, average in size and features. We lived free, out in the Northlands away from the enslaving forces of the Empire. I spent my formative years learning how to hunt and fight. That was my existence. All members of the Northland tribes were expected to fight but that duty fell heaviest on the berserker clan. Be that as it may, I started off subpar in melee combat with handheld weapons. I just never really understood the underlying concepts of swordplay. At best, I was average in most other areas. The weapon I had the most affinity for was with the spear. So my trainer and I abandoned the other areas of midrange fighting in lieu of trying to become proficient at one combat form. I still try to use daggers and bows in order to cover the changes of battle, of course, but my primary area of practice is spear work.

The strange thing is, I have a natural affinity for unarmed hand-to-hand combat. None of my peers had ever come close to beating me at hand-to-hand. In fact I don't remember having to go beyond a minute with any of them.

My teacher, Master Bui, is a great fighter; it has been an extraordinary privilege to train with him. He is an old battle brother of my father's so despite my incompetence at close weaponry, he agreed to train me. Both my brothers have become shaman and my father would like at least one warrior in the family. Normally Master Bui only takes the very elite of the crop, but he tells me the scar over his eye would have cleaved him in half if Father hadn't displaced most of the axe's momentum. So despite having to explain the moves two and three times more than to the other students, he puts up with me.

Then there is my one truly unique attribute. I haven't decided whether it's a blessing or a curse. I emit no aura. Thus, I can't be influenced by magic. Magic wards, enchantments, glamours, charms or any other incantation can't detect me, lock onto me, or work on me. The drawback is this applies to all forms of magic not just those that could be harmful to me. When I was born, the shaman thought I was a stillbirth because he could not detect an aura. For months before I was born my mother was dying from a demon's curse. She actually died eight months into the pregnancy, so they had to remove me with a knife. They were sure I was not going to live. I am told the shaman had a fit when I started moving. He went through half a dozen procedures to make sure that I wasn't an inhabiting spirit.

Ever since, the shamans have been a little perturbed by my presence. For example, I can't see when they're trying to scare the class with a vision other than taking my cues from my other classmates. And, if anyone is too close to me, their magic can be interfered with. Plus normal magic healing spells or other helpful spells don't work on me.

I have a very difficult time when I am injured. My non-magic attribute won't let the shamans' spells work on me. The first time I got badly hurt, they were able to stop the external bleeding by cauterizing the wound; but I was still bleeding internally. At the very last minute they came up with a plan. Using a plant that grows in our area, they were able to cause clotting inside the wound. The plant is full of little crystalline filaments that it normally uses for pollen collection from the air. It can be used for internal clotting as long as it is still alive and can grow into the wound. The shamans were able to manipulate the plant far enough from me that my negative field didn't affect the processes they used on the plant. The rest of the world may consider us barbarians, but we are actually better adept than even the Empire at treating wounds without the use of magic.

The Northlands are a strange place. Storms and strange magical tempests constantly occur that can interfere with the normal casting of spells. When we are in the midst of a storm, the shamans use conventional non-magic methods to treat wounds and ailments. They have taught me that the causes of most illness are minute animals. They are thousands of times smaller than I can perceive with my eye. However, the shamans that are proficient in divining are able to see them using their magic. If one is ill, the shamans know different herbs and fungi that help the body fight the sickness. If you are wounded this means you have to kill the tiny animals with boiling water, or poison them with alcohol, or burn them with fire. This is the same when you are removing an arrow or any other injury. The tools you use must be boiled first or else the minute beasts will cling to them and attack you once the tools are inside. After a wound is treated the shamans use a type of plant fiber to seal the wound. The fiber kills the animals on contact and keeps the wound closed so that they can't get into it.

Master Bui, my teacher, actually is very blessed by our god Vili. He can transform himself into animals and other things. The most important thing, though, is that Master Bui has unique power that can affect me. For magic to work on a subject, it must lock onto that being. Since I don't emanate an aura, magic cannot lock onto me. However, if a spell is used that changes the magic energy into a non-magic energy, then I can be affected or hurt. Master Bui has such power.

This is not to say my non-magic trait doesn't come to my advantage sometimes. The first time my father let me go out on a raid against the encroaching elves, I was only supposed to watch from a distance. But, being a curious eleven year old, I decided to explore. While my father's party was flanking from the right, I decided to flank left for a better view. While I didn't know it at the time, I was walking through elven proximity wards and other magic fields designed to disintegrate a victim instantly. I walked through a whole field of these traps without even noticing. My noisy walking did catch someone's attention, however. I will never forget the look of shock on the elf's face. He tossed a spell at me. Then another until others realized I was there. They had come with golems; those magical constructs of animated metal and stone, that contend with the world through enchantments. They kept telling the golems to attack. Finally the elves gave up on that, and two dozen elves started casting every spell they knew. My father's band heard the commotion and began to close the distance. One of the elves said I had to be a ghost or an illusion because he couldn't see a soul.

Elves weapons, armor, and even their homes are made out of living material as are most of their possesions. They don't use metal and earth the way we do. They actually grow their weapons and armor, making them vulnerable to poisons and other harm. Just as the elves were closing in on me, my father's band attacked them from behind with arrows. The elves had the foresight to put on armor so they weren't decimated but a few did go down. They all were dying by the second round. We tip our arrows with a poison that is especially effective on elves and within moments the elves would die.

What was intended to be a hit and run mission turned into a full blown fight. Another group of elf guards came out and met a volley of arrows. All a sudden everything slows down. An elf is actually coming for me. He has his organic sword out ready to strike. My father sees, but he is too late. Without thinking I dodge the thrust and slide underneath the thin elf legs. I don't know what came over me to do this, but I grab the heel of his ankle with both arms and crank. Before I knew it the elf is on the ground missing a usable knee. He is moaning and rolling around on the ground. The battle is almost over. We caught them by surprise, thanks to my unplanned diversion. Seventy-five elves died or fled.

My father hands me a knife and says proudly, "You earned this son."

I took the knife and with one slash, I slit the elf's throat. But I felt the strangest sensation; it was as if I had done this before.

Don't think too harshly of us humans, the elves wish to enslave us. There was a time long ago when the surface of our world was almost entirely domiciled with humans, dwarves, and other relatively peaceful beings. I say the surface because the shamans tell me the world is at least three-quarters hollow inside with many different creatures below. Then many millennia ago, the elves came from another world. At first they told mankind and our gods not to worry; they only needed a small amount of land. The elves promised just to develop what wasn't already in use. Our race has coexisted with many other races and species from the beginning of our time, so we agreed to help the elves establish a colony. This is how it was for the first few thousand years.

The story is told that one day the elves' gods invited our gods to a party. Most of our own gods, the old gods of our world, agreed to go; but when they arrived they were ambushed. Those gods that were alive and that could, ran. They didn't just run from the ambush, they ran from this world. The old gods betrayed us by leaving us on our own. We had worshipped them for as long as there have been tribes of humans. We have heard there may be other gods still around; some say there are other large colonies of free humans. None of that matters to us. We don't believe that an unknown god would help us if we've never prayed or worshipped him?

According to our legends, of the handful of gods who stayed on this world, only one survived. That god is Vili. He is a war god. He stood up to the entire pantheon of elven gods and struck down over a thousand. When the elf gods begged for their lives he did not even acknowledge them.

Vili was not like the other gods. He came from a different place. He was immeasurably old and a traveler at heart. He had taken a liking to this place and had decided to stay for a while. When he heard us pray to him he actually answered back, but through clues. He said he didn't want to give away an answer completely because then you could not tell if you had learned anything. What he explicitly did pass down was a code for one to follow. He has many suggestions but only three rules. None of them even involve worshipping him. To live in his favor you must never betray a friend; you must fight against any that would attack you; you must never attack or take from those who do not intend to bring you harm. From these precepts many notions may be found. For example, one should die rather than surrender, but if retreating is the strategically sound action then it must be taken. You would betray your comrades who would have to fight them the next day if you died for no good reason today.

What occurred to Vili next is identical in both our books and the elven books. The elven gods attacked Vili, but each attack was parried and sent ricocheting back at them. So the elven gods manipulated many millions of

Vili's followers to shield them from the ricochets and any of their attacks on Vili would kill millions of his own followers. So Vili was forced to retreat. This led him right into their trap. The elven gods had used the life force of all the gods that Atlas had slain to create a rip in existence. They knew they could not kill him so they trapped him. He has been imprisoned ever since. That is the difference between the elves and us. We do not practice the art of deceit like the elves. To an elf, the elf gods are praised and honored for their cunning.

Vili's prison is not perfect. A tiny fraction of what he is still can reach outside his cell. With that, Vili is still able to give gifts to his people. While these gifts can take many forms, the most common gift to humans is to become a berserker. A berserker is able to enter a trance that makes him go into a murderous rage. The enraged berserker has superhuman strength, stamina, speed and the ability to regenerate. Once in this state the berserker does not retreat or come out of the trance until the entire group of enemies is dead and gone. As berserkers age they tend to grow in strength and gain new powers. It depends on the person but common powers are the ability to transform into an animal, heightened senses, and resistance to elements such as fire and acid.

As I mentioned, I was born to a berserker clan; if Vili so chose, he could grant me the honor of becoming a berserker. Vili grants the gift to those that deserve and desire it. While he still prefers to grant the gift based on merit, Vili has decided that the talent of berserk can be petitioned for. So he gives all the tribes a communal vision where each tribe may set up a clan within the tribe whose sole purpose is to train and fight as berserkers.

Those that are born into the berserker clan or ask to be admitted undergo a variety of training and testing in order to be selected to become berserkers. First, there is weapons training. Then meditation techniques that allow one to control the body and mind into and out of the trance state. With practice you can control normally involuntary actions like heart rate and sweat. Then there is a miscellaneous group of training techniques like torture to teach pain tolerance, memory exercises, tactical and strategic techniques. For a human like me who has certain unique talents, the trainers may spend time on that specialty. For example, Master Bui has taught me many stealth tactics like quiet movement, blending into the surrounding area, climbing walls, and methods to trail and lose a pursuing enemy; all of which are enhanced by my not having an aura.

The final stage in becoming a full berserker is a set of surgical procedures. First, a creature is implanted in the stomach that feeds on the host but transforms it at the same time. Over the course of weeks the stomach begins to process food more efficiently such that one meal will give you the strength of three meals. You can eat almost anything that any natural animal can eat. Grass and leaves can be digested like an herbivore. Putrid spoiled food that only a vulture could eat can be digested without harm. The liver and kidneys change so that they can process the most virulent poisons.

After this gastronomic process begins, the various senses are operated on. This is done, as are many of the procedures, through a process similar to the filament healing I alluded to earlier. The shaman uses a series of lenses cut from crystals that enhances his vision to supernatural levels in order to see what must be operated on. The ears are made much more sensitive so that one can hear a whisper through a shut door as if it were a scream. The range of hearing also is expanded. Sounds that are normally too low or too high to hear become audible. Then the inner ears are operated on so that balance and orientation become substantially increased. All the senses are manipulated in such a manner. Senses adjust to conditions almost instantaneously. The eyes become much more acute, vision increases 100 fold both for near and far vision. The nose can track like a dog's. The tongue can taste the residual taste of a known person on clothing. The nerves for pain are dulled while the nerves for sensitivity enhanced so a blindfolded man can tell the direction of an attack based on the change in the air.

Then the lungs heart and trachea are operated on. Filters remove toxins and smoke prior to entering the lungs. Air intake is increased so the average person can hold air in excess of 30 minutes. The heart becomes more efficient. It oxygenates blood at enhanced levels. The muscles and bones are then operated upon. Both become much stronger and heal tremendously faster. Both a chemical and the aforementioned surgery are used. The shamans force the muscles to create more mitochondria which is the part of the muscle that creates energy. The final step is to manipulate the glands, brain, and spinal cord. The spinal cord is given various electric shocks and chemicals. It is then able to communicate with the rest of the body much quicker. The same is done to the brain and glands. The end result is one can force unnaturally high levels of hormones to be produced or dispersed into the system. One can force or prevent sleep. Memory and thought are enhanced. Combined with the aforementioned mental training any function of the body can be controlled. The end result is an enhanced person created without the use of magic. In battle, a clansman uses his psychological training and his new abilities to dump the hormones needed in combat into the body.

The berserker controls the trance needed to bring on all the changes used in battle as a berserker. When the murderous rage is brought on, one becomes immune to pain or fear and strength and speed become greatly enhanced. Once this transformation occurs, the berserker lusts only for combat and will fight until either the berserker or his enemy is dead. Of course, berserkers specializing in forms of combat such as archery do not fully transform or it would be counterproductive. Furthermore, in the fully transformed state the berserker hungers for hand to hand combat even if that is not the best tactic for the moment.

This is but one part of the library of knowledge Vili has given to our people. The procedures can be taken at any point in a man's life and are considered enhancements with only one side effect: uncontrollable rage. It is available to any member of any tribe. The only part that is reserved for members of the clan and the worthiest of the other tribesman is the final procedure: the granting by Vili of the berserker spirit. The shaman communes with Vili in a sacred ceremony to achieve this final and most important attribute. Only this part directly uses any magic. Therefore with my immunity to magic, I can never achieve this final stage. I cannot even attend the ceremonies of others because the shamans cannot detect Vili's presence while around me.

While our methods may seem outrageous and cruel they result very rarely in fatalities. In reality, shamans are always there to treat the wounded. And, there is no pressure to accept this gift. In fact, the shamans counsel each applicant thoroughly to make sure he understands the implications of the process. There is no way to reverse the process. You are a berserker until the day you die. Because of your savage potential, you can become a hazard to your own society. While on the one hand, you are vital to the tribe's survival, under certain times of stress and illness you may transform to berserk. More than once, a berserker has been found weeping by the side of his dead wife. A stressful domestic argument can bring out the berserk and after that the berserker has no rational thought. He is simply a weapon. Despite this, few tribesmen decline the offer.

If one chooses not to go through the spiritual binding ceremony to become a berserk then there are two other options. First, you may become a regular member of the tribe, a worker, or a farmer. Between the training and natural alterations you still are respected as an elite warrior. Second, you may petition for magical power instead. While a shaman normally trains from an early age the mental training they receive has some overlap with berserker training. All tribesmen receive some magic training. Other than me basically everyone can cast minor spells. So, if you are given a gift of magic then this will offset the inexperience you will face in the craft typical for becoming a Shaman.

Having berserkers in a tribe is necessary for our survival. The elves wish to enslave us. The elf is a strange being that cannot be reasoned with. They are not from this world, originally. They are beings of magic who do not think the same way we do. Their eyes and hair are pale while our eyes are slanted and black and our hair is straight and blue-black in color. Elves are a uniformly pale paraffin color, inhumanly gaunt, whose eyes have vertical pupils while ours are round. Their ears are pointed and elves do age at about a three hundredth our rate. The nobles of their race do not seem to age at all. They have a thought process that is alien to ours. It is true they are more intelligent than us but their thinking is constricted. They are not a creative race and they see us as both a threat and a source of slaves. The logical solution for them is to enslave us or destroy us. While their approach may be brilliant they are incapable of thinking of a different option. Thus there is no compromise. They do not even think of us as people. We are like a pestilence problem they need to eradicate or control.

There are three elite groups in the human Northlanders' society; the Berserkers, the Shaman, and the Ogden riders. Each tribe has their own unique ratio of these three elite groups. Some of the most Northern tribes are almost all mystics and Shamans, while the nomadic tribes tend to be mostly Ogden riders. Our tribe is in an agricultural belt and so the ratio of the three groups is relatively balanced. Although all tribesman fight for our people in times of battle, they have other roles as well. They must support themselves and the tribes so when not at war they are blacksmiths, carpenters, farmers, workers of all sorts. They are the base of society which we Berserkers protect. The tribes are also gathered into three loose factions containing various mixes of the three elite groups. Regardless of the faction or tribe, it is difficult to maintain peace. We fight each other even more than we fight the elves. But with time we are changing. The increase in encroachment by the elves makes us all aware that we must band together to survive the upcoming war. And, we will need a leader to unite us or winning will be impossible.

The shamans are one of the three elite groups. Among the shamans are mystics or those that have use solely of their own unique powers. Then there are full shamans, those whose spirits are tied to Vili and that have been granted additional power from Vili. It is also possible to gain extra power by defeating and absorbing someone else's spirit into your own power base. However, while this is not unlawful it is also not encouraged. There have been occasions where the shaman was been thought to have won but the reverse happened and the spirit possessed him. What is encouraged is to seek benign spirits as companions. They can provide a source of energy. Besides this there are dozens of types of magic. A shaman will only specialize in a couple forms if he wishes to become a master. Unlike the elves, we are a natural race. We do not need magic to survive, but we use magic as an added tool or weapon. We can create some energy that can be used for magic.

    The last of the three elite groups is the Ogden riders. These tribesmen are a group telepathically linked to their remarkable mounts, the Ogden. These are not just any mounts, however. Originally, the Ogden were non-magical or natural bear-like creatures, and were subjected to experimentations by an unknown god for use by his followers. Due to an attack from one of the god's enemies the Ogden were able to escape through the same dimensional rift that the god's enemies used to reach his domain. Now they have formed a symbiotic relationship with the humans in the Northlands.

    These incredible animals, the Ogden, form the basis for much of the tribesman's schooling in nature and biology. Teaching about them opens up so many areas of science for discussion it is of great educational as well as cultural value. The result of the experiments by that god, is an intelligent eight-limbed, ursine creature with extremely unique gifts. These gifts include a prehensile tail roughly the same length as the body and tipped with a venom-injecting barb. The Ogden can inject a neurotoxin that kills in seconds. They are roughly ten feet tall, twenty-two feet long, and on average around 12,500 lbs. Their design is so precisely tailored to their riders that there is even a stepping knob on their side for a rider to mount. The Ogden have many powers. They have a maximum speed of roughly 75 miles per hour. They can maintain a 45 mph speed indefinitely. They use all eight limbs to run if not in combat. If they are in a battle, they often will use weapons with two or more of their limbs. All their limbs look essentially the same. Each hand-like foot has an opposable thumb so when playing they will use all eight feet like hands. They regenerate body parts at an amazing rate. They are highly resistant to cold, poison, radiation, and heat. The Ogden can expel a highly deadly mist from their mouths that is both flammable and acidic in nature. They have a number of pockets in their throats containing substances benign by themselves, but when exhaled together the chemicals mix; with the slightest amount of friction the deadly mixture becomes a blast of heat intense enough to melt a 5000 pound solid metal golem. Their regenerative properties are rarely tested because they are so hard to injure. They have thick hides that are substantially tougher than steel. They also have massive ivory horns curled like a ram's. Both their pelts and horns are rarely found but highly prized and are used by the tribes. Due to their regenerative properties, the Ogden grow both horns and skin back in a matter of hours. Even my own, Mitais Haldane's spear, is tipped with the ivory horn of an Ogden. And, in addition to their enhanced senses, the Ogden have a variety of senses we do not possess. Their hearing extends into both ranges greatly and is extremely acute. Ambushes have been avoided by Ogden hearing the draw of an arrow long distances away. They have extremely acute vision, able to make out faces from miles away. Their vision also extends into the infrared and ultraviolet spectrums. They also have ultrasound like a bat or dolphin, and can swim like fish. While in the water they open up an air hole their rider can breathe from. Their tail flattens and moves side to side like many aquatic reptiles. They shut a second clear eye lid they posses so they can see without interference from water. They can hold their breath for over an hour and can use an ultrasonic burst while in water to stun or kill anything up to a large size fish. Their creator did a good job.

The last major attribute of the Ogden is how efficient their digestive system is. They process 95% of the food they intake. Any excess gets turned into fat but unlike most of us it is easily converted into fuel. They also can store water.

One might ask why the Ogden accept riders. Oddly, they only will accept riders from a natural mammalian race, such as humans or dwarves. It is almost unheard of for an Ogden to have a supernatural rider. But it does happen. We had always assumed that the dwarves were supernatural like elves are, until we found out about a small clan that resides within one of our tribes. They have incorporated themselves completely into the tribe. Some of the dwarves have even become berserkers and some, Ogden riders. They accept Vili as part of their pantheon of gods. The dwarves say that Vili is one of three brothers that saved them many years ago and ever since they have revered Vili. Though they may appear to be creatures of magic, the theory is that dwarves merely are able to contain large packets of magic energy.

The strangest thing about the Ogden is there is a one in ten thousand mutation that is born with wings. And many times, the wings are actually functional. However, these Ogden are smaller and tend to be weaker since they have to commit so much muscle to flying. The dwarves love them. It's probably because dwarves cannot swim and don't seem to take to flying spells very well. If an Ogden is born and it takes a liking to a dwarf, the dwarf will trade everything he owns for it.

The Ogden, like the humans and dwarves, can live just fine without magic. Whereas, an elf is a supernatural being requiring magic to live; without magic an elf would eventually die. It's like oxygen for them. But for us, we may not require magic but without it we don't stand a chance against the elements of the Northlands and the elf invaders.

Ogden are so much a part of our tribes that they can maintain their own abodes and even going to the store is normal without a rider. But, both rider and Ogden get many benefits from bonding to each other. It takes several months for the initial bond to develop. Within three to five years they are permanently linked. If they are not bonded, the Ogden have intellects roughly equivalent to that of ten year old children. Once they are bonded they become as intelligent as humans. The bonding catalyzes a process that does this. Both rider and Ogden can use any unused mental energy to reason. They say one should never play chess with a rider whose Ogden is asleep. Both can look through each other's eyes so the rider effectively has the Ogden's extra senses. They can do this when separated as well so a rider is able to scale up a wall the Ogden could not and the Ogden would see through his eyes. A rider, while in physical contact with the Ogden, can heal like the Ogden can. The Ogden can pump its blood into the rider and the blood apparently learns to assimilate itself so the body does not reject it. The Ogden also have certain psychic abilities such as telepathy, empathy, and the ability to build mental shields against mental attack or possession. These are substantially enhanced by the bonding.

At one time I considered bonding with an Ogden. But when I approached a young Ogden it could not sense me at all. I've tried more than once, but they seem to want to avoid me. I'm told that they don't believe I have a soul and I can't be trusted. Master Bui has told me to dismiss this as nonsense.

The most important weapon used by an Ogden rider is the bow and arrow. The most important part of the Ogden and rider team is that the rider navigates the battlefield for the Ogden. In battle the Ogden can completely concentrate on the battle while the rider takes care of steering its direction. The biggest threat to the Ogden are flying attackers. Although they can spew a caustic breath a distance of 50-60 feet, this is nowhere near adequate to handle a giant flying roc or dragon that can attack from hundreds of feet in the air. All riders are excellent marksman. Somewhere in the Ogden genetic code is the ability to upload all skills involving marksmanship into a riders mind. Riders normally receive the best enchanted bows a tribe can produce. The riders, as do most tribesmen, undergo physical enhancement so hitting a target 2000 feet away is not considered difficult.

I actively started going on raids when I was thirteen. I noticed that I was becoming much stronger and faster with each passing month. There was also a noticeable increase in my perceptions. I was part of a squad of fifteen. Master Bui was the leader. I and his eleven other students comprised the twelve. Plus, we had one shaman that specialized in combat magic and one that specialized in healing and divining magic. This was the standard compilation of a squad in all tribes to my knowledge. Our squad started off in an auxiliary role to the experienced units. However, we were getting very good. Within two years we had started to do small missions on our own.

My father died around this time. He had been on a raid. The elves must have found out because they had five times their normal troop level and over fifty of their demonic plant machines. He had died bravely according to all reports. His last act was to strike down an organic war machine and overload its weapon system so it exploded. This gave the rest of his team time to escape. It was an honorable death. It also made my resolve to rid the Northlands of the Elven Empire's minions all the more strong. Knowing that I would soon have to compete with my friends who would be granted full berserker capabilities, I started spending most of my time training with the spear. My best friend of the group, Svinglar, took turns with my other friend Sillus to train with me. I was getting increasingly good at the spear. I was able with ease to read the movements of my sparring partners in advance. By this point, I had thirty-two elf deaths under my belt. It was tradition amongst berserkers to preserve the ears of all the elves he'd slain and wear them as a necklace into battle. Master Bui had thousands of ears. So many, he no longer could bring all of them into battle. The sheer weight was simply too heavy and cumbersome, so he wore a token of his victories.

About this same time, I started having bizarre dreams. I was seeing flying pieces of metal and giant glass buildings. It always came along with a language I didn't recognize and could not understand. I voiced my concerns to the Shaman.

The Shaman told me, "You, Mitais Haldane, are by far the smartest of your group. It is only natural that you have an active imagination. I just wish I could make you shaman. It's probably for the best that you won't be a full berserker since without an aura, you cannot partake of the spirit of Vili ceremony. Besides, you have a sound tactical mind that would be wasted while under the trance of the berserker."

I suppose he was right. I was learning to use my power to the advantage of the group; I was acting as the nearly undetectable group scout and becoming very good at it. It seemed like I'd learned somewhere to be completely stealthy. There was another strange occurrence. I was on a raid when an elf cast a sphere of darkness over us. Other casters were with him and they cast a life draining spell on us. He'd tried to cast a spell on me and nothing had happened so they were trying a new approach. The sphere of darkness was half a mile wide. Those weird metal and stone creatures, the golems the elf was commanding, didn't need any light to function. But in this total darkness, our night vision was useless. We needed a modicum of light and now we were completely blind. I considered running to the edge of the sphere because my negative effect on magic might disrupt it. But at the time, I didn't know how wide a swath of darkness the elves had created. It all seemed like I was recalling a memory. Fighting in complete darkness seemed like the most natural thing in the world. I could hear and feel the changes in the air as the golems came in. A spear was a useless weapon against a golem. I just naturally dropped my weapon and fought them with my bare hands. Master Bui, unlike the rest of us, could see in many spectrums of light from the ultraviolet to the infrared. He was busy holding off four of the creatures with his axe while instructing the blind men in his squad what to do. Both shamans tried to dispel the dark field to no avail.

Master Bui developed a new ability that day. Just as a golem went through his heart he realized that the golem had gone through him entirely. He was like a ghost. While to hit the golem, he had to be substantial, so he would go in and out of solid phase at will. Meanwhile I was fighting two golems with no problem. I was too busy to contemplate what was going on. And just then, at the same time, the rest of my team went into full berserker mode. They ran around with superhuman speed and strength. Even, as much as possible, my berserker strength and speed kicked in. I don't remember much but when I came to I had beaten to death two golems. The other berserkers had ripped the elven mages in half with their bare hands.

Despite our best efforts the Elf Empire was getting a bigger toe hold on the Northlands. They unleashed their genetically mutated war machines out into the land. We were going on a mission every couple of days. We'd quadrupled both our raids and the number of berserkers, but it still wasn't enough. Master Bui was changing. Constant fighting was making his powers increase rapidly. His ability to control his transformations into berserker was astounding too. I was the only one in our squad who could not fully transform into a berserker.

We'd lost three men over the years. I was twenty-two now and the dreams were getting worse. It was like I was trying to forget something that just wouldn't stay buried. Then one day we were out on a raid with other squads. Sillus and Svinglar were by my side as always. We attacked and out of nowhere appeared an army fifty times our number.

Their leader said in a magically enhanced booming voice, "You dare defy the Empire? We let you be before, but the notion of free humans living outside our control is distasteful. So we've decided to round up all the wild humans for domestication."

I knew that voice. I saw a face in my mind; it looked human. Whoever he was, I felt the cold chill of death and all I wanted was him dead in the next couple of minutes. The whole squad went berserk and me as much as I could. If we were going to die it was going to be in glory. I remember my friends and tribesmen fighting and dying beside me. My blood surged through my brain and all I wanted was to die fighting. I grabbed an elf and ripped his throat with my teeth. Then the elven war machines were brought forward. Acid from the war machines spewed out over the battle field. It was dissolving people.

Master Bui's love of his men pushed him, both out of the berserk and into his supernatural powers. First, he made a shield that redirected all the acid. Then he reached out with his mind. He grabbed the five members of our squad first then the twenty-five other men that were still alive and teleported them. He didn't know where but anywhere was better than here. His magic could not work on me and I was still engaged in the battle. I decided on one straight charge at their leader. He was cowering in the back. I charged, half berserker half something else. I gave everything I had but it wasn't enough. I dove through a dozen soldiers; killed two with daggers. Their leader tried to use his magic on me. Of, course it was useless. He looked scared and started running. My murderous intent was clear on my face; then just before I reached him, I got cut by a sword. He'd been standing behind a house. I struck him right in the throat damaging his trachea. Then a dozen soldiers grabbed me. They still couldn't hold me down. More hands wrapped around me and finally I could not move. Knowing that he was safe the leader turned around.

It all started flooding back.

"Eric, you fucking bastard!" I cried out.

I remembered Evelyn's body smoldering. Her beautiful face battered. I tried to use my ability to bend space so I can attack him, but I am too damaged.

Eric tried to use his Noble Powers to end me. It didn't work of course. He grabbed a knife from a soldier.

Just as he was about to strike I screamed out in English, "You fucking coward. You wanted to be a Noble so bad but didn't have Ace's balls or Magnus's determination so you snitched on me, threw your wife out like garbage and in the end got us both killed. Now with all the Imperial Source's

Power you're still standing back. It's taken you twenty guys to hold me down before you'll make a move. Fine, do it! When I come back, you'll be begging me for death."

Eric was taken aback, to say the least, but after a few moments he regained his composure, saying, "I don't know how you keep cheating death but it can only work so many times."

Just then Master Bui charged into us. He had transformed himself into a gigantic bear. He pushed twenty guards off of me without slowing down at all. Finally we fall into the river below us. Everything goes black.

Convergence VIII
Enter Eden

> Sometime a keeper here in Windsor Forest,
> Doth all the winter-time, at still midnight,
> Walk round about an oak, with great ragg'd horns;
> And there he blasts the tree, and takes the cattle,
> And makes milch-kine yield blood, and shakes a chain
> In a most hideous and dreadful manner.
> You have heard of such a spirit, and well you know
> The superstitious idle-headed eld
> Receiv'd, and did deliver to our age,
> This tale of Herne the Hunter for a truth.
> —William Shakespeare, The Merry Wives of Windsor

Odin had to admit the dwarves had outdone themselves. He had given the parameters of the weaponry needed and they had come back in two days with an array of natural organic that was as tough as anything he could have expected. They had made armor out of spider webbing that was stronger than Kevlar. They had produced edged weapons made out of ivory and wood. The wood had been treated in various herbal mixtures that made it as hard as steel. Odin assembled the team and they all grabbed what gear they desired. Longinus and Vlad were adamant about bringing in their keepsakes however. For Longinus, it was his spear. He had spent a very long career in the Roman Legion and had killed a god with it. Needless to say he was rather attached. Vlad refused to remove his family ring. It was the order of the Dragon, a group his family had belonged to for generations. They all put on the spider armor. Longinus wore an accurate version of his Legionaries uniform. St. George and Kveld both wore bearskins over their spider armor. Quan Li wore his traditional monk robes effectively hiding his armor. Sir Kay and Vlad wore ivory plate mail and the rest wore some form of camouflage. Odin wished them strength, courage, resolve, and, of course, luck, and sent them to the edge of the Garden of Eden.

The Garden did not prevent Longinus from entering with his spear. One of the sentient trees bowed to the spear out of respect. They must have thought Vlad's ring was inconsequential because no mention was made of that either.

"So where in the Garden of Eden are we? It looks pretty nice to me," Vinh said.

"If everything that ever lived is here then we should hurry up and figure out where we need to go before we end up fighting T-Rex. I'm already uncomfortable going into this place without any guns," said Tom.

Ern agrees motioning for them to follow. Ern in his furs, wielded his two clubs that had been carved out of the tree of life. The team moved through the woods, led by Ern. He was like a ghost. Vinh who was considered a master jungle fighter by most was the only one able to truly appreciate Ern's level of skill. He made no sound even when walking over leaves. The team traveled through a jungle with trees from the Jurassic period. There were flowers the size of car tires and some insects were a foot long. They saw a number of amazingly different animals from this period; a stegosaurus and other enormous herbivores. The animals did not pay much attention to the diminutive travelers.

The team traveled for about half a day before they ran across their first hostile creatures. It was a pack of giant cave lions; currently extinct outside of the Garden as were all of the other creatures they had seen. They were similar in looks to modern day lions, but were twice the size. With his remarkable sense of smell, Ern had caught their scent first and motioned for the team to hide. Unfortunately, the cave lions had caught the group's scent and charged. Kveld, upholding the berserker's reputation for insane responses, opted to charge them head on. The others had no option but to engage against the lions. Kveld was inhuman in his response to the cave lions' charge. He began mowing into them, screaming unearthly sounds, reminding them that between the two, he was the predator and they were the prey. A cave lion tried to bite him. Kveld grabbed it, sinking his teeth into the lion's throat, he ripped it out. He was pure berserker now; no rational thought was left in his mind; he attacked like the wild thing he was.

Ern was laughing his head off at the fool. He'd been sent to lead this team and that was exactly what he was going to do. He took out his clubs. With his Neanderthal strength and over one hundred thousand years experience, engaged the cave lions. He was a whirlwind of death. Four died in as many seconds and he was just getting started.

Vinh went into the same quiet meditative state he had entered when he fought at Khe San in Vietnam and the other thousands of battlefields he'd been on. Compared to the 500 lb bombs exploding next to you during the war, these cave lions were nothing. He had used a bow more than once in his career. There had been a number of times he'd run out of ammo and had no option but to craft a bow. He calmly brought his bow to aim and shot a lion through the eye and then another. Red Cloud set up next to Vinh and started firing arrows in sync with him.

Longinus had fought gods, monsters, and men of all sorts in his service to Rome and Lucifer. A cave lion was no different. Just as a cave lion charged him Longinus ran back a few steps; at the moment the cave lion was upon him he spun around, planted the butt of his spear into the ground, and let the cave lion impale itself on the spear.

Tom Horn was a little bit out of his element. He'd lived life by the gun not by the sword. However, he had never been afraid of a fight or for that matter, death, and today was no different. He surveyed the land and saw his opportunity. He positioned himself by a tree located on a ridge and tossed a rock at one of the cave lions in order to bait it to come. He took out his lasso and threw one end over a large branch. He twirled the lasso and threw it around the cave lion's neck. Clinching the rope he swung intentionally missing a lower branch twenty feet below he used the branch as a fulcrum in order to swing in a circle. He landed on the lower branch quickly made a tight knot. The cave lion was hanging from the original branch slowing strangling to death. He scrambled up the tree to a higher vantage point. He slowly took aim and started firing arrows into a nearby cave lion.

Vlad and Sir Kay were fighting back-to-back both dressed in ivory plate mail. They had both died in combat after a lifetime of battles. They fought as experienced men do, neither left an opening; they made small wounds on the group that was attacking them. Slowly the cave lions were being whittled down. One by one a cave lion would go down, the result of dozens of small-calculated wounds. St. George had already slain two with his ivory battle-axe by this point. He charged after a third. He swung and missed. The cave lions came in and he barely sidestepped the bite. He never saw the cave lions behind him. Just as it pounced, an arrow flew at him. As he saw it out of the corner of his eye instincts born out of millennia in Odin's service kicked in. He immediately dropped to the ground. The cave lions had no time to stop its bite. It sunk its fangs into its pack mate's neck. St. George rolled to his feet and cleaved the cave lions in half. He looked to the direction of where the arrow came from and saw Aaron Burr giving him an apologetic gesture. Being that the missed shot had still saved his life he really could not complain.

Quan Li lived up to the Shaolin Temple's reputation. Wielding a wooden staff, he twirled it with expert precision landing blow after blow. Half a dozen cave lions lay dead around him. Shimbe proved to be a cave lion slayer as well as a manslayer as he slew cave lion after cave lion. He had yet to break a sweat.

By this time Kveld had gone fully berserk. He was fighting the cave lions with his bare hands. He'd already killed three with his hands and teeth. This entire time Vinh, Red Cloud, and Tom Horn had been picking off cave lions with their bows. There were more than 60 dead and only one left. It was right next to Burr. No one was close enough or had a clean shot to help. He was a dead man. Despite this there was absolutely no fear in the man's face. As the cave lion got within 15 feet of him he placed his hand into his jacket pocket. At ten feet his hand moved faster than any gunslinger or bowman any of the men other than Ern had ever seen. He threw a knife, hitting the cave lion in the throat. In just as many seconds, five more knifes plunged into the cave lion. In its last dying motion it came at Burr who with a stiff right cross slammed into its jaw. The last of the cave lions laid on the ground in its death throes.

The group decides to rest for a little while.

During their break, Vinh asks Aaron Burr, "Where did you learn how to do that? I've read about you and as famous as you are there should be some mention of your skill with knives."

Aaron responds, "Of course not. I knew how to throw knives before I died but I got to this level through centuries of practice afterwards. I love being dead. I've debated with philosophers ranging from Aristotle to Nietzsche. I've learned to paint, sculpt, and a variety of other art styles from the Renaissance's masters. Since Tom showed up we duel each other whenever we have the chance. He's joined me in the art lessons. His pastels are up there with any of the masters. What have you gentlemen been doing with your afterlives?"

Kveld replied, "I've fought and feasted in Valhalla for millennia. When Odin desires I go on missions such as this." St. George said roughly the same thing.

Shimbe responded "I've spent every day perfecting my sword craft." The others responded similarly.

Aaron replies to their answers, "So most of you have done more or less the same thing as you did in life. Have any of you heard of diversifying? Anyway let's keep going."

The Team kept journeying for months. Ern always took the lead and his skill kept them out of many natural dangers that could have killed the group. Everything from sinkholes to geysers that spurt out boiling water that would kill a man in seconds. He never seemed to get tired. The rest of the group was in awe of him.

They had a few inconsequential battles along the way. It seemed to the group that they were traveling through time. The cave lions they had encountered where a relatively new addition to the Garden as they had been extinct only a few thousand years of modern time.

Odin had briefed Ern on the shortest route to where they could find Ve. The Garden was built much like a series of rings. Each ring consisted of a period of time in history. Being that the Garden held all of Earth's wonders; had they not been given some directions, they could have spent thousands of years traveling through the various ecosystems and not found Ve. As each week passed the flora and fauna kept changing. Finally they came to a seemingly endless ocean. Ern informed them that if they tried walking around this ocean it would take years.

Kveld, ever the berserk Viking, says, "We could build a boat and cross this ocean. Think of the glory we'll find battling sea monsters from years past."

Ern replies, "Actually, I have another plan. Odin and Hecate knew of this barrier but any other route would have put years on to our journey. This is why Red Cloud is here. In life, he was able to charm animals to let him ride them. Since death his abilities have improved. Right now we are in the Late Eocene period. The ancestors of proto-whales and sea lions left the oceans with all other mammals, and we're now in the period when the mammals began to return to the sea. At this point they still had legs so they were prone to travel between the land and sea. Odin instructed me to have Red Cloud tame enough of them that we could ride on them for the several week journey to the other side of the sea."

The team began to look around for their potential mounts. After a pains taking week they found the remains of a land-sea mammal, roughly half a mile away from the beach. Unfortunately it appeared the animal had been eaten by some predator stationed along the well worn path made by many similar trail marks. For more than a week, they lay in wait camouflaging themselves in the brush several hundred yards from the path. They wanted to keep a good distance so as not to scare away the herd before Red Cloud could commune with them. Finally, a herd of the animals came walking towards the sea. At the same time several giant animals came charging from afar. The attackers were *Andrewsarchus mongoliensis* according to Ern, the giant mammalian predator and the largest carnivorous mammal ever to live. The face bears a strong resemblance to wolves. Their maws have rows of unusual immense triangular teeth and the legs ended with hooves. Their jaws were the strongest of any animal that had ever lived on Earth. From what we could see there was a mother and two cubs. She weighed close to six thousand pounds and was over 25 feet long. The cubs looked the same but were substantially smaller. One, presumably the younger one, was about a third the mother's size. The other cub was about half its mother's size.

The team was approaching the herd of proto-whales. They looked rather more like smooth-skinned mammalian crocodiles that had short two-toed legs and long, thick tails that dragged behind them. Ern directed Red Cloud to go "speak" to the proto-whales and direct them away from the animal attackers. Aaron Burr was to go with Tom, Longinus, and Vinh to attack the mother predator. The larger cub was left to St. George, Kveld, and Quan Li. The smaller one was for Shimbe, Sir Kay, and Vlad whom already had showed they fought well together. The enormity of the mother was causing the group to have problems dealing with her. Ern decided to face the mother head on while Aaron and Vinh attacked with projectile rounds from opposite flanks. Longinus was instructed to attack from the back. His spear had pierced the Christ, hopefully it was enough to stop this prehistoric creature.

Vlad and Sir Kay attacked the cub from opposite flanks. Shimbe attacked from the rear. They took well timed slashes at the cub. The cub would inevitably charge one of them when it took a solid blow. The first time it charged, Vlad dove out of the way just in time. By charging Vlad, the cub had exposed himself to Shimbe's and Sir Kay's sword. Kay drove his sword deeply into the cub's exposed side; too deeply. While the thrust had injured the cub gravely the sword became lodged in one of the cub's ribs. The cub bucked with Kay trying to hold on to the sword. Kay's grip was insufficient and he was flung a dozen feet. Shimbe was also hit and stunned. This left Vlad momentarily alone. He had time to slash at the cub tearing apart its leg muscle before the cub turned its attention on him. The cub charged on to Vlad and this time Vlad did not have time to dodge. He barely raised his shield up in time to defend against the cub's bite. The force of the bite still knocked him to the ground. Pinned to the ground despite his plate mail and shield he could feel his ribs crack. He was a dead man. Then out of nowhere an arrow flew with uncanny accuracy. It struck the cub right in the eye. The cub lurched in pain giving Vlad just enough time to scramble away. Shimbe had come to just enough to give aid to Vlad. Kay had recovered by now but his sword was still lodged in the cub's side. He pulled out a mace and a hand axe and charged. He charged right into the cub. Shimbe, Vlad, and Kay knew the beast was severely wounded and slowed. They kept making small cuts in the cub's hide. Eventually the cub began to slow until finally it collapsed entering into its death throes.

Meanwhile Red Cloud was communing with the proto-whales. This involved an intricate series of dances, songs, and chants. After a few minutes the proto-whales began to accept him. He led the proto-whales to the edge of the beach away from the fight. Kveld, St. George, and Quan Li were fighting the other cub. They had taken a much different approach than the others. Kveld, in his berserker way, had simply charged the cub with his battle axe. Each time he would get thrown back. St. George and Quan Li began attacking from the flanks. Every charge gave them enough time to get a few blows in. Finally, the cub charged Kveld. The cub pinned Kveld against a tree. Kveld was frothing at the mouth fully berserk at this point. He had placed the handle of his axe in the mouth of the cub in order to block the cub from biting him. The cub was so incensed by this that he continued his charge ignoring the attacks. Finally, St. George was able to slash his axe into the cub's jugular. Within moments the cub bled out. Meanwhile, Ern's complement was battling the mother. The mother was easily two times the size of the larger cub. Ern faced the mother head on. If he had met this animal in any other place he would have been able to strike the animal down with a single blow or kill it with a spell. However, in this place he did not have his normal god-like power so fighting this beast would take savvy. He engaged the mother only to the point it was required to draw her attention from the others. With expert skill he dodged every attack. By drawing attention from the others Vinh, Tom Horn, and Aaron Burr were able to pelt it with everything they had. However it shrugged most of these attacks off. That was not the point of the attacks however. Longinus had climbed up a tree and everyone else's actions were simply to herd the mother towards that tree. After minutes of repeating this process, they were finally able to get the mother into place. Longinus had climbed up about fifteen feet. He jumped with his spear tip down. He impaled the mother through the neck. The mother died almost instantly.

By this point Red Cloud had tamed the proto-whales. Each member of the party climbed aboard a proto-whale and rode for several weeks across the water. Intermittently they found islands that were useful for both the proto-whales and themselves, resting and replenishing. After a time they realized they were nearing the time circle that held dinosaurs.

With only a couple days left according to Ern's calculations they got caught in a huge maelstrom. They had no option but to go under the sea's surface. Fortunately the last part of their mission also required underwater breathing so the dwarves had provided them with breathing tubes made of ivory. Even underwater the huge storm's effect on the current forced them off course. By the time they reached the coast they were lost, not able to pinpoint their location relative to Ve. They could walk around for years without finding Ve's home. There was only one alternative. Odin had instructed them to find the Spirit of the Forest if they got truly lost. When he had free time he occasionally visited Earth so he was present in every culture's mythology in one way or another. He has hundreds of names most notably the Green Man, the Horned Beast, Hermes the Hunter, and the Spirit of the Forest. He was the Garden's caretaker and controlled it however he saw fit. And, he was Gaia's son and as old as all life on Earth. Odin had told the team only to do this as a last resort because the Spirit wasn't particularly fond of human-like creatures. However, Odin and Atlas had both joined him in Elite Wild Hunts on occasion so they were casual friends with him. Hopefully that was enough to sway him to help the team locate Ve. The odd thing about the Spirit of the Forest was that while looking for him anywhere in the Garden, you would soon find his house. The group just started walking and within a few hours they came across a house carved from a living tree. The problem was it was surrounded by half a dozen of the most dangerous predator to ever live, *Tyrannosaurus rex*. The Spirit of the Forest's dwelling attracted all sorts of animals for some reason. And since The Garden was connected to all time circles, fauna from all of history were there for the T-Rexes to dine on. Normally the T-Rexes would have fought for the territory but the bounty was so great they apparently just tolerated each other's presence. Each weighed roughly eight tons and stood 43 feet long, and 16 feet tall. Each had a massive skull filled with huge teeth balanced by a long, fulcrum-like, heavy tail. They had huge hind limbs and small, razor sharp fore claws, and there was no way in hell the group was going to take them. The team retreated to form a plan.

Vinh was the first one to suggest an idea. "We can beat them the same way we Vietnamese beat the U.S. and French. We are going to build caves."

Vinh elaborated on his plan. They would build caves from roughly 1000 yards out which were far away from the T-Rex's senses. Then they would build six caverns large enough to trap a T-Rex. The ground above the caverns would be designed to collapse when roughly a ton of pressure was applied to it. Far less than a T-Rex's weight but far more than any of the Team. They'd have to make the caverns roughly 15 feet deep in order to ensure the T-Rex could not escape. They'd line the bottom with sharpened poles that would skewer the T-Rex. Using an old trick he used often in his fight against the Americans and French, Vinh also planned to coat each sharpened pole with human feces. Human feces are highly toxic and would begin poisoning the T-Rex almost immediately. They would build man-sized tunnels connecting the caverns so when the surface collapsed the trapped T-Rex could be attacked from all angles. Since they didn't have enough manpower to attack all six at once they needed the tunnels to connect in order for the group to travel to each cavern to finish each off. While it was true they could simply leave the T-Rexes trapped, the possibility of even one escaping was too great a risk.

The problem would be luring the T-Rexes towards the caverns. Ern volunteered to act as a runner and so did Aaron Burr. The actual excavation took several grueling months of labor. They finally finished. Ern and Burr both got ready. They stripped themselves of everything but their clothes and ran into the opening where the T-Rexes resided. They attracted the attention of the huge lizard and started running. One by one each of the T-Rexes fell into a cavern. The other team members methodically began butchering the already wounded T-Rexes until none remained. They got themselves out of the tunnels and approached the house.

Ern opened the door to the home and they entered cautiously. They saw a being not born of this earth with a man's torso that had the head of a deer whose antlers were outrageously large. Other than this it was completely green and plants sprouted out of it.

Ern respectfully informed the group, "This is the Spirit of the Forest."

When Ern approached him the Spirit shouted "What the hell do you want?"

Red Cloud and Quan Li also approached, bowed, and Red Cloud said, "Wise Spirit of Nature, we ask you to guide us to the dwelling of Ve."

The Spirit rustled its greenery demanding, "Why the hell would I want to help any of you humans? You are the biggest nuisance I have ever had to deal with. I used to be able to take vacations. You can predict a natural disaster and most other things that will cause a race to die but humans; you have made me work harder than I have since the last ice age. You're whole species should be categorized as a walking natural disaster. Do you have any idea how hard it is to make a working ecosystem?"

This tirade continued until Aaron Burr finally had enough. All of the others had pleaded with the Spirit or simply not joined the conversation.

He was a god in his place of power. Aaron Burr looked much different from normal. All the others saw in front of them the elder statesman that had nearly argued his way to leading a country. He exuded an aura of self-confidence despite standing before a god. Even Ern was impressed.

Aaron calmly stated, "I'm Aaron Burr. I don't give a damn who or what you are. I've been in this Garden for months and I want out. You are going to tell us where to find Ve."

The Spirit replied, "The Aaron Burr? You're the only man to kill an American President in a fair fight. Why didn't you say so in the first place? Of course, I'll help you. I've read dozens of biographies about you. I have a painting of you in my house, and I even took human form to bid on a rifle you used during the American Revolution."

The Spirit actually seemed positively star struck. Then The Spirit pulled out a digital camera and had Ern take a picture of the two. Since The Spirit was the ultimate controller of the Garden apparently the provision against technology did not apply to him. He offered to transport them to where Ve resided. Needless to say, they agreed.

The Spirit of the Forest also resolved a problem the dwarves had not been able to solve. Ve resided at the center of the Garden which is the first circle of time and life on earth. The center replicates the conditions of the beginning of life. If those conditions didn't exist the early organisms would obviously not be able to survive anymore than a lion would be able to survive under the sea. The problem was, when life began, the atmosphere was much different. The earliest atmosphere consisted of volcanic emanations alone. Gases that erupt from volcanoes today, however, are mostly a mixture of water vapor, carbon dioxide, sulfur dioxide, and nitrogen, with almost no oxygen. It wasn't until hundreds of millions of years later that oxygen levels increased due to plant life. Plants breathe in carbon dioxide, the same way animals breathe in air composed partially of oxygen. The plants exhale oxygen as a byproduct of their energy system. The Spirit provided the team with organic face masks that would breathe the air, exhale oxygen and combine it with the other elements necessary for the team members to breathe. The dwarves had made scuba tubes of ivory, but they were only good for up to a day. After taking one more picture with the whole group The Spirit transported all of them to where Ve resided.

They found Odin's older brother meditating on a ledge overlooking the middle of the Garden. This part of the Garden was nothing like the rest. It was a vast desolate wasteland. No plant or animals had evolved yet just a few one-celled organisms residing in a pool where a meteorite had struck all those billions of years ago. The group approached him. He had a striking resemblance to Odin but he was gaunt from years of living the life of an aesthete. He opened his eyes and greeted them.

Ern explained who they were and that they were there at Odin's bequest to ask for Ve's help in performing the Summoning Ritual.

Ve replied, "I've put away my old warlike ways after hearing the teachings of the Fully Enlightened One and now strive for Enlightenment myself. I cannot be a part of my brother's war."

Quan Li motioned for the others to back away.

Ve said to him, "Ah so you're a monk of the Shaolin. I once admired you for your marital spirit but now I admire you for your dedication to Lord Buddha's teachings."

The two discussed Enlightenment and the sutras for hours finally Quan Li backed Ve into a corner, saying, "Would any of those on the verge of enlightenment, the Bodhivistas, let a bandit kill a helpless woman? You know the answer to that, Great Ve. We of the Shaolin embrace that precept. We must fight Yahweh not because we enjoy killing but because we love life. We cannot stand idly by while billions die for one being's desires." Quan Li bowed his head deeply, in reverence.

Ve acquiesced to Quan's argument. "I should have known I would have to wield my axe again." Ve had mediated so long in the Garden that he could commune with it; sensing his desire the Garden transported all of them to the Garden's edge. He bid the Garden farewell and left.

When he arrived at the meeting place, Odin greeted him "I knew you'd come to your senses brother".

Chapter 10

> "I fear all that we have done is to awaken a sleeping giant and fill him with a terrible resolve."
>
> —Admiral Yamamoto. Leader of the Japanese fleet in WWII

I wake up with nothing but some clothes and a strange feeling in my head. I am being drawn to some place. I keep following the sensation. A mountain appears ahead of me. I have to go around in order to follow the energy. I arrive at a cave surrounded by sparse tundra. Inside the chasm I can feel the emanation of a great power. I know that I stand before Vili's prison. I hear a voice.

I feel I know who it is and ask in my head, "Lord Vili?"

"How is it you can hear me, a being that is out of phase with everything else?" Vili asks.

"I think it is your brother, Odin, who gives me the ability and has sent me to you. Odin set up a series of events that has led me here," I said.

"My brother does not have that sort of strength. He must have paid dearly for such help," Vili said. "Are you to be my herald, my avatar?"

"If that is my purpose, but why me?" I question.

Vili explains, "The bits I can free up to give to my people are just breadcrumbs of what I am and what they need. With you I can transform into any shape, take on any persona directly."

"What are the terms?" I ask, the lawyer in me seeping through to this reality.

"Tell me what are your plans right now?" Lord Vili asks.

"Kill Sadas, kill Eric, and then destroy the Empire." I hiss.

I feel power coming into me. My essence is getting pushed and pulled from a dozen different directions. I am being filled with energy. I see memories that are not mine flooding into my head. Vili's memories have come to me.

He is an ancient being, and the memories even though attenuated a million times, seem almost as real as my own. I feel my mind being inundated with information about the Northlands and its inhabitants.

Vili pulls back, just before the surge of energy destroys me. I am powerful. I feel every atom in my body. I reach my arms to the heavens and focus. A lightning bolt crashes down.

Somehow I know what I need to do. I go to find Master Bui. With my new powers it isn't hard to travel to the northern regions. I need to reunite the tribes. I find my way back to my city in the Northlands. I need help. In reality there are hundreds of millions of human tribesmen. This world is twenty times bigger than earth and the tribesmen are dispersed over huge distances. So uniting the tribesmen is a lot easier said than done.

I manifest Vili's power and begin to control the skies. I form clouds into three interlocking drinking horns. It is Vili's sign here in the Northlands and it is Odin's sign back home. As I demonstrate Vili's sign, the shamans can feel Vili's power surging through me and they know I am truly his herald. They believe me and promise to start bringing together the tribes. My problem is I need to go to the farthest reaches of this continent and contact the shamans there. In those cities reside the most powerful mages and casters of the North. The Northlands' groups rarely have contact with the rest of the tribes so merely word of mouth will not be enough. I have to demonstrate my skill to them.

Vili has filled my head with information that will help with my mission. There are two types of mages in the Northlands. They have separate civilizations. Each have between 50-60 million people spread over an area the size of North America. Both areas have their own capital city. If I can convince the leaders of the capitals that I am real and that we have a chance to lead all the Northlanders against the Elven Empire, the other parts of the populace will follow.

The two schools of mages use two different methods to acquire magic. The first one gains magic by seizing it from the outside world. While this can involve taking it from living beings, most mages simply take it from the residual magic in the world. This is mostly because living things have instinctive defense mechanism to prevent a serious drain of magic. I thought about introducing them to Martin but the idea of 50 million Martin-like energy drains was a bit much for me. The second school of the Northlanders believes in increasing one's own innate magic energy levels through a process that apparently involves a lot of work and meditation. I was a little unclear of the details, but suspect it is just a different more passive way to gather the residual magic.

Most of the population of Northlanders looks like the average member of my own tribe. They practice the art of magic but they also have primary occupations apart from magic. Most of them are farmers. I discover farming is essentially impossible on the surface. So farming is done underground in caves.

The leaders are much different however from the average tribesmen. They appear like emaciated shells glowing with power. I approach the leaders of the first group of Northlanders and identify myself as Vili's actual avatar and an emissary of Odin's. Not surprisingly, they don't believe me. They want me to prove my claim as Vili's and Odin's agent. But since my essence is still out of phase, I can't show them Vili's mark on me. I try to con them and say that I am immune to magic due to Vili, but they don't fall for that. I try another approach; I use my new powers to do everything from cause lightning bolts to rain down around me to juggling three 10,000 pound boulders at once. But, they match every one of my feats. Before making any more of a fool of myself, I realize that I need to learn more about their magic.

The Northlander's magic is based on three things: the ability to gather magic from the world around them; how much of it can be retained; and how efficiently it can be used. The Shaman went off on some metaphysical tangents, but I didn't pay much attention. Then, like one of my own lightning bolts, I realize that these mages have had centuries to efficiently use magic energy while I have only had a couple of weeks. After a long talk, they begin to believe it is plausible I am Vili's avatar.

Even though they want to rid the Northlands of the elves, they don't want to die in a futile effort. They want assurances that I am competent to lead. To prove myself, I must accomplish three things: I have to contact the other tribe and get them to join me; I have to contact Ragnar of the mountain and if he joins me I am definitely a good leader; finally I have to slay a dragon that has plagued them for centuries.

I opt to approach the Hoa tribe first, since that is the least likely to get me killed. The Sanh tribe members are noticeably fitter and healthier in general. They also dabble in magic but are primarily tradesmen. The average citizen still is as strong as a journeyman shaman from my tribe, though. I get an audience fairly easily. The best way to describe the leaders is they look like stereotypical martial arts heroes and can do all that stuff too. They are generally amicable, and explain to me that their view about depending on an outside source for magic leaves one inherently dependent and therefore weak. They spend years in meditation and martial training in order to harness their own powers. They can do magic, but they also can do incredible feats with their bodies. For example, they can hold their breaths for hours, sit in fire and not be burned, and a hundred other impossible feats without the aid of any augmentations.

They tell me that if I want them to join me then I will have to prove myself against one of their masters. Master Sung is my opponent. He is a man of average height but has incredibly toned muscles. He exudes an aura of power. He is so fast that he hits me before I even react to put my hands up. Driven back 20 feet I do a summersault in the air and land on my feet. We fight fairly equally for nearly an hour. I decide to take a gamble. In fighting turning your back to a person is generally considered a very bad idea. You can get suplexed, choked, or hit without being able to defend yourself. But, there are a limited number of moves that aren't very well known. I dodge a kick and intentionally overreach on a spinning back fist which exposes my back. As expected he reaches for my back with his hands and grabs for my waist for a suplex move. However, I thread my right hand underneath his right hand. Then I grab my right wrist with my left arm. This creates a lock. I kick my legs up jumping 180 degrees as best I can. The result is I push his wrist behind his back and past his neck. This rips his rotator cup in half along with every ligament inside. I disengage and he acknowledges his defeat. After this, the leaders recognize my martial prowess and agree to aid me.

Having accomplished my first task, I go to the mountain to seek Ragnar. Vili has imparted the memories of Ragnar to my mind. Ragnar's story is a sad one. Fifteen thousand years ago, before the elves came, he was the greatest fighter in the land. His axe slew dragons, demons, and monsters of all sorts. He had been a mercenary by trade. However, he was rather fair in his fees. If the client was a lord he'd charge as exorbitant a price as he could get away with. However, if he was hired by peasants he'd find a bag of barley and a night's rest sufficient consideration. Ragnar was born into a fishing family. Fishing in this world inevitably involved fighting sea monsters as well. Even before the elves came to this world, there were hundreds of sea monsters dwelling in the oceans. As such, fisherman would hunt the monsters as well. One large sea monster was equal to a week's worth of fish. By age eight Ragnar could tie any knot known to man. By age thirteen he could throw a harpoon with impeccable aim. By nineteen he was considered one of the best fishermen in the village. Killing sea monsters was and still is a dangerous job. He was the eldest of nine brothers. Only five survived to adulthood. He'd watched the others die at sea. As such he was very protective of his other siblings.

One day he came home after a fishing expedition to the sight of his youngest brother being beaten by elves. He had just been rescued from a giant sea serpent through the quick actions of fellow crewmen. A can of oil and a torch was all that had stood against him being swallowed whole by the creature. Needless to say he was already on edge. He recognized one of the two assailants as the first born son of the Duke that ruled all the land in the area. The Duke's son had a reputation for beating up commoners and raping local women. His royal blood gave him immunity from prosecution. The other one was one of his servants.

Ragnar pulled his fishing knife out and told them, "Get off my brother."

Instead the two youths drew out swords and the Duke's son asked, "Do you know who I am?"

Ragnar replied, "I don't give a damn who you are. Back off!"

The two bad boys introduced themselves and stood at ready with their swords. While Ragnar had spent his youth fighting for his life on the seas, these two had spent theirs receiving private tutoring. This included years of fencing lessons. Therefore when they saw one commoner wielding a knife they laughed at him and attacked. Ragnar used his blinding speed and superior strength to put an end to them. They died in seconds for which Ragnar was brought to trial. The only witnesses were his brother and two life-long neighbors. His brother's testimony was deemed inadmissible. The court ruled his familial relationship with Ragnar made him a subjective witness. Therefore the probative value of this testimony was substantially outweighed by its prejudicial value. The other two were bribed with ten times what they normally made in a year. They told the court Ragnar had killed the two without any provocation and his brother's bruises had come from Ragnar accidentally striking him during the course of the melee. Needless to say, Ragnar was convicted. The Duke wanted Ragnar to suffer so under the pretense of generosity the Duke requested that the court not execute him. Instead, he suggested they send him to the gladiatorial arena. For most men this was a de facto death sentence. The only difference is you got to brood over your death for a longer more miserable period.

Ragnar was built out of hardier stuff, however. He was given a three month course in fighting. The trainers found the axe suited him the best. For sixteen years he fought every form of monster the arena made available to him. All the while he received the best hand to hand instruction the arena offered. He went to the brink of death hundreds of times but the healers always brought him back. One day after a bout where he had slain a flock of a dozen harpies, the arena masters informed him he was free. The rule of the arena was after a thousand victories you were free to go. Ragnar had been aware of this but he had long ago lost count of his fights.

They let him keep his axe. Then they gave him an emerald ring and a small severance pay to live off until he could find employ. The ring was the symbol of his freedom. A badge of honor very few ever received. Moreover, it was enchanted to protect against a variety of spells and allowed the wearer to cast a few minor cantrips as well. It is a symbol of strength only one in eighteen hundred and eighty gladiators ever survived to receive the award. After becoming reacquainted with the world, he traveled to the Duke's estate. He found out the duke had placed a bounty on a pack of fire drakes that had been ravaging the local area. Normally fire drakes, which are small, fire-breathing bat-like dragons, did not go into the civilized lands. But this pack apparently had grown bold. While they slept in packs it was common for them to go hunting alone. Ragnar saw one flying by after several days searching. His aim with a harpoon was impeccable. He struck the fire drake through the heart and found where its body had fallen. He carefully removed a gland from the body and placed it in a sealed bag.

He carried the carcass to the Duke's home. After being paid by a seneschal accountant of the Duke's, he asked for an audience with him. He met the Duke in the open courtyard of his castle and he noticed two dozen archers trained on his position. The Duke didn't recognize him. Sixteen years had gone by and Ragnar had taken efforts to conceal his features. The Duke thanked him for his efforts and asked him if he was willing to remain in the area in order to hunt the rest of the drakes. Ragnar agreed. Then he pulled out the gland and offered it to the Duke as a souvenir. At the same time he made a small incision in the gland. Using the power of his emerald ring, he subtly let some of the glands pheromones rise up into the wind. He told the Duke the gland made excellent cologne. He placed a little bit of the gland's hormone on to the Duke's hand to show him. The Duke was pleased by the scent from this gland, but he did not realize that the scent will draw the attention of any drake that smelled it. Meanwhile the Duke's court wizard saw what was occurring and tried to cast a spell of paralysis on Ragnar. Ragnar was not even aware of this but thanks to his ring he was protected. Before the wizard could issue a warning twenty-four fire drakes had descended upon the castle. Ragnar had led the fire drakes close to the castle with the corpses of several animals he'd slain. Ragnar told the Duke who he was. Moments before the fire drakes descended.

The Duke, the wizard, and most of the guards died quickly. The Duke's sons had come out to see what the commotion was about. Ragnar grabbed a bit of sand that had soaked in some of the gland's hormones and furtively tossed some on them. In the end Ragnar was actually commended for his bravery as he fought off most of the fire drakes. Being that all of the Duke's direct heir's were dead the Duke's estate went to a distant cousin, Walter. He had contacted the Castle and had asked Ragnar to stay so he could reward him. While Walter appeared to be a timid small man in his mid 20s he had a scar of a wound that had gone down to the bone on his face. His hands had the calluses of a man constantly using a sexton i.e., a navigator's hand. They also had the marks of one that regularly used a harpoon and net. Ragnar recognized it as a mark caused only by the tentacles of a mollusk found in the most dangerous waters in the North. Walter saw Ragnar's inspective look. Walter was rather self conscious of holding what was normally a commoner's position.

"I'm the youngest son of a minor noble family. We are nobles in name alone. Our lineage is three times removed from the old Duke. The only reason I'm inheriting this land is my brother agreed to split the land with me and all the closer relatives got themselves burned to death six months ago at a masquerade party. Our family was too base to be invited, according to the host. My father is a blacksmith. My elder brother was lucky enough to marry a wealthy merchant's eldest daughter. The merchant wanted to become a member of the aristocracy and is rich enough that he couldn't care less about my family's finances. The only reason I could even afford the schooling to be a navigator was because of the sizable dowry my brother received," continued Walter.

Ragnar replied, "I was just impressed that a timid-looking fellow like yourself has traveled to the far waters where a markow mollusk resides. Losing a quarter of the crew is not uncommon in those waters."

Upon realizing only a person that had been to those waters would recognize such a scar, Walter tossed Ragnar a harpoon he had brought with him. He grabbed another one for himself. He pointed out a small knot on the beam. Walter was challenging him to an old mariner's game. The closest person to hit the object won. Walter threw it and hit a quarter inch away from the dot. Ragnar followed course. When they tried to measure the difference between their throws the distance was too small to accurately measure. Ragnar was happy to leave this place to a fellow mariner. Walter gave him a sizable bag of coins and bid him farewell.

For the next nine years Ragnar worked as a bounty hunter and a mercenary. He killed every type of monster you could imagine. He quickly became a legend and his axe was the inspiration for quite a number of skirl's songs. Then one day he met a woman by the edge of a river. She was a beautiful woman with the green eyes and the blonde hair of the southern races. Apparently lost, she asked him where she was and told him she didn't know who she was. Thinking this was a begging ploy he tossed a few coins her way. Thinking nothing more of it he walked off. However, after a couple miles curiosity struck and he decided to return. Once he got close to where he had met her he heard her screaming. He ran towards the direction of the sound and pulled out his axe. Nine bandits surrounded her. One was ripping off her clothes in order to rape her. Ragnar didn't even bother to elicit a response from the bandits. He struck them down in fewer blows than there were bandits.

He helped her recover herself and he talked to her for awhile determining that she truly didn't know who she was or where she was from. Her first memory was standing by the riverbank. She begged him to let her come along with him. She promised to cook, make fires, and any other chores required. They traveled for a few years. During that time she named herself Abigail, and she carried out her promises. She picked up some of Ragnar's skills as well. Within four years Abigail could track prey, shoot a bow with precision and was fairly good in melee combat as well. They worked as a team now. Abigail used comely looks to coax their bounties into leaving with her while Ragnar waited for them outside. When battling monsters, often times Ragnar would fight them at close quarters while Abigail would launch arrows at the quarry.

More importantly, Ragnar and Abigail fell in love and were wedded. Eventually Abigail became pregnant. They settled down to raise a family. They built a house in the woods a mile from a small city. Ragnar still took bounties within the local vicinity but their wandering had ceased. They ended up having four children. For the next 15 years, life went on fairly uneventfully. One day their youngest child, Lucas, was playing near their home in the woods. A mountain lion attacked him. Abigail was nearby and ran to save Lucas. Abigail pushed Lucas out of the way just in time, but she was mauled by the lion. Still a fighter Abigail pulled out her knife and began slashing. Ragnar, who was close by chopping firewood, heard the commotion and ran towards them. He yelled for Lucas to grab his axe. Upon arrival both the lion and his wife were dying. He kicked the mountain lion off and attended to his wife. At that moment a figure appeared. It was a man in form at least. He was a tall, impossibly handsome being that he exuded a supernatural presence.

The figure said "Back away, this is none of your concern mortal. I am Lamar the God of Reason. What's about to occur is the business of gods. Leave now."

Ragnar's voice and eyes filled up with murderous intent. "Did you have anything to do with this?"

Lamar laughed, "I warned you mortal." Lamar lashed out with his mind. He was trying to bend Ragnar to his will.

Ragnar spat in Lamar's face, "I asked you a question. Did you have anything to do with my wife's death?"

Enraged Lamar unleashed his full might at Ragnar. Right now, simply being in his presence would make most mortals kneel and grovel before him. Lamar was focusing his entire will directly at Ragnar and yet could only sense an iron resolve filled with murderous intent. Lamar had never met a human whose will was strong enough to resist his might. It defied all reason. For just a moment Lamar was caught off guard. Ragnar charged and swung his axe. He connected and drew a single drop of blood.

Then another force stopped him. "Ragnar stop." The voice came from where Abigail's body lay. He looked back and her body had disappeared. In its place was a preternaturally beautiful woman. "Ragnar it's me, Abigail. When we first met I had been banished. The other gods punished me by forcing me to take human form and erased my memory as well."

Ragnar pondered the situation for a moment and asked, "So is it over? Are you no longer my wife?"

Abigail replied, "Only if you want it to be. You're still my husband. I'd like you and our children to come with me to the realm of the gods."

Ragnar went of course. All their children became godlings the moment Abigail changed to her true form. Abigail invested a portion of her power into Ragnar in order to make him immortal. They spent three thousand happy years together. Abigail was the patron god of magic. Abigail taught Ragnar magic as he had taught her to fight. The combined private tutelage of the patron god of magic and the divine essence Abigail had instilled in him made him surpass the power of any mortal mage. He was close to a god in his own right. His combat experience and will compensated for his lack of actual raw power. He took up his old job and became a bounty hunter for the gods.

Then Ragnar met Vili. They happened upon one another in a tavern frequented by the gods of the various pantheons of this world.

Vili told him, "I saw you kill that Balrog some months back. You're quite skilled but your axe needs to be sharpened." Vili touched his finger along the edge of Ragnar's axe. He bled slightly. The blood merged with the axe.

Ragnar felt his axe had been infused with Vili's divine power. They quickly became friends and they sparred often. Both of them were axe wielders. Vili would lessen his strength so that it was competitive.

Then the elves came.

In order to prevent war the human gods agreed to a nonaggression pact with the elven gods. Vili was furious. He knew this was simply a ploy by the elven gods to stall until they became strong enough to attack. However, despite being more powerful than the entire pantheon combined, Vili was not officially a member of the human pantheon. Therefore, he didn't get to vote on the nonaggression pact. He and Ragnar adamantly opposed it but they didn't get a vote. When the elf gods finally ambushed the pantheon nearly all the surviving gods fled. Ragnar and Abigail stayed along with a handful of others. Despite Vili's urging them to flee they stayed to give their children a chance to flee. Ironically, the god that bought the others enough time to flee was the self-proclaimed god of cowards, Jinx. He was resurrected by Vili to help Ragnar. He threw himself at the elven gods and was destroyed. He gave the others just enough time to flee. Ragnar's children were not full gods so they didn't make it out in time. At the end Vili attacked from the front while a cadre of gods attacked Abigail and Ragnar who were defending the wormhole the gods had constructed to flee. The elven gods outnumbered them. Abigail could have fled but that would have meant abandoning Ragnar. So instead Abigail fought and was mortally wounded. Abigail's dying act was to use her magic to fling Ragnar as far to the North as she could. Around the same time Vili was being captured. With his last act Vili infused as much of his power as he could into Ragnar.

Ragnar became a hermit living on a mountain close to where Abigail had thrown him. For 12,000 years Ragnar has been practicing his magic and axe work, waiting for a time when he can get his revenge against the elves. He is now ridiculously powerful. He is as strong as the Emperor using the entire power of The Source now. The elf gods are actually afraid of him because if they want to attack him that means going onto the mortal world where they'll have to fight him on equal ground.

It was time for me to find Ragnar on his mountain. I approached cautiously. I've heard stories of people going up on that mountain. All are tested. Those found wanting are never to be seen again. Those that pass either are granted powers beyond any normal berserker or are allowed to study magic alongside Ragnar. I have no idea what test I'll have to pass to get an audience. My senses are at their peak. What I see I don't expect: a heavily muscled, six foot, grey haired man wielding a huge axe waving at me jovially.

I shout back, "Hail Ragnar, the people have need of you."

Ragnar throws his axe at me with impossible speed. It misses me by an inch and goes through several trees before returning to his hand. He's laughing with great amusement.

"Just kidding," says Ragnar, "I've been waiting for you. Vili told me you'd be coming. Come on in."

I am graciously served a horn filled with mead and we immediately fall into the warrior's passion: discussing the details of my plan.

Weeks later, I see Neriss, Michelle, Martin, Harvey, Rodney, Linh, and Bobby.

Neriss steps up, "So I hear you've got a dragon to slay. Want some help?"

Now I know who was responsible for my reincarnation. Damn it, I knew he wanted to gloat over whatever great act of magic had accomplished it. He wanted me to ask though.

I was so damned curious I finally broke and asked him. "How did you do it? How did you know it was me?"

Neriss replies, "Perhaps it's because I'm the greatest wizard you know?"

"Yes, Neriss, you have defied the laws of nature, man, and the gods and not only found the secret to my immunity to magic but were able to bring me back from the dead as well. Now could you please tell me?" I insisted.

"Remember those experiments I asked to do on you? Well they weren't for research? It was for exactly one spell," confessed Neriss.

"You don't know when to let things be," I complained.

Neriss continued, "I knew you would get yourself in trouble again, so I wanted to have a safe guard when you got caught. I labored for months over the matter and I made no progress. I contacted a dozen Powers and they had no answer. One day, I finally traded something of great value to lock on to the connection between you and your essence. Using that information, I constructed a device that could capture you, at the moment of death before you could go to where ever it is your essence was. I used the samples I'd taken to clone a body. When you died, I captured your soul and placed it in a human womb. It wasn't an exact science. I just threw you out at random for any potential tribeswoman that was capable of bearing you. I had made some alterations to the body so that you'd fit in with the tribe. It wasn't hard since I just needed to suppress the half of your genes that aren't from that race. You were supposed to remember roughly five years ago. Then I assumed you'd track me down. As best as I can determine the reason you didn't is simply because you didn't want to. Your subconscious was blocking your revival. I tried to track you down but without knowing where to start Martin and Rodney went to the place where you died and saw the residual aura of my spell. That's when we began to make progress. I had the knowledge, Martin had the math, and Rodney acted as the magical battery. We began with the premise that all of you had been sent here for a purpose because if it was just random chance there would be no possibility of figuring it out. We determined the minimum amount of distance dimensions would be involved. We decided that we'd take a guess and assume your soul had either been moved one dimension that the rest hadn't been moved."

"Whoever sent you was so precise the act of integrating your persona into this world had destroyed any residue. That fact alone narrowed down the list. But it wasn't narrow enough. The list also wasn't of people you talk to unless invited. It was enough to go ask one of the wisest beings in existence; one of the sages that helped defeat the old ones. He asked for a price. I expected him to ask for my eternal soul or eternal penance. Instead his price was, if I figured out who did this and for what, that I must tell him. The implications of him not knowing are more than you can comprehend. With the information he gave us we were able to track you down."

"You're still connected to your essence but it's not detectable without instruments so precise you can measure the exact moment a quark will flux. By this point I was out of money. I didn't want to draw on the family assets because that would attract suspicions. Martin went to ask Linh for a loan. So I get to Linh's secret lair. That being the basement of the bar he and Bobby bought. It's nice; they have a mural of you killing a demon with your bare hands. It moves and everything. Linh said help yourself to whatever you want and feel free to come by anytime you like for more. Linh has stolen practically every devise that is purported to not be stealable. Just because he was told it couldn't be done. Martin took some exceedingly rare objects from the vault and traded them for a device to see the aforementioned link. We found it and in the process found that your soul seems to be traveling randomly through an infinity of planes within a huge number of dimensions. There was one dimension where it wasn't moving. One day Martin realized the movement isn't random. It is based upon the relative movements of billions of bodies and forces. It is an equation. It is most likely an equation that gives you a roadmap to your home world. There's no way it's solvable though; it requires calculating trillions of constantly changing variables with only one constant. Only the greatest of god's could do that," concluded Neriss.

I replied, "I know." Then casually I said, "Have I mentioned I'm the living incarnation of Vili, Odin's older brother now?"

We have Cory travel ahead to the tribes that specialize in watercraft. He's going to be in charge of modernizing their tactics.

We go ahead and take on the dragon. Apparently dragons here are exactly what the legends say they are: giant flying reptiles that are highly intelligent magic-using immortals. We approach the lair of the dragon. Hoping to catch it by surprise we sneak up on the lair. Martin and Linh slowly disengage the wards while Neriss, Michelle, Rodney, Bobby, Harvey, and I prepare. What we don't count on is the dragon not being in there. As we crept into the lair we saw the corpses of many would-be dragon slayers but no dragon. We plan on leaving and putting the wards back into place. Much to our luck, good or bad, the dragon returns just as we were leaving. It is over a hundred feet long and fifty feet in girth. It has two foot long teeth and a forty foot tail.

It roars out, "Why do you dare disturb my abode?"

I shout back in a booming voice, "We've come for your life."

Harvey puts up a barrier just as the dragon breathes fire on us. We split up. Bobby immediately transforms and takes to the air. Martin turns into mist. Harvey merges with the earth. Rodney teleports off and I bend space just a tad so I'm a hundred yards to the left. Martin rematerializes on the dragon's back and tries to suck the life out of it. The beast just seems to get mad. It flings Martin off and breathes a cone of fire right at him. Bobby flies at Martin to push him out of the way. He partially succeeds but some of the flames hit Martin. It apparently makes him too woozy and he lands hard, unconscious. The dragon dives in on Bobby. It has Bobby in its maws crushing him. Rodney is flinging lightning bolts at the dragon but the dragon has wards against them. Michelle makes some vines try to ensnare it while Linh does the same with some shadows. This gives Harvey enough time to make a pillar of stone and attempt to drive it deep into the dragon. The pillar crumbles like butter against its magically reinforced hide. Neriss summons up a batch of demons and commands them to attack. The dragon summons a pack of his own. Bobby is still being crushed. I use the power Vili gave me and lash out. A bolt of pure kinetic energy rips into its body. The bolt tears through its scales and exposes some of its flesh. But he doesn't let go and Bobby has only seconds left. Rodney and Neriss are desperately trying to summon magic to aid Bobby. Then the most curious thing happens. Bobby's fur starts turning gold and he begins to become visibly larger. I think I know what's happening. I look at his tails and more are emerging. He has become a nine tailed fox demon. He still can't quite free himself however. I use another blast directed right at the dragon's maw. This is enough to let Bobby pry himself free. Bobby breathes a gigantic cone of foxfire right into the dragons face. It stings the dragon who lashes out with a blast of magic. Bobby raises a shield of magic and blocks it. Apparently his transformation has given him new powers. The blast still forces him back. He flies again at the dragon. He elongates his tails to fifty feet a piece. He starts stinging the flesh in the raw areas. His poison should have worked but this dragon was more powerful than anything we had encountered before. Bobby's speed and strength had tripled but it wasn't enough. Finally as he darted in he was caught by the dragon's tail. Linh came in with his shadows to catch him. He was too focused on that act to see the cone of fire come from the dragon. It looked like he was dead when Michelle dove in front of her lover. She raised some plants from the ground. It blocked the flames just enough to singe the three but they were clearly out of the fight. With her last bit of energy, Michelle has the nearby plants absorb all three of them. Hopefully it is enough to heal them.

Harvey meanwhile has a novel idea. He constructs a seesaw from the ground and forces a dozen boulders on the other end.

He heats his armor screaming, "Yippy Kay Yi Yay, motherfucker," as he flings himself towards the dragon. He misses his mark by a bit. Instead of the dragon's body he hits the right wing of the dragon. His armor thousands of degrees hot, burns right through it. Unfortunately he goes right through the wing and is heading towards a hard landing on the ground. The rest of us are still caught up fighting the dragon so there is nothing we can do. But Harvey is able to manipulate the earth turning it into soft sand. Still the landing knocks him unconscious. Harvey has done his job however. Without a right wing the dragon careens towards the ground. It is no less dangerous, however. The three of us, Neriss, Rodney, and I, fling all of our powers at it. Between the three of us we manage to break down its magical shields. The dragon is hurt, tired, and fading. But we were fading faster. Neriss is beginning to cough up blood and Rodney is panting heavily. I throw one more bolt but it is substantially weaker than the previous ones. For the time being, I've spent my powers. We can't take it. I grab my spear.

I yell at the others, "I'll distract the dragon while you grab Martin and run. Neriss still should have enough power to summon a minor demon to fly you off."

They both in unison tell me, "We either live or we die together."

The dragon is walking towards us. We muster what energy we have left and make our final stand. Suddenly out of the east arrows start pelting into the areas of exposed flesh. Every second, six or seven arrows strike it. When it faces that direction to meet its attacker two arrows penetrate right throw each eye. The arrows penetrated so deep you could not see them. Piercing its brain the arrows killed the dragon!

I sit down and open a flagon of liquor. I already know who it has to be but how and why he found us I have no idea.

Magnus walked up to us looking me straight in the eye, "I knew you couldn't be dead."

"How the hell did you find me?" I queried.

"Once I noticed Neriss was missing from court, I went looking for everyone else. I hear about a nut trying to unify the Northlands so I follow the stories until I hear the guy is going to slay a dragon," says Magnus.

"No way was your timing that good," I say.

"Oh, I've been here for a bit. Since I didn't see anybody dying I figured I'd see whether you guys could take him on your own."

If he hadn't just saved my life and if I weren't so tired I couldn't stand, I would slug him. Upon inspecting the remains, the Northlanders' mages join us. We have the dragon's body transported to the main facility to prove we killed it and to let Neriss experiment on it.

Preparing for Battle:

Finally, I have united the tribes of the Northlands. Now I have to figure out how to use them to beat the Empire. I think about the elves' powers and weaknesses. There are many who would argue the differences between an elf and a human are really not that great. They base this on a concept that the elves' exterior bodies resemble humans' bodies. I have studied the elf and it is nothing like us. Apparently The Source keeps them young nearly forever. Mind you, we live several hundred years here in the North. Master Bui is 117 and likely will see 317. We have herbs and treatments that sustain a body unless it dies in battle.

I know the elves came from a different world and I believe their world was much more forgiving than ours is. We are a far hardier race than they are. We can beat them based on the following reasons. Firstly, we breed roughly 250 times to 1 child of theirs. They live a long time and they take a long time to reproduce. The gestation time for elven women is between 38-42 years. Secondly, Elves will get ill in environments that have a minimal effect on us. Thirdly, they have much less strength and stamina, and cannot handle changes in temperature. An elf will die of exposure in a day in weather that would merely leave a man cold. The same applies to heat, and to things like elevation and barometric pressure. The reasons for this are their entire body is an open system to the environment. They have no heart, lungs, or any other organs at all. If you cut one it bleeds blue green. I have observed the blood under Neriss' lens. It has no mitochondria so it can't process energy like us. The cellular outer layer, the membrane, is much harder than ours, like a plant's. I assume it has some other method of producing energy most likely magical.

The most bizarre thing is that an elf has no centralized brain. Its nervous system is open. Outside the senses, everything is evenly distributed throughout the body. This is why I think elves move so much faster, more coordinated and balanced than us. What if your nervous system just had to go to your closest body part which is where the neurons are in an elf? This is also why elves seem smarter than us. They have a lot more nerve tissue to work with proportionate to the size of their bodies. Yet why aren't they creative? An elf cannot adapt to a new random situation immediately. It can't come up with those logical leaps and gut instinct decisions humans can. This is in part because its brain is not centralized but distributed over its entire body. It just can't splice together information right away. There are probably a number of factors for that but the neuron thing has to be a big one. Another is probably that an elf doesn't have the same level of oxygenated blood going to that one part of its body. The blood is always distributed evenly. This is probably why it heals substantially slower but, like a lizard, it can regenerate body parts. It also appears that elves are cold blooded. It appears that they need to intentionally expend energy in order to stay warm. This process is not nearly as efficient so it causes a huge drain in energy.

Finally, the last thing I have found is that Elves have more heightened senses than humans but they don't adjust as quickly. So if you turned on a light it would be blind four or five times as long as a human. Same goes for hearing. The trick to beating an elven army is to take it where it does not know what to do. Facing it head on leaves it able to use its enormous magical reserves to kill you. Make it march to the north for six months then that's another story. Just ask Napoleon and Hitler.

The dwarf is the near opposite to an elf. It has redundant organs for everything but its brain. It has two hearts, a third lung that filters first, a four level stomach. Its kidneys and liver are off the wall. It can process most poisons like water. Its muscles are denser and heal faster along with its bones. Its immune system can repel diseases that will kill a human in a day. I have noticed that it cannot cope with heat. Its body just doesn't have enough surface area and it's just so dense, physically. It can't swim because of its density. And because of all those extra organs, they need 10 times as much food as a human. I wonder why dwarfs tend to have excessive plant allergies.

As I'm musing about dwarf allergies, suddenly I have an idea.

I explain my plan to everyone. But they don't believe it's possible. First we would have to build a thousand aircraft carrier-sized ships. That is assuming that we can develop airplanes and guns in time. I explain to them how and what I plan on doing. During World War II a scientist by the name of Geoffrey Pyke invented an interesting substance. It was part ice, part air, and part sawdust. It was light and strong (as strong as concrete), and it was a fairly good thermal insulator. It was super-strong ice which melted very slowly. Pykrete was a secret weapon. The British intended to build really gigantic aircraft carriers of the stuff. Just make the hull thick enough and any torpedo damage will have almost no effect. If your ship is made of super-ice rather than steel, you could build mile-long floating islands. They never finished the project. By the time the ships were ready to be built it was 1944. The island hopping campaign was already going smoothly in the Pacific, so they decided to abandon the project. Only one small test-ship was ever built. It was in an English lake and took three sweltering summer months to melt. Had it been built to size it would have taken a decade to dissolve. For a permanent ship, I simply needed to have ice elementals and spirits bind to the ship to keep it from melting at all.

In a little less than two years the elves are having a centennial festival celebrating their navy's destruction of the human's navy. I plan on using every available resource and borrowing from every single successful military plan that I knew in deploying against the elves. I leave everything else up to the others. The Pykrete ship will be my base for planning and staging the battle.

While we are in camp I notice a young winged Ogden playing with Harvey. Throughout the entire time we are in camp it is always following Harvey and Harvey does not seem to mind. He is constantly feeding it and playing with it. He actually is playing fetch with it by creating a tall pillar so the Ogden which Harvey had named Bruin had to fly to go fetch.

When I ask Michelle about Linh she blushes and mutters something about preparing for the war. I pat her shoulder and tell her a good balance of shadow and light are necessary for plants to pollinate, and maybe Linh can help with that. She disappears into the ground. Good for them.

Anyway it is time to get to work. I actually need Michelle and Cory for this next part. We travel to the North bringing several thousand seeds. Michelle uses her gift and 5000 mature trees grow 500-800 feet in height 2-3 hundred in diameter. Now it is time for me and Cory to get to work. I use my power to turn the trees to dust. I start willing piles of snow into the ocean. Cory and I use our respective powers to start mixing the saw dust with the snow through a gigantic tidal wave of snow. Big piles of snow melt very slowly. Compressed snow is a thermal insulator. It's like Styrofoam made of ice. This was going to take awhile. We mix the snow and sawdust in the subzero temperatures of the North. A huge floating snow-pile begins to build up. The weight of overlying layers compresses it into a solid mass of Pykrete. After we make a few million tons of it, we begin to form a ship. Then dozens of smaller ships are made.

Ragnar calls out to all of the spirits of the North. He summons all those spirits that have been abused by the elves and their gods. He offers them a chance at vengeance if they will follow him. Millions of spirits of all sorts are gathering. Some will be used initially. Others are to bide their time and attack when the elves invade. When Ragnar explains the plan, they are willing to follow him on faith. All of them can sense Vili's mark on him. Some are old enough to remember Vili's final stand. It saved many of their lives. Many others have heard of him through stories passed down through generations.

Rodney is in charge of designing a combustion engine and designing the aircraft to be built. Nearly all patent lawyers have a hard science degree of some sort. He has a double major in mechanical engineering and chemistry, so he is the best qualified for this work. Making the engine is not the difficult part. He is having a problem with a fuel source. A steam engine would work for everything except the planes. But the planes are the most important part of the operation. He cannot find any oil and it would take too long to develop a refinery system for an ethanol-like mixture. Then one day he comes across a girl lighting a lamp filled with heavy oil.

He asks her, "What is this oil?"

She replies, "Its oil made from gamlin root. You must not be from around here. It's used by everybody in the North for heating."

He purchases some from her and does some testing. To his astonishment, the unrefined root fuels an engine as well as gasoline does. All you need to do is just squeeze the root and the oil seeps out ready for use in the airplane engines.

Bobby is building guns and bombs. He's been doing this as a hobby for years so this comes as second nature to him. It takes him about a month to instruct the tribesmen working for him. First, he shows them how to make black powder. Then he shows them how to rifle a barrel and how to make a bullet. The bombs he makes use gunpowder and are designed to explode through a timer mechanism. Once a bomb is released from a plane, a needle will start spinning. After a number of revolutions calibrated to equal five thousand feet, the needle lights a fuse, which will cause the bomb to explode.

Production goes smoothly. All this work is being done in giant caves protected against divination. More importantly the caves are occupied by bat-like animals that excrete guano. The guano has the potassium nitrate necessary to make gunpowder. In the U.S., bat guano was used as a source of nitrate in the production of gunpowder during the War of 1812 and the Civil War. Gunpowder is made from sulfur, potassium nitrate, and charcoal in the following proportions; 75 percent potassium nitrate, 15 per cent charcoal, 10 per cent sulfur. The bats have occupied the lower recesses of the caves for thousands of years. Therefore thousands of tons of guano are available for use. But, all of this gunpowder requires a great deal of iron and sulfur. Acquiring it is no problem since the voles have no problem trading with us. The main problem is the nearest mine large enough to supply us with the hundreds of thousands of pounds we need, is several thousand miles away.

That is where Harvey and Michelle come in. They build a train system. They bring together several thousand shamans in order to use their magic energy. Michelle creates the wooden cross ties and Harvey uses his power over earth to mold the tracks. Once the shamans understand what needs to be done they learn quickly how to replicate the feat. With tens of thousands of miles of track laid, every city and industrial site in the North is now connected. The trains are designed and built prior to Rodney's discovery of Gamlin oil, so we opted for using steam engines. Being that the North was abundant with combustible fuels, I was curious to see what they were using to power the engines. It turned out they had taken a page from the Himalayan tribesmen. In the Himalayas dried yak dung is used as fuel for fire. While the Ogden normally process food extremely efficiently, an addition of an herb to their food reduces their digestive abilities. Thereby they create more dung. Hundreds of thousands of Ogden are contributing. The entire railroad system is being fueled by Ogden poop pies.

The trains are transporting materials to Bobby's site where they upload the nitrate-rich guano. They send the guano to the far North where our main agricultural operations were occurring in the Northern caves. Guano is not only a good source of nitrate for gunpowder it is also an excellent fertilizer for crops. The tribes had already known this but they had never had a feasible method of transport before. Tracks have been laid at all locations where large deposits of guano can be found and they are transporting guano to all the different agricultural sites. The bats are very common, and since their guano has never been seriously harvested before, there are millions of tons available.

Neriss is working on the corpse of the dragon. He reanimates it so that it can fly and then he infuses it with the most potent explosive compound available. Unfortunately the compound is hard to come by so it is impossible to get enough for the bombs. That's why we need to use gunpowder for the bombs. After he is done, Neriss returns to the Imperial Capital. For the next year he scouts out elves that are easily susceptible to his geas or controlling spells, and have access to secure locations. After finding a particularly safe place, he casts a geas on them and gently touches them to infuse them with his explosive compound.

Meanwhile Martin and Linh are trying to break the hardest equation on the planet, the protective enchantments that guard the Capital city's Arcane Tower. That is where the greatest of the Elven Empire's mages reside.

Master Bui is training the shamans on the aquatic skills their portion of the mission will require. They can hold their breaths indefinitely and already have knowledge in stealth. However, they will have to swim for miles while transporting giant logs tipped with poison in order to accomplish their mission. They won't be able to use any magic to remain undetected either. That would trigger the alarms of the bay they will be attacking. The alarms don't detect non-magic people because it is infeasible to screen all marine life coming into the bay. Besides the monks are going to be swimming to a facility that normally does not have much traffic anyway. On the day of attack, this facility will contain a small auxiliary fleet. Unlike the main fleet this fleet will have their weapon systems ready. So attacking them head on will not be wise. That is why we are taking a chapter out of Vietnamese War fighting and use of stealth.

The planes are being built in Bobby's caves under Rodney's supervision. Rodney's crew is rapidly learning the mechanics behind the engines and propellers. After a few months they can handle the operation on their own. Rodney then leaves to do more research on the upcoming attack. After each plane is completed it gets loaded onto a train and is sent to Ragnar. Ragnar binds a spirit to each one. Each plane now has a spirit's protection and has an auxiliary source of power. More importantly the planes don't need to take off. They can vertically lift like a helicopter or a harrier jet craft. This will maximize the number of planes a ship will be able to carry.

The Attack:

It is game day. We just have to have faith in everybody to pull their end off. I am running through the dark with Master Bui and the other berserkers. Martin and Michelle are getting ready. It is as much them as me. The Emperor is there at the annual float show. Nearly all the ships in his navy are standing there with the sailors saluting. Little did the Emperor know another vessel made of frigid ice was deploying its cargo of fearless fighter pilots captained by Cory, the ex Navy Seal turned Nix. Today the Empire will be displaying every major military maneuver that can be done all in one day. And, today was my world's Tet offensive. In the Capital and a few other cities, people are having the mysterious urge to go someplace else where they are unknown. Neriss has cast his geas resulting in around six thousand elves deciding to take a walk.

On the main continent in the coastal cities that have been safe for millennia, people don't even notice the metallic shapes on the horizon.

An auxiliary brigade officer was bitching to his executive officer, "Why? This is supposed to be my day off? Why am I on guard duty?" All the while he's complaining, he doesn't notice the hundreds of spiritual shamans and huge pointed logs approaching in the water. He would have laughed if anyone told him a human could do that. He still doesn't believe those ridiculous arena stories about humans.

On the back of an undead dragon, ride two men whose minds are born and molded to see patterns and holes in algorithms. Inside a certain extraordinary Tower Arcane, ten thousand arch mages are viewing everything from supernovas to women, and in their own little worlds they don't feel a mind reaching out. They would have laughed if you had told them what is about to happen. In their hubris they think their wards are impenetrable.

On the North Continent are the villas of those Nobles that displeased the Empire, forcing them to take their titles on that remote Continent. These Nobles are part of the Emperor's plan to colonize the North. But this day they are busy celebrating as well. They do not see the 100,000 Ogden riders darkening the horizon.

The audience overlooking the naval maneuvers sees the little wooden boxes in the sky that do not look very menacing. The laughter ends when a number of the planes fly past. Then another sortie of planes starts dropping bombs. One by one the tribesmen start dropping bombs on ships and buildings. Only three people know what is going on. A fourth notices but has no idea about the potential for sneak air attacks like at Pearl Harbor. The planes manage to get to one of the elven earl's provincial palaces. The shields are up now so the planes can no longer approach. Those planes that are already under the shields decide to go for the palace. 50,000 pounds of bombs carried on essentially overgrown trees will do the trick. They still have bombs left but there are no ships left to bomb. 12,000 ships sink in less than an hour.

Harvey mans the next group. Destroyer after destroyer unleashes its enchanted armaments on towns that aren't important enough to get shields. All the occupants can do is die. The cities don't know what's hit them.

At that very moment, the main refinery for food production in the empire is attacked, right in the heartland of a world that is 80% hollow. A group of berserkers is being led by Caspian and his voles through the hollow earth towards the main food processing refineries of the Empire. They emerge at the surface. I give my thanks to Caspian and lead my troops towards the refineries.

500,000 berserkers literally go berserk. With Vili's power, I focus in on the refinery gates. It doesn't take much. The bolts of lightning shower down again and again. Eventually the refineries for the commoners' food are destroyed. Michelle reaches out to every weed in the area and spreads a field of pestilence that begins devouring the crops. With each passing moment the crops begin to be overtaken by weeds that will burn easily.

Then the berserkers set fire to it all.

The remaining 10% of the elven fleet are given the command to come to aid the city. When they sail out, their ships are pierced by the poisoned spikes placed there by Master Bui and the monks. The Elves' living ships are slowly poisoned to death. The ships come in at high tide and now it is approaching low tide. The shallow water exposes the spikes so that the bottoms of the hulls are pierced by the poison logs. It had to run like clockwork. Any later and the spikes would be visible; any sooner the spikes would be too far beneath the surface and unable to pierce the hulls.

Linh and Martin teleport out of the Arcane Tower just in time to arrive at a safe spot to watch the death of this world's M.I.T. As the tower collapses, Martin smiles.

The Emperor lays there injured. "Help me up, Sadas. I didn't see the bombs coming so my auto defenses were just barely good enough to keep me alive."

As Sadas reaches out with one hand the other hand plunges a poisoned blade into the Emperor's heart. Sadas feels the power of the Empire and The Source flow into him.

"One hundred seventeenth in line, my ass!" he protests, then raises his fists to the air, "Now Sadas rules!"

All of our troops regroup in the Northlands at one of the larger cities. All of my friends and the warriors are exhausted despite our triumphs today. I congratulate everybody and tell them to celebrate and rest.

Chapter 11

> "You curs!" Odysseus cried. "You never thought to see me back from Troy. You ate me out of house and home; you raped my maids; you wooed my wife on the sly though I was still alive—with no more fear of the gods in heaven than of the human vengeance that might come. I tell you, one and all, that your doom is sealed."
>
> —Homer's The Odyssey

General Hill and the Nobles in charge of each section of troops meet with Sadas at his request.

"We must plan a response to this brash attack on our Northland colonies," demands Sadas. "Bring me that fighter, Ace, who knows these arrogant humans."

Ace enters the room and bows deeply to the gathering of High Nobles.

Sadas speaks, "You know these humans. How could this have happened?"

Ace replies, "John is back; all these attacks are plays on methods from our home world. You might say he is dead but I can smell his hand behind this. The barbarians used strategies from historic and famous battles fought on our former world. For our sake, I hope they can't pull off the finale."

Ace began his breakdown of the battle. "One of the most important aspects of the battle was to attack when least expected. His timing was perfect just like that of the Tet Offensive from Earth's Vietnam War. They made a full on attack on a day when the people felt safe and their guard was relaxed. Then the main attack was obviously like that of Earth's Pearl Harbor which is what got the US into World War II. But the spikes that destroyed the remaining ships were from a strategy used by the Vietnamese at the battle of Bu Tran to sink all of the Chinese ships thus winning the war. That is the part that amazes me. Do you have any idea how precise the timing of that entire operation had to be in order that they take out those last ships? He had maybe a half hour time frame. Before the tide would have been too high so no effect. Too late, someone would have noticed. Finally, he has to lure the rest of us into the war. This is his last gambit. But what I can't understand is that you killed him. He's died. That's for certain. However it wouldn't be the first time coming back from the dead for any of us.

General Hill says, "The humans are drawing us in. They know that we can't let the loss of ten million dead go. But it's a trap, an obvious one at that. They are mocking us because they know we have to attack. I am in awe of his troops; so many that are well trained and efficient. Just to have 1000 men like his that could carry out orders with such timing, I'd march through Heaven's gates."

"Do you actually admire this man, General?"

General Hill replies, "My Liege Sadas, I know that you have never been on a real campaign, but to not respect one's enemy's will, desire, and tactics is to leave oneself mortally exposed."

"These are humans. They are not ageless the way we are," says Sadas.

At this point the General knows that Sadas' troops are in trouble. He excuses himself from the meeting and orders an immediate special operations mission for himself, his second, Sergeant Major Grimes, and the entire Special Forces, especially the non-elven combatants. The General leaves a note of warning for Sadas and cites an obscure statute telling Sadas that despite the General's wish for glory, national security comes first.

General Hill knows that without ships they will have to use magic. The Source and the Nobles are not used to battles requiring The Source's powers like this.

Sadas believes that it would make great military strategy to come into the ports and raid the coastal towns for supplies and staging sites. But, there are problems with his plan. The human townsmen anticipated that he is coming and burned their cities to keep the elves from capturing them. Sadas' downfall may be that he is too stubborn and won't believe the humans can defeat his efforts.

The Nobles in their planning the war originally thought to use human conscripts. That idea is rejected because the magic used by humans will disarm the collars controlling the human slaves. The Nobles then draft many other beings numbering well over one hundred times the actual elven force. The enslaved conscripts all have control collars on, so they can't even think of rebelling.

Once enough of the elves and their conscripted troops are transported into the Northlands, they start building a base camp. To the elves shock and dismay, the coastal Northlands' towns are all burned to the ground. This is the way the elves whole campaign would end up; much like Napoleon so as not to be able to use the city for supplies and rest, the Russians burned down Moscow. The Northlanders did the same. Every town enroute to the battle grounds are razed. And the entire population of each town was transported with the Riders, weeks ago. The invaders would not find a single home to loot. Moreover, little did the elves know the ground in this part of the Northlands discharges a gas that attracts bugs. These insects carry a virulent disease. Within a week most of the elves fall ill. Their remaining troops show up to find sick elves bedridden and being treated for an unknown disease. After two weeks the elves and their conscripts finally start to march towards the capitals.

Frequent storms of fist-sized hail and bitter cold sleet hit the troops along with sixty mile per hour winds. Ragnar added to their misery by raining down more and more of the horrible weather. The first complaints come from those whose mounts were getting weaker and could no longer fly. The elves complained about the indignity of actually getting saddle marks from riding on the ground. These were enlisted elves mind you. Even they were supposed to have a minimum of a flying mount. Of course, all units use magical heaters and cookers; heaters that attract spirits that feed on magical energy. Instead of setting up a basic security ward or simply appeasing the spirits with an intentional offering, the elves fought them. The legions were starving and weak. The magical food devices could only be used for so long before damaging spirits began to converge. The devices were beginning to break down. So food rationing had to begin. The conscripts were a problem as well. To make matters worse, the troops were coming to the part of the North where the ion storms, magical kaleidoscopes of chaos, began to occur with increasing frequency. The control collars on the conscripts' necks would malfunction and cause the conscripts to go insane. The elves were not designed to deal with this. Neither were any of their war machines. The whole elven effect was the elegance of swift and immediate action. They were not designed for a forever winter where it stormed constantly, where illness was a way of life, and food was becoming scarce. Even the priests were dying. None of them knew their limits because they had never been pushed to these extremes.

In spite of the weather, the troops began closing ground on the Northlanders. But the elven troops are surprised when they reach the mine fields laid out by the humans. The elves are horrified as their comrades are blown up by mines right before their eyes; the whole area is laced with landmines. The elves search for a magic signature left by the mines, but there is none. Ace tells Sadas what the mines are and what is needed to be done to disarm them. But Sadas thinks that sending huge pressure waves over the next few hundred miles in order to explode the mines in advance of the troops would be a waste of their waning magic powers. The elves are using The Source to its capacity for the first time in many hundreds of years. So instead of using pressure waves, the elves force the slave conscripts to run across the fields tripping the mines. As each one falls, a foot or pincer or talon is blown off. The injured beings lay there bleeding, attracting predators and scavengers, of course. What the Nobles don't know is that mass dying causes psychic vampire spirits and possession spirits to be summoned and these too must be fought off by the troops. This results in more days of fighting before they even reach the Northlanders.

As the elven troops and their remaining conscripts approach one of the capital cities of the Northlands, the guns created by the humans and stationed at the edge of the city fire away, hammering at the elves. The 155 millimeter artillery pieces rip through conscripts and elves alike until the elves finally put up shields. The Source is stressed to its maximum capacity.

A certain shadow, Linh, and a certain tree, Michelle, begin conducting reconnaissance of the elven approach.

The slaves all either run or start dying. After the last of the conscripts flees, a peculiar thing happens. A dwarf on a winged bear, of all things, shows up from behind the elven lines. The elven troops pay him no attention as they are being pelted with artillery shells. Harvey has wrangled a considerable amount of magical power from the combined forces of two rival northern schools of magic. He decides to use his power and make a hundred foot high stone wall roughly fifty feet thick. The elves and the few remaining slaves try to bore through the wall. They try their best but then one more blow happens; the berserkers start arriving through a carefully concealed short-range teleportation device. There were hundreds of thousands of them. The elves had only enough strength to shield against the shells, not the onslaught of berserkers.

The carnage of the minefields; the screams of the dying sentient slaves; the suffering of the elven troops all hits Ace with a jarring effect. Ace begins thinking to himself how Sadas humiliated the humans, enslaving so many of them, killing his friend and former human colleague. He reminds himself of his life on Earth and that it was his former race that was now being enslaved and butchered by Sadas and his troops. It can't be a coincidence that the elven push to civilize the North brought this on; this conflict of cultures; the human Northlanders versus the elven Nobles. And now the humans are uniting here in the farthest part of the world. The rumors swirl that Ace's friend and former colleague has been reincarnated here in the Northlands and is trying to live a new life. Is that also a coincidence that the rumors are about Sadas' arch enemy? Is that why Sadas must at any and all expense continue to push into the deepest reaches of the North? And now after this devastating march, the troops are at best a fraction of what they were.

Ace notices the man approaching from a distance. As he is getting closer Ace feels an odd shock of familiarity. But at the same time he does not recognize him. Ace starts to engage, because if he waits any longer he'll be too winded to fight.

The man is wearing Ogden skin armor and a helmet that intentionally obscures his face. He sees Ace and waves his men off, challenging Ace to a proper fight. Carrying his spear, he squares off with Ace. He can tell that Ace's skill has grown to new heights as he feints a move to the left then he dodges while throwing a concealed dagger. The man narrowly dodges it. The two fighters gracefully maneuver around each other. Two masters, neither one willing to commit first.

Every time the man attacks, Ace leaps or literally summersaults away. Ace wants him to think he is being played with so that his opponent will make a mistake. That's exactly what appears to happen. But unbeknownst to Ace the man does a clever acting job. Ace comes in with a straight linear charge thinking that fatigue has made this otherwise skillful man clumsy. The man with the grace of a ballet dancer steps to the side and sends a spinning heel kick to the jaw knocking Ace unconscious.

The berserkers descend upon the elven troops. The elves are doomed. At this point Sadas and the 24,000 high nobles thought this was a brilliant time to teleport away from there. All they could do was to pray to The Source and to all the elven gods. For once prayer worked. The elven gods manifested themselves for the first time in millennia. They were so impressive you wanted to bow. Beautiful beyond compare their flawless features made the fairest elf look mundane and they were about to rip my heart out. With some of Vili's memories imparted to me I know what their capabilities are. The images are terrifying and we don't stand a chance. Just as I think we're done, another unknown force from below comes storming in. The combined might of the attack takes the elves off guard. I see images in my mind. It is my friends, the Ripplers, from below. They tell me that most of them had listened to my message of self improvement and discovery and had left to explore the universe. A few had stayed behind because the elders predicted I would need help. They had sent the elf gods back to their dimension but they could help me no more. The only reason they had succeeded was because they had surprised them.

Now to stay was certain death. They had one last gift to impart to me. My mind was ready to take the next step. They poured their command of reality into me. My mind and control expanded exponentially.

By the time Ace woke up, the berserkers had slain over 30 million troops. Out of 8 million elves, roughly 25,000 came home.

"You're getting careless bro," I joked with Ace extending him a hand.

Ace snapped, "Was it necessary to do that?"

"Yes, your fault for getting soft, Ace." I had the others take him to Michelle to tend to his wounds.

"Well I think I might finally be able to do this," I said to myself. My mind didn't just see it controlled reality enough that I could reach out and connect with Vili's prison. I expanded my mind as much as I could. I could see the prison with my peripheral senses. The prison walls were pulsating in dimensions and angles I could not have perceived before. Still I pushed and pushed, calling out to Vili. At the same time Vili was pushing with all his might. The walls were beginning to budge. Minutes were like hours in this five dimensional demolition attempt. We were almost there. Vili refused to believe that he could be this close and fail. They kept pushing but they both knew they were weakening.

Meanwhile:

A wizard and a barkeeper were having a beer at the bar. It happened to be owned jointly by a caveman and a Keystone cop. The caveman had journeyed into the Maze accidently and then realized by the 12th level of the Maze, it was a whole lot better than a cave. The bar was located in the Mall of a Gnomish Mine that is inside a place outside of reality called the Maze of Menace.

The Wizard said, "Watching these guys try to break Vili out has been fun; too bad they aren't going to pull it off."

The shopkeeper replied, "You know we could help them, they are so very close."

"You've always been too soft, Izchak," said the Wizard.

The truth was, a mere thought from either of them could rip through the prison like tissue paper.

At that point a certain repeat customer wearing a Hawaiian shirt entered the bar. Then a crowd of like-dressed beings entered the bar. They all had expensive cameras and were taking pictures of everything in sight. A poor Balrog got blinded and bumped his head into one of the balls.

Izchak said, "What is he doing here?"

The Wizard says, "I gave that monkey a good deal of leeway as to how he'd get the amulet."

The Wizard continued, "You're that fellow that had heard of the Maze and thought it was an elaborate game show. He thought putting your life on the line was a really novel concept and the object was to get the amulet. Monkey explained to him that he shouldn't have kept the amulet. It was just a prop for the game. The prize was getting turned into a demigod. Monkey told him he needed the amulet back so they could start the new series and apologized for the mix up. He asked him if there was anything he could do to make up for the mix up. He wanted free and safe passage for his friends and family. He'd act as the tour guide."

"Izchak, get them to tour some other level and I'll take care of the prison. God, I hate tourists."

Chapter 12

> "In the underworld, Abode of the Accursed . . . Tityus lying stretched out over nine acres, exposes his entrails for the vulture to tear. Here Tantalus reaches for the water he can never catch, and the overhanging tree forever eludes his grasp. Sisyphus now pursues, now pushes the stone that always comes rolling back. Ixion whirls around, following and fleeing from himself, and the grand-daughters of Bellus . . . continually seek again the waters which they always lose."
>
> —Metamorphoses Ovid 8 CE

I was on the verge of breaking. Both Vili and I were pushing but the effort seemed futile. Then it seemed as if an outside force bolstered our efforts, because the prison finally broke without any added effort on our part. I could feel Vili surge back into this world.

He spoke to me and Ragnar, "You both have done quite well. Ragnar you come with me. I think we have some unfinished business with some gods, my boy."

Then he addressed me, "You won't have any more difficulties from the elves' gods." Before I leave let me explain what's been done to you. I wasn't able to fully understand what my brother, Odin, had done while I was imprisoned. Your soul was placed out of phase with this dimension so that it could act as a homing beacon back to your origin, your home. Is there anything you need before I leave to deal with the elves?" he asks.

I tell him, "It would help if you could expedite our journey to the Western Continent."

Vili nods assent and he adds, "Call upon me if you require anything else."

Then Vili transports my entire cohort to the next staging area of the operation. This literally saves months on our time table. I tell Linh to go on ahead and tell Magnus of our early arrival since Magnus' part in the plan is vital. The Western continent is much more heavily fortified than the Northern continent ever was. In comparison, the North was an outpost relative to the fortress which is the West. While it is nothing compared to the main continent it still has twenty times the forces of the Northern colonies which we destroyed.

All of the towns are heavily warded with security spells. Now that the elves know we are on the warpath, every elven town and city is on high alert. For this to work, Magnus will have to deactivate the security wards for the entire continent. Even then we alone do not have nearly enough resources to succeed with the attack. However, Harvey has been in negotiations with the Dwarf Republic. I contact Caspian and ask him to petition the Vole leaders to join forces with us. The Dwarves and Voles agree to join us. They are more than happy to rid the West of the elves' presence but both are skeptical of our chances. Since we have demonstrated our ability to face the Empire and win, they are open to the alliance.

For our plan to work, we must hit every major city at roughly the same time. Magnus' deactivation of the security wards will give us maybe a forty-eight hour window at best. After that, certainly at least one of the high nobles will figure the wards are down and fix them.

I assign a unit to each city. Everyone is surprised that I am opting to lead the raid on one of the smaller cities.

Master Bui approaches me after I assign him to lead the assault on the capital city of the West. "Why is it you are not leading the charge on the capital city? You made this happen. It should be you to lead the hordes into glory."

I tell him about Evelyn dying and explain, "Eric is head of the city I am going to attack. I plan to torture him until he begs for death."

Master Bui has not tried to pry into my past life since I regained my memories. I decide to tell my teacher everything that has happened from home all the way to now.

"You have an amazing tale." Bui replies. "I understand your need for vengeance. I want you to know it has been my greatest honor to have you as my student. I hope you remember your torture and interrogation techniques. His suffering should last at least three days."

I smile at my teacher. We both know I failed that exam two times before passing. I had always been a little squeamish towards some of the more esoteric methods of torture. I assured him that that would not be a problem this time.

Rodney is in direct communication with Magnus in order to coordinate the timing.

Meanwhile the battle between the gods has begun. Vili and Ragnar caught the elven gods by surprise. Vili has by then, infused enough power into Ragnar to make him a true god. I could sense them attacking the elves' pantheon. They were attacking them with impunity. They were meting out a vengeance saved up over ten thousand years. The gods were trying to escape but few of them could. Vili was held in that prison for a long time and he was ready to make them pay.

My vengeance hasn't been brewing for nearly as long but it is just as fierce. The dwarves and voles are staged to strike their respective targets. A third of the cities for each group has been assigned. Caspian is personally leading the attack. He uses his expertise to come up with a rather effective plan. The voles are underneath their target cities. They plan to attack from below with explosives. Their knowledge of the caverns tells them exactly where to set charges to bring the cities down. Then their forces will hit any survivors. They haven't been able to do this before because of the wards. When Magnus deactivates them it will be simple for them to do their work. If we time this right, Magnus will not even need to blow his cover. Linh is working on a way to wipe any evidence of Magnus' disarming the security system. Linh has given a sample of his own aura which the Empire knew all too well from the destruction of the Tower Arcane. The Empire's wizards will likely assume he is responsible for this break-in as well.

The hour is nigh and my unit is ready to strike. Martin receives the signal and we attack. Pounding the city with 155mm rounds, our artillery is laying waste to the walls and town. Eric is in his castle, ever the coward; he's already trying to leave. I use my ability and transport myself right into the Castle. I find him just before he is able to escape.

I growl, "Come on, fight me, you son of a bitch! Do you even know how Evelyn died? You don't even care."

Eric doesn't try to fight back. Instead he just begs for his life. "I surrender, please don't kill me. I'm a Noble now. I'll be a valuable bargaining chip."

"Don't worry I'm not going to kill you." I say.

By this time Martin arrives.

I tell Eric, "We have a special place we're going to send you." Then turning to Martin I say, "Do it, Martin!"

Martin casts the spell Neriss has prepared. It sends Eric to the same demon that Daloch has gone to. This time the demon was going to get to have all eternity to torture his victim.

The raids are a complete success. All the cities in the West have been destroyed.

Magnus has not been caught. In fact, he is praised for his bravery for staying behind and helping some escape. Much to everyone's surprise I order all of our troops to return home. While there is a lot of grumbling amongst the men I explain to them we are not going to make the mistake Sadas made. We would suffer exactly the same fate as his force, if we try to enter the main continent. We would need a thousand times the force we have including our allies to even stand a chance. So we march to the shore and the ships transport us back home.

Vili contacts me. He sent the elven gods running or killed them. Vili tells me that Ragnar is now a god and will remain to protect the tribes. Meanwhile Vili is traveling to earth, as Odin has requested his help. He asks if I want to return to earth with him. I tell him I have to stay to ensure the North remains stable.

Over the next few years I engage in the process of modernizing the North. One day I get a letter addressed to me in English. It is from Leah. She says she wants to leave Sadas. We correspond using her carrier pigeon over the course of several months. Finally she agrees to meet me and leave Sadas for good. She will be arriving in a week.

Today Martin gives me a report saying that he and some of the more sensitive shaman felt a huge loss of life. I don't really pay attention. I am so excited, to say the least, to see Leah. While I normally don't care about my attire, today I spend more time and money than I have since coming to this world. I have the best in the city make dinner and enchant it so it will stay fresh until she arrives. I use the rest of the day training, trying to get rid of my nervous energy. I get myself dressed and I wait for her. You know I've been burned, stabbed, shot, sent through a wormhole. Since then I've under gone more injury and suffering than anybody you could name. On top of that, I set up an entire education system for a serf society in poverty and just liberated a continent from occupation. Things just have to balance out sooner or later. This is my day to get things right.

Leah shows up in a shower of light. Teleportation at this distance, she always was a fast learner. She is beautiful, dressed in a silk gown with a jade necklace around her neck. The sight of her puts me in a state of euphoria. We have dinner and talk about old times with the occasional reference to the happenings of late. It is prefect and no one is going to take this from me this time. I have waited for almost 150 years for this. I'd fought hosts of demons, impossible odds, a god, and won. I'd bled for her in the arena to get the funds to pay for her entrance into the School Arcane. I've taken more than one wound that should have been fatal, defending her. This moment made it all worthwhile. I'd give up every bit of power instilled in me for this to be the start of the rest of our lives. I make a song play and we dance. It seems like an hour has gone by.

Then the moonlight falls on us through the window and I know it is the right moment. I kiss her deeply. As I took off her dress I notice a glimmer from her wrist. I haven't seen any jewelry on that arm. I guess I must be slipping.

At that moment I feel a blade pierce through my heart. I can feel something eating me from the inside. I know what it has to be, a scarab beetle.

Oddly, my thoughts spin down to the weapon. It is the most difficult and expensive assassination tool to find. Its ability to hide itself from magic is only surpassed by mine. It is invisible to practically any means of detection. It has no scent, radiation, heat, visible image; you name the detection mechanism it has a method to camouflage. The only way to obtain one is through contact with the race of beings that has evolved alongside it. Outside of them, only the few Powers like The Oracle can find it. Even Odin has to actively be looking for one in order to detect it. The price they charge for one is enough to buy a planet and the souls of everyone on it. In order for it to attack it has to begin a biological mechanism that slowly kills it. The beetle only reproduces once in its life. Normally this mechanism is in place to catalyze that process and create an undetectable nest where its offspring will be safe until matured. The beings have engineered the beetle to constantly stay undetectable by forcing it to stay dormant until triggered. The process of creating one took the ability to harness the power of a dozen supernovas and the ability to sculpt subatomic particles at once. It took 200 millennia of flawless subatomic crafting to create one beetle. Move one quark wrong for a fraction of a nanosecond and the whole effort is wasted. Sometimes it is worth it.

It was one of the sure ways to kill practically anything, even immortal gods. When it attacks there is no stopping it. It latches on to you and nothing can get it off. Teleportation, dimensional shifting, nearly any attack is foiled. There are only a few accounts I had heard of where defeating one involved using a black hole to suck it out. Only Atlas, who regenerates fast enough to survive exploding suns and strong enough to escape collapsing quasars is known to survive an attack without removal.

I knew I was dead, I just hoped the next life wasn't going to be as depressing. I really had tried. I was just always a day late and a dollar short despite whatever I tried. The beetle took its time. It was designed to figure out any anomaly before it attacked just in case the being had a way to feign death. I was honestly quite honored. I had never heard of a beetle used on anything short of a Power or a god. On the other hand the only thing valuable enough to purchase one would be lives. Suddenly, I remembered several of the others saying that they had felt the simultaneous death of several million souls. To do that just for one wretched life was something I could not understand. I lit a cigarette and chanted the sutras of the Lord Buddha. I could have killed her with a thought but despite all of it a part of me still loved her.

I ask aloud, "Am I such a bad guy?"

Leah is crying. "No, you're just a fool. You could have been powerful and rich beyond belief. You had a god offer you anything and you asked him to call you when needed. You were going to destroy the Empire and with it civilization."

I respond, "Civilization is not based on how pretty your statues are. It's based on the purpose, morals, and philosophy that guide a society."

I lurch over in agony. It was starting. Then I ask her, "Could you just tell me, do you think Sadas loves you like I love you? I mutter my words through bloodied lips. Would he have bled for you? Would he have risked everything just to hold your hand? Do you even love him or is it just your station you love?"

She was holding my head in her lap. I feel her tears landing on my face. She replies, sobbing, "It wasn't supposed to be this way. I just wanted to be somebody important and every time I considered you, something came up. He's a living god. He has worlds at his command. Even if I didn't love him, how could I or anyone hope to defy him."

I take one last drag of my cigarette and reply, "Even if we couldn't beat him, what sort of beings would we be if we didn't at least try? Maybe in another life I'll make it work. Goodbye my love." I hope I'm not lying to myself again, but I think she told me the same in response. Everything goes black.

Martin is the first to find the body. He uses his powers looking for a trace of who had done this. He knows that aura. He jams his fist through two feet of granite and cries out for the others. When they get together, Neriss and Ragnar examine the body.

"This is a scarab bug, the most deadly assassination tool known to any god I've ever known." Says Ragnar. "Once it hits, you are dead."

Neriss adds, "It's incredibly rare; in the past million or so years it's been used less than ten times according to Vili. It's a weapon designed to kill gods."

Ragnar continues, "One thing is, it needs skin contact in order to work."

Martin interjects, "My senses are a little more sensitive than most of yours so look through my mind and see the aura I see."

They all either recognized it or realized who it had to be.

"It's making sense now." Neriss says. "We know the only person that would want him dead and who would have the resources to spend on this. That massive death of 10 million lives was his payment for that thing."

The funeral was the largest display of might the Northlands had seen in millennia. Dragons, giants, demons, and sprits of the light all stood side by side. Millions of tribesman stood at the ready chanting the songs for departed heroes. A hundred different races, some at war with each other were there. Hundreds of thousands of dwarfs were in attendance as were a vast horde of spirits of all kind filled the sky wailing in sorrow. Ragnar was at the head of a host of gods and godlings who stood in the back making sure that their presence did not take attention away from the service. All the gods of the voles and dwarves were in attendance along with a number of others that respected the sacrifice. A Buddhist monk that had obtained Enlightenment recently was asked to perform the services. Before they began, an array of narcotics and alcohol was passed around.

Among the gods were those that advocated doctrines of complete sobriety even they drank out respect for the mortal that had been instrumental in freeing this world. Linh was playing his flute until Martin started playing a list of his favorite Manowar songs. Out of nowhere a small group of the Empire's Special Forces arrived. They would have been killed but someone noticed they had the banner of truce waived high. It was a standard that had not been flown for thousands of years. General Hill marched his men towards the funeral. They were wearing full dress uniforms and the only weapons they carried were ceremonial in nature. Colonel Hague carried the standard while Sergeant Major Grimes carried a medal of opposition. It was an ancient medal that the young had mostly forgotten about. It was the greatest honor their military could give to an enemy. It was only given to someone that had fought with outstanding bravery and showed the military resolve that only another soldier could understand. The Emperor couldn't even comprehend the concept. The Battalion with Grimes was the real elite of the Empire. They killed the demons and monsters that plagued the night while the Noble High Guard put down little disputes so that their families could brag. These were the Special Forces units that did the work the Noble High Guard always got credit for. These were Sergeant Major Grime's and General Hill's troops. They fought for them and country. The Emperor was just a necessary evil. Ace was with them. He was a captain now.

General Hill and the Sergeant Major Grimes marched with precise military cadence.

"There was a time my Empire was better than this." The Sergeant Major spoke. "He was a brave man. I dreamed of fighting him one on one on a hundred occasions. I'm sure you already know the details but I joined a couple centuries before the General. I was his first platoon Sergeant. I swear upon my rank that we had no knowledge of this and don't condone it either." The funeral lasted a few more hours and slowly the different groups left to plan what revenge they would have.

Bobby, Martin, Linh, and Magnus went to the Imperial Palace of the Capital.

"Are you here to celebrate the barbarian leader's defeat? I see you brought guests." Says Sadas.

Magnus had in his hand the fiddle he'd been given so long ago. "If you don't mind my liege, I was planning on entertaining the other Nobles with a song."

"Of course, your musical talents are rivaled by none," replied Sadas.

Magnus began playing an ancient Celtic ballad about unrequited love. The haunting music was so enchanting that many of the nobles began to weep. A flute started to play in harmony. The song continued telling the story of rejection and betrayal. The flute's melody extenuated the dirge to a Gothic beauty never before heard in these halls. Then another instrument began playing. Normally it played songs of death and war but today it was simply accompaniment to an already ethereal tone. The song told of the man's sacrifices in her name. This moved nearly all in the Hall. Even many of the Noble High Guardsmen were visibly weeping. Finally, the song moved to a scene of betrayal. The woman came to him with promises full of lies. The song finally ended with the woman standing over the man's corpse to fulfill the schemes of another.

The crowd could not pull themselves together.

Magnus spoke to them, "I haven't decided how to end the song. I've been thinking I should have the man avenged so that it does not leave the crowd so sad."

A voice came out from the crowd, it was Ace. "Any woman is deserving of death, at best, that would do that to someone."

The crowd roared its approval.

General Hill, full well knowing where this was leading said, "Any man that would have a woman do his work is a coward. I hope this story is not true."

Magnus spoke out, "Unfortunately it is true. It is about the Emperor and his Lady."

The Lady Leah was visibly shaken. Sadas asked, "What proof do you have of these allegations."

Magnus spoke, "We knew of the secret meeting that night. He'd never failed to inform us of a meeting before. Furthermore, the deadly device used could only be obtained by a select few. The only way anyone in this room could have gotten one is if he had sacrificed a great number of lives. Didn't you recently order the execution of 10 million prisoners? Oh, you failed to mention that to anyone? Moreover, the man could have killed his assailant with the time it took for the device to work. Other than his friends, who else would he have not at least tried to kill?"

"He was a threat that was going to destroy us," the Lady said. "He could have been rich and powerful in his own right but chose to rebel. This place is no different than our home on earth; they just don't lie to themselves about it. Back home there is an aristocracy; they just don't call it that. The truth is we were part of it."

Magnus replied in English in his real voice thick with his West Virginia Appalachian accent, "If that place of our origin were an aristocracy, then how is it that a man raised in the backwoods of West Virginia could became Senior Partner at the biggest firm in town."

She had no reply, too shocked by this revelation.

Magnus bellows out, "Let's get on with this. I challenge you as a high noble to your right to lead the Empire."

Sadas replies, "Do you truly think you have a chance? I have complete control over The Imperial Source. If I deem it, your access to The Source will be blocked. Besides you need two nobles of Duke or higher to support you. Is there anyone in this court that will support this motion? I thought not."

Magnus scoffs at him, "You are so cowardly. You will not accept a fair fight? Not even with The Source as yours alone to control."

Sadas replies, "You are not a true elf. You are an elf in body alone. In truth you were born human."

Magnus demands, "Do you deny I am Earl Magnus McCullough? Do you contest I am the one who earned his nobility by defeating an arch demon in single combat?"

Sadas snarls back, "Regardless, you do not have any one to support your bid, therefore you are guilty of treason. Seize him."

Knowing that their positions were at stake, the nobles and soldiers go to seize Magnus. General Hill, Sergeant Major Grimes, and their troops stay back from the attack on Magnus.

It was the easiest thing for Magnus to use the commanding Power of his voice, gently whispering to the crowd to back away and be silent. Amongst the crowd were some of the most powerful wizards in the Empire, yet they could not resist his voice. Everyone in the room immediately backed up against the walls. With a whisper he had bent over 10,000 soldiers to his will. The only ones not affected were the Sergeant Major Grimes and General Hill. Magnus was not particularly surprised. They had over 16 millennia of combat experience. Gods, monsters, and demons had met their fate by their hands.

The Sergeant Major was quite disgruntled his elite troops were up against a wall, quiet. "We obviously need to start training harder come tomorrow. If I remember correctly I am qualified to vote on this matter as I am the Command Sergeant Major of all the Empire's Army. I represent the voice of all enlisted men in the military. I vote for Magnus."

General Hill knew that his friend and comrade had just signed his death warrant and he wasn't about to let him die alone. They gestured to each other to get ready. One way or another, Sadas, this false leader, was going to die. Besides he had nearly killed that bastard himself after he assassinated the old Emperor. That would have led to civil war, however. A military rank might give you the right to vote, but it was not enough to challenge the Emperor.

Sadas prepared himself. He knew of Magnus' great command of elven magic, his powerful swordsmanship, and his profound voice, the voice that could compel dragons to lie down and purr. He raised his shields. He was completely protected by The Source against all this. He waited for the attack. Unfortunately for him, he didn't know about a certain type of magic that was still practiced in the Mountains of the Appalachian. A subtle magic, that came over with the Irish. It was Celtic in origin but was influenced by the Cherokee and the Hoodoo magic brought by African slaves to the America's. So while he waited for an attack able to shake a god, a little peasant charm snuck in underneath the backdoor. Sadas felt disoriented.

"I reckon if granny were here now she'd be laughing at me using the evil eye against someone like this," Magnus chortled.

Sadas tried to focus his magic to attack but he was under the influence of this simple charm. He'd never seen the like but he could tell it was a bit of human magic. He just didn't know how to break free. It was like the common cold's affect on the first Indians.

Magnus managed to speak with his accent transposed to this land's language. "You see, boy, we country folk use a little music in our charms; let me show you." Magnus started playing an old Confederate battle song his people played in the war against the Yanks of Earth.

Sadas started dancing to the tune of the song. He couldn't control himself. Despite his best efforts, he couldn't understand this magic from a dimension and world so different from his. The music changed, it turned into an old Irish jig. The pace of the music was getting faster so was Sadas' dancing. The crowd was in awe and beginning to snicker. There were many ways they could have seen this fight go, but they could all see this magic. It was simple and utterly alien. It was fueled with the power of country folk that had made a living hunting and farming the land. This was the music Magnus kept playing; the music was coming from childhood memories and ancestral dreams. For all he'd fought the traditions he was still a country boy from West Virginia. An hour passed and the music changed to an ancient Celtic song from around the time of the Romans. Sadas was getting visibly tired; there was vomit covering his chest but he still had to dance. As the next hour went by the music went to an impossible pace. Magnus was playing an ancient song from when Stone Henge was erected. Sadas's body was about to break. Sinew began snapping and ligaments tore. Four hours of dancing at this impossible pace was killing him but he could not stop. Sadas collapses to his knees but he couldn't stop. A couple more hours went by and even his supernatural enhanced body was on the verge of death. Finally his body gave in to exhaustion and he began to die. As he lay dying, Magnus showed him his true essence. It was of a West Virginia country boy catching fish with a branch he'd tied some line and a worm to.

Sadas' last thought was how could he have failed to protect himself. He had warded against magic that would wound a god, yet here he was defeated by a human peasant's crude mountain magic. Sadas dies.

Magnus feels his own connection to The Source become more refined and malleable. At the same time the conduit begins to expand exponentially. It has been designed for an elve's essence, however and Magnus is still human at heart. He is in a struggle with The Source. He is slowly molding it to his will as all the Emperors before him had when they took over the Empire.

Meanwhile, one of the elven Nobles sees Magnus is incapacitated due to his struggle for control of The Source. The noble signals to his clan and the Noble High Guard to attack Magnus. General Hill sees the dishonorable display and moves to intervene. Including Sergeant Major Grimes, the General's troops only number fifty; but that is more than enough. 20-1 odds only matter when fighting real soldiers, not fops in costumes. The Sergeant Major, the oldest and finest elven soldier in the Empire starts going through nobles like heat lighting. His patented morning star-axe combo was killing them off faster than they could register.

Of course Linh, Martin, and Bobby aren't about to let the General's troops have all the fun. Bobby's nine tailed, eight armed, winged form nearly makes the guards faint. Ace gets in the melee as well, enjoying fighting side by side with his comrades once again. When it is all said and done 1000 lay dead without a single death on their side.

Magnus finally has remodeled the conduits. Now any being can access The Source if it is connected to it, and he is about to make that much easier.

Magnus, now in control of The Source, proclaims, "I came here to avenge my friend. Becoming Emperor just is an incidental consequence of that. Regardless I am the controller of The Source and the leader of the Empire." Magnus announces, "The gods you once worshipped are dead, slain by Vili, one of the gods of my people. There shall be a temple built in honor of my people's gods. My brother in arms, Linh, shall instruct the building of a temple to his gods. From today on there will no longer be Nobility. There will be no distinction between elf and man. All races will be equal under the law. Any citizen of the Empire now will have access to The Source. All people currently in the Empire, the Dwarf Republic, or the Northlands are citizens. For others there will be a petition process to be determined later. For all of you that are worried about the decrease this will have in your powers."

He calls to his comrades. Immediately Neriss, Ragnar, Harvey, Linh, Bobby, Martin, Rodney, Cory, and Michelle appear.

Neriss states, "We have figured out how to use the residual energy of the slain gods to open the hole between worlds exponentially. That undead fiend, otherwise known as Martin over there, along with this dwarf and dryad, aka Harvey and Michele, determined a method to create a construct that will be able to hold thousands of times more energy. So we're going to see if this experiment with The Source actually works." Says Neriss.

"So what do we do with Lady Leah?" Asks Bobby, with a sneer.

"I think I'll drink her soul, being that she killed my friend," replies Martin.

"He could have killed her had he wanted to, Martin," Bobby says. "What do you think should be done with you?" He asks the lady.

Leah whispers, "I don't know."

"Give her what she wanted in the first place, status." Bobby says.

Magnus begins, "Our friend didn't want her dead, so let's put her to work. Leah you are now in charge of creating a real judicial code. Afterwards you'll be the Attorney General. We're just going to put a little spell on you to make sure you do a good job." Magnus then places a geas on her that will force her to work to the point of exhaustion until the day of her death. She still will get respect and her place in high society, but at great cost.

Magnus continues, "Actually all you guys are getting jobs. You can embezzle however much you want but I need your help. Harvey you need to set up a police force. Michelle you're going to make an E.P.A. Linh you are going to design the security systems for all the important facilities and I'll need an intelligence agency as well. Neriss and Martin you guys are doing weapons development. General Hill, Sergeant Major Grimes, and the Colonel, it is good to see you. From your actions I take it I have your support. I request that you make whatever changes you see fit to streamline the military. Cory will be along to help you with the Navy. You think you freed humanity here. Maybe, you freed us too. The Empire has become distorted and corrupt over the millennia, perhaps this is a chance to start anew." Magnus stops and looks over his friends and comrades, then smiles one of his great earthy smiles.

Requiem

I heard the fourth beast say, Come and see.
And I looked, and behold a pale horse.
And his name that sat upon was Death
And all Hell followed with him

—Revelations 6:7-8

"My brothers, Vili and Ve," Odin speaks their names fondly. "It has been too long since we have seen each other. I am heartened to have you here with me; Ve from The Garden and Vili freed from your prison. You know why I am calling upon you; Yahweh and his hordes are planning the obliteration of all things through his Armageddon. Only we and our summoning of Búri, our Grandfather, can prevent the end times. We have our fellow gods, the many immortals, and the brave mortals to thank for this reunion. And now with all of you we must begin this war against Yahweh."

Ve, Vili, and Odin begin the summoning ritual. Each starts the part of the incantation he was given to summon their grandfather. The ritual takes hours. Upon completion, each takes a knife and slashes his own hand. As the blood pools together it forms a pentagram. Then a figure appears within it.

"Well Grandsons, what sort of trouble are you in this time." It is Búri in all his power and glory. Búri's Power compared to most self proclaimed gods is what a star is to a grain of sand. With Búri they assemble all the gods of the Aesir. The Asgardian dwarves and the elves arrive next all decked out in their finest armor. Out of the distance a huge host descends upon them. It is Loki leading the Giants along with the Midgard Snake. The Midgard Snake has brought his many dragons from different worlds to come aid in the cause.

Initially, Odin raises his spear against the monsters.

But Loki looks directly at Odin and says, "Today is a day to put aside our differences. I've grown to enjoy this world and I don't want it destroyed."

Odin agrees as do the Giants.

The snake, Midgard, hisses, "I don't really care, I just want to see if Angels taste as good as they look."

Then come the Vanir. They are led by Ngord, lord of the seas. They have brought with them all the fairies and other fae folk of the British Isles. Everything from Banshees to brownies has come to fight the good fight. Atlas has returned with Ern, Hecate, The Hundred Handed Hecatonchires, Menoetius, and a number of other comrades. Atlas also has brought with him Schrödinger's cat. He'd taken so much crap from Lucifer about not being able to catch him that he had decided to prove Lucifer wrong. It is riding on his shoulder.

Atlas approaches and says, "Its been a long time, Búri. I hope you haven't gone soft on me."

Then comes the Fenris Wolf. Fenris is accompanied by Cerberus, the three headed dog of the Greeks. The Legends never mention that Cerberus is a female hound. Since the Greek gods left, the Elysium fields have been free for anyone's taking. Many of the dogs of myth have taken up residence there. It's a perfect place for dogs. Open fields for them to roam around forever. Together Fenris and Cerberus have had many pups. Some have come to join their parents. Most notable are, Hati and Sköll. In Norse mythology the former chases the Moon across the night sky and the later chases the Sun. After finding that a whole civilization of dogs were gathering, Barghest of Yorkshire, Black Shuck of East Anglia and Cusith all decided to convince all of the black dogs to stop haunting the British Isles and join them in the Elysium fields. When Cerberus was born two other dogs were in the litter Orthus and Garm. Her brother Orthus is a two headed dog that once guarded cattle for the Greek gods. Now that they are gone he's free to roam the universe. Garm is the other. He took up Cerberus's job for the Norse gods. Both guarded the Hell the respective gods made for those that really pissed them off. The Foo Dogs have taken up residency there as well. After a tenure of faithful service they are allowed to retire. When on vacation even the Foo Dogs that still work go there to hang out. The Wild Hunt of the Earth has become a bit passé over the years so the Cŵn Annwn who are the white, red-eared ghostly hounds of the Wild Hunt have taken up residency there as well. There are hundreds of thousands of dogs. Some of them are supernatural. Others, like Argos, who was Odysseus' faithful dog, are just good dogs that weren't ready to be reborn yet. They are led by Charon. He was the boat master that ferried the Greek gods, favored and disfavored, across the river Acheron. He is a thin immortal man. He wields a double hammer and looks ready to use it. After the Greek gods abandoned Earth, he was free from his bondage so he decided to follow his favorite dog, Cerberus, to the fields. After all what is a dog without its master? They have agreed to fight as well.

Meanwhile, Lucifer summons all of his Angels. They are his warriors.

He addresses them saying, "Many of you have stood with me since the early times of my mortality. Today we may very well lose our immortality and die, but if so we die for a righteous cause. Yahweh wishes to slaughter billions for no other reason than hubris and power. But for our failings he would never have been able to marshal the strength to even dream of attempting this slaughter. That is our sin and today we must pay our penance even if it is with our lives. For those that joined me after I came to Earth, I understand if you do not wish to join me in this fight. Step away now if you do not wish to fight. You did not create this evil."

Not a single one moves.

Lucifer continues, "For the rest of you, I am still the one you followed on a thousand battlefields. You are my warriors and today we fight our brothers in arms, from the schism created long ago during Heaven's Great War. That is unfortunate. We fight against those whom we bled beside on countless battlefields. While it is a regrettable thing, it is a necessary thing. Moreover, I would rather see our brothers die in honest battle than to continue to be manipulated and brainwashed by that monster, Yahweh. I have one last order. Gabriel betrayed us. He is the only one that I believe stayed with Yahweh for no reason but power. Many of you wish to slay him but his demise is promised to another. Let no one here fight him for he is Judas's to slay. Judas's right for vengeance is greatest of all of us."

Lucifer raises his arms, "Gird your weapon and don your armor brothers for today we ride into glory."

The Jade Emperor supreme god of East Asia arrives with all his gods. At the forefront are the Eight Immortals. Immortal Woman He (He Xiangu), Royal Uncle Cao (Cao Guojiu), Iron-Crutch Li (Li Tieguai), Lan Caihe, Lü Dongbin, Philosopher Han Xiang (Han Xiang Zi), Elder Zhang Guo (Zhang Guo Lao), and Zhongli Quan. Each has a unique power and martial arts skill. Behind them are thousands of gods. The Great Spirit of Native Peoples and the Monkey, and the other Asian gods have all arrived. There are billions ready to fight.

The Lord Buddha is not with them. Despite pleading by all the gods he still will not engage in violence.

The battles are on the horizon. The gods will fight separately from the mortals. They will engage the Angels and Yahweh while the mortals will face the mortal hordes of Yahweh.

The head General of the mortals is none other than Vo Nguyen Giap, architect of the Vietnamese War. He has divided up his army of mortals into different divisions. The Mongols are led by Genghis Khan and his top general Subutai. Subutai directed more than 20 campaigns during which he conquered (or overran) more territory than any other commander in history. His last campaign was at age seventy and he still was considered the greatest general of the Mongols. He would have been put in charge of the whole campaign but he never familiarized himself with more modern weapons.

St. George is put in charge of all of Odin's mortal warriors, known as the Einherger from Valhalla. The greatest generals from history are being divided up to lead the campaign. The first emperor of China, Ying Zheng, and his advisor Li Si lead a contingent. Between the two, China was unified through a series of bloody battles. Sitting Bull is leading both the Native Americans and other Aborigines into battle. Field Marshal Yamagata and Admiral Togo lead the modern Japanese while Mushasi leads the Samurai of old.

The berserkers of earth will be subdivided into a separate group led by Kveld. His leadership is likely to be a direct charge at anything that moves.

King Arthur, Merlin, and his warriors are there ready to fight as well. A figure appears to approach them. Arthur recognizes him immediately. It's his son.

Mordred joins them saying, "Hello father. If this is the final battle I'd like to join. I suppose it's time to let the past go."

These are but a few of the many generals brought to lead their armies against Yahweh. For most this is their chance at vengeance. For others it is justice. Even so, the force they go up against is legion.

Yahweh's mortal hordes are led by the greatest general humanity had ever produced. Confederate General Thomas J. "Stonewall" Jackson. For many on the other side it is a sad thing to have to face Stonewall. He is a good man that simply chose the wrong side, yet again. The hordes are similarly divided into various components. Richard the Lion Hearted leads a huge contingent of knights. Joan of Arc is by his side along with a number of other notable Christian generals. Saladin, considered by many to be the greatest Muslim General to live, leads an equally large contingent of Muslim warriors. David who still wields the sling he slew Goliath with, leads the Jews.

Behind all of his warriors are the chosen of Yahweh. Among them are of course the Christ and his Disciples; other notable figures are Daniel and Sampson, Joseph Smith, Muhammad, and Hitler, Abraham, and Emperor Nero, and many of the Saints. All have been infused with the power of gods by Yahweh. He would rather not lose them so he has kept them from the battlefield.

The armies clash. A million battles are fought once more. The Vietnamese and Japanese fight against the Western forces they fought before. The Native Americans engage those troops that once took their land. The Mongols are facing off against the Europeans that they faced long ago. The Norsemen are much less selective with whom they face; they take on any and all comers. They slam into Saladin's army with their combined might. Kveld's berserker's storm right into the middle. For them this is the Ragnarock, their Armageddon, that they have been training for. While it appears to be mad chaos the respective generals of both armies have their respective situations under control. Stonewall and Vo Nguyen Giap move their troops masterfully against each other. They counter each feint and attack with precision.

For the time being, the armies are equally matched. However the mortals Yahweh commands vastly outnumber their opposition. Had their general been anyone else it would not have mattered but Yahweh's hordes are led by Stonewall Jackson. Slowly the tide begins to turn and Yahweh's hordes begin to win.

All the gods are engaging the new Angels. These are all the Angels that came after the original host. Thousands of former gods attack but they hold their own. The Great Spirit and the Asian gods ride in. Atlas is fighting side by side with Ern, Hecate, Hecatonchires, and Menoetius. They have joined forces with Odin's warriors. They are taking on the combined gods of Mesopotamian's, South American's, and all the others gods and spirits including many of the Egyptians and African gods. Atlas and Menoetius meet them head on while the Hecatonchires and Hecate launch boulders and spells, respectively. Atlas alone is holding off hundreds with his club; oldest amongst those there, save Búri, his strength and skill are unmatched. Odin has already taken down a dozen with his spear, Gungir. To his left is Thor and to his right is Tyr. Búri sees that his sons and friends are holding their own so he goes after the main target, Yahweh. He motions to the Eight Immortals to engage the Apostles while he breaks the line to face Yahweh. The four Hitokiri of the Bakumatsu join in.

All the while, Judas is infiltrating the line trying to get to the Christ and rescue him. Búri has given him a salve that will restore Christ's memories. At the same time he looks for the betrayer, Gabriel.

The original Angelic Hosts, led on one side by Lucifer and on the other by Michael, engage each other. Although outnumbered, Lucifer insists his men, and his men alone, fight them. They slam into one another. Former comrades, who once fought back to back in thousands of campaigns, now face each other as enemies.

Lucifer finds Michael. As they clash swords Lucifer says, "I'm sorry it had to come to this."

Michael replies, "As am I, Lucifer."

Michael calls out, "All of you fighting could still come home to us."

Tears well in Lucifer's eyes as he responds, "I'd rather we stayed in that fucking bubble prison for all eternity than to go through this, but it is not just our lives at stake. It's the lives of a whole planet and I can't let Yahweh obliterate the human race."

As Michael replies the tears flowed down his cheeks, "And I can't betray my oath."

Across the battlefield similar conversations were occurring. Both sides are fighting, but now half heartedly; all but Gabriel. He revels in the power given to him by Yahweh and strikes down an Angel that had saved his life a dozen times while he was mortal.

Just then Judas finds Gabriel saying, "You're dead, you son of a bitch". Judas and Gabriel clash. Such is the intensity of their attacks that it cuts a hole in the fabric of space. They fight in their own dimension for a day and a night. Gabriel, more skilled by far, but Judas is driven by thousands of years of hatred and guilt. Gabriel is fighting to kill and live on while Judas makes no attempt to block. He simply attacks and accepts what blows he suffers as a result of his own hate-driven recklessness. In the end Gabriel begins to falter. At the same time Gabriel thrusts his sword into Judas, Judas summons the combined strength that has been given to him. For one moment he is a god. He grabs Gabriel by the head and drives all that power into Gabriel. Moments later, Gabriel is nothing more than an empty, withered husk.

Judas is mortally wounded from the sword strike but he doesn't care all he has left is one task and he can die happily. Judas uses the last of his strength to go to the Christ's side. With the others engaged in their own battles no one pays attention as Judas finally gets to the Christ and makes him remember with the potion Búri prepared. All of Christ's memories start flooding back to him. He realizes what has been done to him and what is about to be done to the world. Christ tries to call out to the horde to stop. Yahweh realizes what has happened; he throws a bolt of energy at Christ. Judas tries to dive in the way, but the strength of the beam is so great that it rips through him and through Christ. The two childhood friends die together in each other's arms.

    Stonewall sees the Christ obliterated by Yahweh and nearly goes insane. His whole world has just been put into doubt. His army is on the verge of victory but he realizes he has been fighting for the wrong side. He gives the order to retreat. Even those that are only nominally following him obey thinking that it is part of a greater plan.
    Surprised by the retreat, Vo Nguyen Giap orders his armies to regroup into a defensive position. He doesn't want to be caught in an ambush. Kveld and his berserkers of earth cannot be reasoned into retreating so Merlin has to step in and transport them back to the home lines.
    Meanwhile Stonewall Jackson just starts to walk off. He lights his tobacco pipe and just keeps walking. He disappears into the mist, walking.
    A figure approaches him, "Hello my name is Lilith. Walk with me; I think we have suffered a similar betrayal." She takes Stonewall by the hand and leads him away.
    Yahweh's army is now without a leader so the warriors are left waiting for someone to take command.
    Meanwhile, both sides of the Angelic host are desperately fighting against those that they fought with for millennia. Both sides are having their doubts, however. Azrael, out of instinct, begins singing the battle hymn of their old order. It is in a language made from an energy mankind has yet to even discover. All across the battlefield Angels from both sides begin to sing. Lucifer and Michael both finally lose their resolve and join in the chorus. The entire Angelic Host is singing the anthem of their long ago military. Tears flow. They are united once more.
    Meanwhile the rest of Yahweh's Angels, those gods and immortals who were not part of the Angelic Host, appear to be winning against the gods. They are pushing them back and the gods look like they're on the verge of retreat. Even Atlas and Odin look desperate. Finally the gods go into a full scale retreat. The Angels sensing blood fall in behind them. That's when the Angels fall for the ambush. Concealed in a dimensional pocket are the Hounds led by Fenris and Charon. On the Right, similarly concealed was the Midgard Snake, the Giants and the dragons. They pounce upon the Angels. They have them cornered and ambushed. They begin to slaughter them one by one. Midgard enjoys his supper.

Meanwhile Adam Alfred Rudolf Glauer, founder of the Germanic Thule Society, has been slowly making his way through the enemy lines to find the man that usurped his country. Glauer believed in his Germany and in the god, Odin. Finally Adam Alfred Rudolf Glauer finds Hitler.

He sees the old Fuhrer and spits, "You destroyed it all Hitler. You betrayed the fatherland out of your greed and hubris. Now you will die for the same." Adam Alfred Rudolf Glauer jams his bayonet into Hitler's chest again and again. Finally his former Fuhrer lies still, for eternity.

The Apostles and Yahweh's other chosen are fighting the Eight Immortals and the Bokusai. Slowly the superior skill of the Eight Immortals and the Bokusai begin to win the day. They are fighting conservatively however, since they are intended to only be a distraction. They have achieved this goal as Búri passes them undetected.

Búri engages Yahweh. Yahweh sees his forces are failing and tries to run. Búri slams into Yahweh from behind sending him flying. Búri hits Yahweh again and again. It is a one sided fight that appears to have an inevitable winner. However, Yahweh has one trump card up his sleeve. Yahweh dreads using it because of its inherent danger to the universe, but it is all he has left. He summons up a power that he coaxes into believing in him. It is the Holy Spirit. Those who oppose Yahweh always assumed the Holy Spirit was just a metaphor or marketing device on Yahweh's part since they have never seen any direct evidence of it. In fact it was a being vast and powerful, paling even Búri's power.

The Oracle of Delphi has been watching from inside the confines of the Maze. She now knows what the Holy Spirit is. She leaves the Maze and appears at the site of the battlefield. She calls out to everyone with her mind. The Holy Spirit is the being that she has been hiding from. She sees that Yahweh has learned how to draw upon it and make it worship him as the Father. It is really the incarnation of several of the Ancients fused into one being. But it is much like a toddler that looks to its Father to meet its needs, ease its pangs. It has been consuming universes just so it can have company. Yahweh promises it happiness and as the Holy Spirit, it has followed Yahweh like a child.

"There is no way we can beat it. Everyone run." Shouts Búri.

Yahweh is infused with the Holy Spirit's power now. He is drawing on its energy and making himself more powerful. Yahweh has been hesitant to do so before due to the danger of the Holy Spirit turning on him and obliterating everything. Now it is his only option. The power the being gives him is beyond anything Yahweh could conceive. He flings Búri back with but a flick of a finger. He commands the Holy Spirit to destroy his enemies. Just as it is about to consume everyone there, the Lord Buddha, Siddhartha Gattma, arrives along with the other twenty-seven Buddhas. Sensing the Holy Spirit's child-like essence and its pain, the Buddhas join its mind with theirs. For a brief instant their minds are merged. The Holy Spirit's mind sees the calm enlightened mind of the Lord Buddha. It realizes how to end its pain. With the Lord Buddha's assistance it obtains Enlightenment. It loses all its fetters to this world and merges with the universe. It is finally at rest.

Yahweh is still a threat however because he has absorbed much of the Holy Spirit's primordial power. Yahweh now has the power of an Ancient. Búri, all the gods, and now the Angels face him. Despite this he is stronger. Eventually they start to falter against Yahweh's might.

At the same time a certain shopkeeper is trying to coax his friend out of his new home to save his former home.

"Look, before I came here that was my home." Says the friend.

The shopkeeper responds, "I understand that you don't want to leave here, but billions are going to die if we don't help them."

"Izchak, sometimes you're more trouble than you're worth, but you're my best friend."

For the first time in ages the Wizard of Yendor takes a tentative step out of his Maze. They both transport themselves to the battlefield. With everyone otherwise engaged they are undetected. They both realize that Yahweh is too strong to take head on. They devise a plan and contact the Oracle. The two begin to build a type of black hole that is designed to draw in only Yahweh's specific energy. It's going to take time however and the forces massed against Yahweh are not going to survive long enough to build the trap. Then Izchak sees Schrödinger's cat.

Izchak and the Wizard contact the advancing force and convince them to stop the charge and simply stay on the defensive. Izchak creates an illusion while the Wizard works on the trap. He gives the illusion of Anu to Schrödinger's cat. Anu was the strongest of the Sumerian gods and had refused to join Yahweh. Instead he left to an unknown realm. Izchak communicates to Schrödinger's cat to take the shape of Anu. Izchak has made a prefect illusion so Yahweh believes it truly is Anu. He focuses all of his attention on the cat, Anu. Yahweh tries a million different attacks that should have killed even a god instantaneously. However the cat cannot die. Every time Yahweh attacks, some inexplicable coincidence saves the cat.

Yahweh is becoming increasingly infuriated mostly because he thinks Anu is taunting him since Anu never tries to attack. In truth the concealed cat doesn't have nearly the raw power even to scratch Yahweh. This goes on for hours and gives the Wizard and the Oracle the time to prepare the trap. Now it is up to the Oracle. The Oracle uses her power to line up causality in such a fashion that the trap appears in the exact position that would give the forces a chance to win. The trap is similar to a black hole in its magnitude but it is keyed only to Yahweh's life essence. Still it is not strong enough by itself to draw him in.

The Wizard commands everyone to make one last charge. All of the forces allied against Yahweh push him into the trap. Unfortunately everyone that still worships him is connected to him, so billions of souls are getting sucked in with him. Seeing this, the Wizard quickly moves to destroy the strand connecting the mortals. But the gods and all the mortals that have been uplifted such as the Apostles are too deeply connected. Since the original Angelic Host is now united and Yahweh's Angels have left him, they are unaffected. But all those that still worship him are drawn in.

They've done all they can. Though Yahweh is already in the trap, if even one being still remains connected outside the trap, then it would create a crack that could potentially lead to Yahweh's escape. Izchak, the Wizard, and the oracle finally cleave the last connection and all of Yahweh's remaining followers are sucked in. The trap is closed and Yahweh is sealed in a prison that is like one that the Wizard had used to imprison an Ancient. Since that being has never escaped and was even more powerful than Yahweh, the Wizard is assured that Yahweh is sealed in forever. The Wizard then casts the prison outside of reality and destroys any trace of where the rupture took place. Even if someone were to look for it the prison is now hidden and beyond the reach of any being.

Now that the battle is over most of the gods and their mortals go off to their respective homes. A few stay behind to loot the battlefield, most especially Monkey.

Atlas and the Oracle are talking.

Atlas says, "It's been a long time Del. You know I've got a little free time now that the fight's over." Atlas pulls out an old ring, "I still kept it after all these years. Would you give a guy another try? I promise I won't even fight back if you want to imprison me again."

The Oracle takes her ex-husband's hand and they leave hand-in-hand.

The Wizard and Izchak are about to depart when a certain immortal cat starts purring at the Wizard.

The Wizard picks him up and says, "Alright you can come."

Odin is addressing Lucifer, "Well, what are we going to do now?"

Lucifer explains, "Now that the war is over, some of us are going to stick around; I've heard some others are going to explore. We're going to make a rotation of it."

Odin replies, "Well all of you are welcome to join my pantheon."

Lucifer waves farewell, saying, "See you soon. Remember we have a visitor coming."

Epilogue

Búri and his grandchildren return to Asgard.

Búri addresses his Grandchildren. "I'm proud of all of you. Summon me if anything of this magnitude occurs again." He leaves in a flash of light.

Ve says goodbye to his brothers. He is still set on trying to follow the Eight Fold Buddhist path but he tells them he's still their brother so be sure to call him if needed.

Vili and Odin are sitting on a ledge by themselves.

Odin asks, "So where are you off to brother?"

Vili replies, "I'm not sure, but I'm going to do some traveling."

Odin laughs, "Well this time try and not get trapped. When are you leaving?"

"In a few days. I figure we have some catching up to do." Vili says.

"Before we do anything I think we have a mutual friend that's about to arrive," reminds Odin.

I wake up and this time I'm pretty sure I'm dead. I see a rainbow bridge guarded by a helmed warrior. The bridge can only be Bifrost, the bridge that leads to Valhalla. The warrior must be its guardian, the god Heimdall.

I walk up a little hesitantly. "Do I have permission to pass?"

Heimdall replies, "Welcome, John Tran, we've been waiting for you. You missed one heck of a battle, however. Yes, of course you may pass."

I cross Bifrost and I see Odin and Vili waiting for me. They offer me a horn of mead. So I take it. I now know I'm destined for Valhalla.

Odin replies, "You didn't exactly make the cut for Buddhist of the year so Nirvana is going to have to wait. Valhalla is an option but Vili and I actually had a different idea. We have a friend that needs someone to go exploring the multiverse with and we were hoping you'd be willing to join in the journey."

"Of course, my Lords, whatever you wish." I bow deeply to them.

Evelyn steps out from behind them and smiles. Odin gives a ring that is a copy of Draupnir, Odin's own ring; Draupnir was forged by the dwarf brothers Sindri and Brokk, and every ninth night the ring drips gold to make eight copies of itself. It is the highest honor Odin can bestow upon one of his warriors.

Odin says, "With my ring you can contact me or Vili anywhere, anytime, should you need us. It also will let us know where you are. When your other friends eventually die they'll be sent here and may join you if they wish."

Odin and Vili both instill us with more power. We are close to gods in our own right now. "Ready my love?" I look into Evelyn's beautiful eyes.

She smiles, "For longer than you know."

I take Evelyn's hand and we set off to explore eternity.

Printed in Great Britain
by Amazon